SPLASH!

Splash!

A Novel

Stephen Glover

Constable • London

CONSTABLE

First published in Great Britain in 2017 by Constable

1 3 5 7 9 10 8 6 4 2

ISBN: 978-1-47212-633-7

Typeset in Bembo by SX Composing DTP, Rayleigh, Essex
Printed and bound in Great Britain by CPI Group (UK) Ltd, Croydon CR0 4YY

Papers used by Constable are from well-managed forests
and other responsible sources.

MIX
Paper from
responsible sources
FSC® C104740

Constable
An imprint of
Little, Brown Book Group
Carmelite House
50 Victoria Embankment
London EC4Y 0DZ

An Hachette UK Company
www.hachette.co.uk

www.littlebrown.co.uk

For Celia, Edmund and Alexander

Chapter One

All over London they are making their preparations. In the flat above Number Eleven Downing Street, the Prime Minister's wife is talking on the telephone to the Prime Minister's diary secretary who is just about to talk to the Prime Minister's driver. Across the city, the manager of Mount's Hotel is checking on his tablet for the third time that three thousand oysters have been ordered, and that the vintage champagne is being refrigerated at precisely the desired temperature. In a hairdresser off the New King's Road known to the cognoscenti who do not want to splash their money around, Lady Evelyn Wherewill is having her hair coloured. Sitting at his desk in the crumbling remnant of what was once a generously appointed episcopal palace, the Right Reverend Bob Butcher, Bishop of Middlesex, is wondering whether he should mention the newly vacant see of Canterbury if he encounters the Prime Minister at the party. The stout figure of Madame Po Chun is embedded in the soft black leather of her limousine as she is driven noiselessly from the Fig Leaf restaurant in Mayfair to the Kensington mansion she shares with Mr Po.

In the editor's office of the *Daily Bugle*, whose centenary is about to be celebrated, Eric Doodle is listening to senior members of his staff describe the next day's edition. His mind has begun to wander while the foreign editor makes a doomed case for 'splashing' with a devastating earthquake in Tibet. The *Bugle* does not greatly concern itself with foreign stories with no British connection, and it is most unlikely that any Britons have strayed into the mountainous regions of that unhappy country where the Almighty has elected to wreak such havoc. The dead are probably all monks. Or peasants. Doodle pats his side pocket again to feel the reassuring bulk of the speech he will deliver this evening. His proprietor, Sir Edwin Entwistle, has told him he must not exceed four and a half minutes, and he has practised his oration endlessly in front of the sometimes irritable Mrs Doodle, who has timed it to the last second. His speech has been printed out in 20-point type so that he will be able to read it easily even if there is little light. The editor of the *Daily Bugle* has persuaded himself that the award of the knighthood which Daphne Doodle and he have craved for so long will hang upon his short performance at Mount's.

All over London people are making their preparations – and none more assiduously than Lady Entwistle, or Caroline as we must learn to call her, wife of the proprietor of what was once the highest-selling newspaper in the world. Caroline regards her naked body in the long mirror with approval, noting the firm outlines and pleasing contours which in her estimation are not often to be found in a forty-year-old. She smiles at herself, admiring her bleached teeth. But then the smallest look of crossness passes over her lovely face as she observes in her mirror the bulging form of her husband standing behind her, clad only in underpants of unseemly briefness, over whose elastic waistband cascade folds of white flesh. Not for the first time Caroline reflects that if she can justly claim that four decades have treated her kindly, the same cannot be said of the six decades during which Edwin Entwistle has sojourned on this earth. Nonetheless, she manages a thin smile of solidarity, which her husband takes as an expression of endearment, stepping forward to clutch her right buttock with agricultural vigour.

A grimace is rapidly converted into a smile. This is not the evening for a row with Edwin. As fervently as the Doodles long for an honour, so Caroline yearns for a life peerage to be bestowed upon her so far merely knighted husband so that she can be the consort of a peer of the United Kingdom of Great Britain and Northern Ireland. She needs him to be on top form and make the speech of his life.

All over London people are making their preparations: the *Bugle*'s star columnist, Adam Pride, who is regarding himself in his mirror; Mount's hordes of waiters, who include more than a smattering of illegal immigrants – a group against which the newspaper has often fruitlessly inveighed; politicians of every persuasion; the Russian oligarch Boris Vrodsky, accompanied by a blonde lady who bears little resemblance to Mrs Vrodsky; proprietors and rival editors; Sir Archibald Merrick, City magnifico and a vice-chairman of the governing party; ambassadors and diplomats, though few of them have ever read the *Bugle*, preferring instead the low-circulation, politically enlightened and more upmarket *Chronicle*; Emmanuele Botti, highly strung owner of London's latest voguish restaurant, the Fig Leaf; Ambrose Treadle, the bafflingly successful City PR king; a brace of fashionable novelists; a sprinkling of film stars and starlets, all of whom have appeared at one time or another not as they might wish in the pages of the *Bugle*, including the veteran actor Tray Nevada, whose drug-fuelled orgies on his yacht have been somewhat misrepresented by the newspaper to his great annoyance; and those who will convey them all to Mount's, as well as those who will photograph them as they arrive. The *Bugle* may not be what it was – it is scarcely making any money, and there have even been rumours that Sir Edwin is thinking of selling the paper – but it still strikes enough fear and loathing into its victims to be treated with respect.

All over the vast unfolding city people are making their preparations – except for Sam Blunt, the *Bugle*'s chief reporter, whose journalistic feats have included naming the original owner of a headless and legless torso found in the Thames (admittedly, with a fair degree of assistance from Detective Chief Inspector Nobby Walters of Scotland Yard) and breaking the story of Lady Evelyn Wherewill's unfortunate adultery with Terence Glasswell, MP.

Uniquely among the hundreds of guests that evening, Sam is not making any preparations whatsoever. In an insalubrious suburb far removed from the fashionable climes occupied by our other players, he is stirring amid the ruckled sheets of a bed that is not his own. He is hardly aware of the identity of the woman whose not insubstantial body is pinning him down. If he was told her name on meeting her a few hours previously, Sam has forgotten it.

Re-entering the eager world, he senses that an important obligation lies before him, and yet cannot remember what it is. His head throbs and he is aware of a dull ache in his groin. He struggles to release an arm so that he can peer at his watch. It is nearly six o'clock. He takes a little time to consider whether it is morning or evening. Outside it is light, but that provides no evidence one way or another since it is early summer. He tries to recall the events that have brought him there, and, recollecting a drunken lunch with the woman on top of him, decides that in all probability it must be evening. In which case, what can the important engagement be?

Then the face of a senior colleague shimmers into his mind. It is not that of Eric Doodle the editor, with whom Sam has little to do, but of Trevor Yapp, the pugnacious, indeed pathologically disturbed, deputy editor. He can see Yapp's snarling face, and hear his sneering voice. 'I'm buggered if I know why that old idiot Entwistle invited you along with all those fucking columnists. You'll only roll up pissed.'

Sam sits up with a start — or rather he tries to, but can scarcely move. The *Bugle's* centenary party at Mount's! He is not a man to take social engagements seriously, but his absence from such a momentous celebration might be noticed, at least by Yapp if not by Doodle, and be used against him. His position at the paper isn't as secure as it used to be. There's talk of Yapp taking over as editor, in which case anything could happen.

Our hero is not unchivalrous. Pressing though the matter is, he does not want to tumble the strange woman out of bed. Besides, there might be prolonged recriminations. The sound of regular snoring suggests she is still asleep. Experienced escapologist as he is, Sam succeeds in wriggling free without waking her. Once out of bed he grabs his clothes without another glance in her direction, and swiftly and silently puts them on.

Chapter Two

It was one of those early June evenings when the world felt as though it had been newly created. The leaves on the trees had that full, pristine greenness of early summer. As he strolled across St James's Park, Benedict Brewster was glad to be young and alive. Glad that he had just visited his father in his club. Glad that he had drunk two glasses of delicious wine. And delighted that the following day he would be joining the *Daily Bugle* as a junior trainee reporter.

On leaving his father at Stride's he had meant to take the tube to his small flat in Hackney, but the gentle beauty of the evening cried out to his youthful heart, and begged not to be abandoned. Buoyed by the loveliness of all that surrounded him, as well as the wine, Benedict only needed a purpose. The idea of visiting the *Bugle*'s offices in Pimlico suddenly seized his romantic soul.

Within a quarter of an hour he was gazing at the nondescript 1950s building that had housed the newspaper since its move from Fleet Street some two decades previously. Benedict knew perfectly well that it was not a beautiful building but he could not have observed the Taj Mahal with greater rapture. At last he would have a job and no longer be dependent on his generous parents. At last he would have a role, though he was not at all clear what it would be.

Two factors had led to his employment at the *Bugle* on a very low salary. Thirty years ago, when it was selling three times as many copies, the paper had only three graduates on the payroll. Now it had a policy of recruiting the mostly highly educated, or at any rate those with the best examination results, and with his Oxford First in Anthropology Benedict had put himself firmly in that category. But this alone would not have been enough to get him a job since there were hundreds of other candidates with just as good academic qualifications who had shown much greater interest in journalism at school and university. What had swung it for Benedict was a chance meeting his father had had with the editor, Mr Doodle, at a shoot in Yorkshire. Doodle, who was new to the sport, had recognised in Sir Cumming Brewster a gentleman of the old school, and one moreover who owned a fair portion of Lincolnshire, where he was said to entertain large shooting parties. Sir Cumming had openly confided his worries about his younger son, who, for all his academic talents, showed scant ambition. The imaginative editor immediately suggested what amounted to little more than a glorified internship on the *Bugle*, for which Sir Cumming professed his thanks.

It was true the baronet had never read Sir Edwin Entwistle's famous newspaper, and might not have much liked it if he had. Nor did he have a very high opinion of journalists as a breed insofar as he had ever thought about them. But needs must. Younger sons are younger sons, and the Brewster coffers were not as replete as they once had been. Sir Cumming would have been happy if Benedict had followed family tradition and joined the army, but Lady Brewster feared for the life of her beloved son in one of the several conflicts in which Britain was engaged around the world, and the boy himself showed little appetite for taking up arms. So when chance presented him with Doodle, Sir Cumming gratefully bagged him.

If the father was ignorant of the ways of journalism, so too was the son, though he harboured unformed hopes of being some sort of a writer, which he thought might be mysteriously fostered on Sir Edwin's organ. Benedict was unfamiliar with the *Bugle*, though his eyes may have occasionally skimmed the sports pages. He was not, in fact, a regular reader of any newspaper. At university he had occasionally glanced at the *Chronicle* as well as the 'page-three girls' in the downmarket *Daily Dazzle*.

Benedict knew nothing about the *Bugle* or its former glories. He was unaware that it had been founded by a Mr, later Viscount, Pepper, and he had no idea that this gentleman's feckless and inept grandson had lost ownership of the newspaper ten years previously to the northern carpet magnate Sir Edwin Entwistle. He had absolutely no notion that this very evening its centenary was being celebrated by such people as the Prime Minister, Lady Evelyn Wherewill, Ambrose Treadle, Madame Po and the Bishop of Middlesex in the art deco ballroom of Mount's Hotel.

As Benedict was inspecting the bland façade of the newspaper's offices, trying to imagine his future there, he saw a tall, hook-nosed man shoot out of the main door, cut across the path of a young woman with a pushchair, and clamber into the back of a waiting taxi. Of all the many things Benedict did not know, perhaps the most important was the identity of Trevor Yapp, deputy editor of the *Daily Bugle*.

Chapter Three

As an eighteen-year-old in the late 1890s, Arthur Pepper got his first job writing social snippets for a magazine with shabby offices in the Strand. Arthur was poor – so poor that he would walk all the way from his mother's humble home in Paddington, and back again when he had finished work in the evening. In this way he got to know the city, and in particular the great houses of Mayfair into whose ungiving windows he would peer with unabashed covetousness. One day, he said to himself, he would own such a house. It was a dream he dared not share with his darling mother.

After six months on the magazine Arthur got a rise, and six months later another one. He could now have afforded to take an omnibus but he preferred still to walk the few miles each way, setting aside the money he might have spent on transport for the magazine he intended one day to launch. He lived frugally, seldom drinking alcohol, and never went to a restaurant or a pub.

Nonetheless, he could not help noticing an establishment called the Earl of Aberdeen in a little side street. Every evening, after passing a row of fine Georgian houses which thirty years later would be erased to make way for Mount's Hotel, he walked past the pub as he cut up from Grosvenor Square to Oxford Street. He would hear the sound of laughter and happy voices, and longed to go inside. One Friday evening he succumbed. He drank only half a pint of beer and left quickly. But having done so once he did so again, and after a while it became a habit for him to pop into the Aberdeen every Friday evening, where he would sometimes linger for half an hour. He got to know the clientele of clerks and shop workers. They did not know it, and nor did he, but they were the people who would read his newspaper when he launched the *Daily Bugle* ten years later – the people to whom he gave a voice. As rich and grand as he became, he never forgot them.

Superficially, the Earl of Aberdeen has not changed much in the years that have beaten past since Arthur Pepper took his weekly drink there. It consists of a single rectangular room whose four walls are gigantic mirrors. Arthur's first thought was that it resembled his conception of a brothel. One mirror was cracked during an air raid in 1940, and later replaced. You can still look into the mirror where the stiff-collared young Arthur would examine his face and follow the movements of a barmaid.

Having taken a taxi from the distant suburb, whose hefty cost he would put on his expenses, Sam decided to stop for a fortifying drink at the Aberdeen before braving the centenary celebrations at Mount's. It was not a pub he had ever visited before, and he had no idea the creator of his newspaper had once sat there.

Sam gripped a gin and tonic. His eye swooped around the pub, and he noticed an attractive woman sitting by herself. In other circumstances he would have tried to chat her up but he told himself this was not the time. He was already very late. He inspected himself in the mirror, and saw a slender man in early middle age, well lived-in, with specks of grey flecking his once raven hair, but still passably handsome.

By the time Sam got to the ballroom at Mount's, Eric Doodle was approaching the final paragraph of his speech. The Prime Minister had already said a few words, emphasising the importance of a free Press, in which of course he did not at all believe, and praising the *Bugle* for its tenacious pursuit of truth. His real feelings about the paper were rather less generous since, although generally supportive, it had been appallingly rude a couple of weeks previously when Trevor Yapp had been editing in Doodle's absence. It had called him a 'weak, vacillating shadow of a leader'.

Doodle's speech was not going as well as he had intended. Jokes that had been amusing even to Daphne in their Wimbledon sitting room had not been spotted. Despite the 20-point type, he had contrived to lose his thread on a couple of occasions. For some reason Daphne's watch did not measure time in precisely the same way as Sir Edwin Entwistle's, and the newspaper tycoon was looking crossly at Doodle, convinced that his editor had already been speaking for five and a half minutes, and impatient to take the floor himself.

Sam surveyed the ballroom. There were many figures he recognised, and a few he didn't. He saw Trevor Yapp, who was observing Doodle with contempt. The Bishop of Middlesex – a well-known media performer who liked to be known as 'Bishop Bob' – was whispering in the ear of a well-built Chinese woman, whose hair towered above him like a missile on its launch pad. Edward Sneed, editor of the high-minded *Chronicle*, looked as though he had smelt a ghastly odour he couldn't shake off. There was the *Bugle*'s star columnist, Adam Pride, standing by the Prime Minister, with whom he had presumably been conversing before Doodle set forth. Sam reflected that a stranger from another era might have inferred from Pride's easy confidence, and the expensive cut of his suit, that he was the Prime Minister, and the limp figure beside him a mere columnist. He noticed Lady Entwistle standing with Lady Evelyn Wherewill, whose dull imperiousness Sam thought attractive. As for the proprietor's wife, she was a corker. She seemed unimaginably removed from him. As though aware she was being watched, Caroline turned her face in his direction. Sam felt himself reddening. He took a swig of champagne.

Doodle was coming to his climax.

'And so, my lords, ladies and gentlemen, whatever happens in the world of communications – and who can doubt great changes are afoot? – we may be confident, with a proprietor such as Sir Edwin Entwistle at the helm, a worthy heir to our founder, the great Viscount Pepper himself, that the *Daily Bugle* will continue to prosper so that, a hundred years from now, our grandchildren and great-grandchildren may, like us, raise their glasses to the greatest newspaper in the world.'

'Hear, hear,' said Mr Po Chun.

'Six and a half minutes,' muttered Sir Edwin Entwistle bitterly.

'To the *Daily Bugle*,' reiterated Eric Doodle.

'To the *Daily Bugle*,' chorused a hundred other voices.

Even Sam found himself raising his glass, whose contents he drained in one go. He cast another glance in the direction of Caroline Entwistle, and caught her eye. To his surprise she smiled at him.

Anyone encountering Sir Edwin Entwistle in a pub, and listening to his views about the world, might reasonably conclude that five minutes would quite suffice for his speech. But a newspaper proprietor is inevitably a great personage – much greater than a mere carpet billionaire. Oracular significance is ascribed to his utterings.

Sir Edwin was not an accomplished speechifyer. Despite delusions of Churchillian grandiloquence he tended to mumble and rush his lines. In a straight run-off with Eric Doodle, fair-minded judges would in normal circumstances be inclined to award the cup to the stumbling editor.

But tonight the newspaper tycoon had something to say. He intended to sing his own praises, though naturally – Caroline had advised him on this – this panegyric would take the form of celebrating the *Daily Bugle*.

When he had acquired the title a decade ago, he declared, it had fallen on hard times. It was a mere spectre of what it had been in Arthur Pepper's day. There was a lack of vision. The *Daily Bugle* had, he was sorry to say, lost its mojo. But he, Sir Edwin, had believed in the newspaper. He had valued its history. And with the help of a collection of brilliant journalists – he did not name any of them, not even Doodle – they had restored the *Bugle* to its proper place in British public life.

Lady Evelyn Wherewill, who was anxious to ingratiate herself with her friend Lady Entwistle, clapped her hands, and Madame Po and Mr Po joined in, as did Bishop Bob and, somewhat belatedly, Adam Pride. Soon a polite ripple of applause was circulating around the ballroom. It grew into a gust of approval as the guests reflected that they were, after all, drinking Sir Edwin's vintage champagne and eating his food. Only a very few pairs of hands did not come together. One of them belonged to the sour-faced Sneed. Another was owned by Steve Rutt, the celebrity diarist of the *Daily Dazzle*, who because he hadn't been sent an invitation had been forced to gain entry into the ballroom through the kitchens after making a small payment to an under-chef. Equally unmoved was Sam Blunt, chief reporter of the *Daily Bugle*.

'Bollocks,' he muttered. 'We were selling more copies before Entwistle bought us.'

This was indeed true, but what is truth on such an occasion? The applause had lifted Sir Edwin's sails. He frankly described the mess he had inherited from the 3rd Viscount Pepper (who was now dead and could be safely slandered) and stressed the many changes and improvements he had introduced for the benefit of the greatest newspaper in the world.

Another round of applause, this time daringly set off by Caroline, spread around the room. Sir Edwin allowed it almost to die down, and then put out his hands, palms downwards, as though to quieten a level of appreciation that was in danger of getting out of control. He attempted to stick two thumbs in his waistcoat but gave up on discovering that the garment was fitted so tightly around his imprisoned midriff as not to admit them. Then he stroked his small moustache with a forefinger before launching his final peroration.

'My Lords, ladies and gentlemen – and, of course Prime Minister – I shouldn't be doing my bounden duty if I didn't mention a concern that has been much on my mind lately. You, Prime Minister, have spoken very finely this evening about the vital importance of a free Press. I won't pretend we haven't had our occasional set-tos, but we welcome you here this evening as a good friend who will always carry with us the proud banner of liberty. So I trust you won't mind, Prime Minister, if I say there are forces abroad that don't share our views – forces which would, if they jolly well could, snuff out the voice of freedom. I shan't name them now, but enough to say we all know who the culprits are. So I am going to lift my glass on this unforgettable occasion to toast not only the hundred years of this great newspaper but also to stress the paramount importance of Press freedom.'

Sir Edwin was so persuaded by his own rhetoric that he was now quite moved. He raised his glass.

'To the *Bugle* and freedom,' he cried.

'To the *Bugle* and freedom,' repeated a hundred voices.

Sam raised his glass, and spoke into it as he drained it. 'Bloody fraud.'

A further round of spirited applause was set off by Madame Po. When it had died down many conversations struck up. It was generally agreed that while Mr Doodle had not advanced, and even possibly set back, his prospects of a knighthood, Sir Edwin had undoubtedly cemented his claims to a life peerage with a formidable performance. That, at any rate, was the view confidently promulgated by Lady Evelyn Wherewill, and endorsed by Bishop Bob. Eric and Daphne Doodle were soon seen leaving.

Splash!

Sam was by now quite sozzled, having drunk most of a bottle of champagne in addition to the gin he had put away in the Aberdeen and the uncounted glasses he had consumed earlier in the day. He was drunk enough to try to engage Adam Pride in conversation as the haughty columnist glided from a tête-à-tête with the Chancellor of the Exchequer to a similar encounter with the Home Secretary. Pride had little enthusiasm for Sam even when the reporter was sober. He now brushed him aside as though dismissing an unwelcome petitioner.

As Sam fought his way aimlessly through the throng he bumped against the saturnine figure of Trevor Yapp.

'What the fuck are you up to now, Blunt?' enquired Yapp.

'Just looking for some room to breathe,' replied Sam.

He found a chair in a darkened corner of the ballroom, a few yards from a whirling chocolate contraption that resembled a gigantic doner kebab. Sir Edwin and Madame Po had taken up residence there. As they ran their spoons along the rotating mound, taking large scoops of chocolate, Sir Edwin grunted like a warthog, and Madame Po emitted peals of airy laughter. Sam watched in dwindling fascination until he fell asleep.

'Tired?'

Sam looked up to see Caroline Entwistle standing above him. She was wearing a tight white silk dress.

'No – yes, I suppose I am.' Sam struggled to his feet.

'We met once before,' she said, putting out a slender hand that felt deliciously delicate. 'At the *Bugle*'s summer drinks party.'

'I remember.'

'My name's Caroline.'

'I know.'

She looked at him with a kind of indulgent amusement. Sam wondered whether she too was not rather drunk.

'Have you enjoyed the party?' she asked.

'Not particularly. I was late.'

'That's a shame.'

Sam was intimidated by this beautiful woman. He had once been lowered from a helicopter into a crocodile-infested African swamp. He had interviewed a serial killer who flushed his victims' remains down a sink disposal unit. He had seen a baby laid out in a mortuary. There was little in life that scared him but he was afraid of Caroline Entwistle. It wasn't because she was beautiful. He had made love to a few women in Caroline's league. No, it wasn't that. It had nothing to do with class either. For all her graces, Sam suspected her background was scarcely more elevated than his, which was far from privileged. That wasn't the reason. He was frightened of this woman because she was so rich. Sam was frightened of money.

Perhaps it was this thought that made him totter, and almost lose his balance. Caroline put out her right arm and gripped his left arm with surprising force. She kept her hand there for a few seconds.

'You should go home,' she suggested.

'I expect I should.'

Caroline Entwistle and Sam Blunt were roughly the same height. Suddenly she leant forward and kissed him lightly on the cheek. It was done so rapidly that he wondered whether he had imagined it. Then she thrust a piece of paper into his hand.

'Take this. It's my mobile number.'

18

Chapter Four

Eric Doodle habitually arrived at Pepper House at nine o'clock, and the morning after the centenary party was no exception. He had left his Edwardian villa in Wimbledon at precisely the usual time in his chauffeur-driven car after an unpleasing altercation with Daphne. Over breakfast he had finally given vent to his suspicion that his wife's timekeeping had not been everything it might have been. He should have known that Daphne would not admit the tiniest degree of fault. She countered that she could read a watch as well as anyone else, and the reason he had strayed so egregiously over the time limit stipulated by his proprietor was that he had lost his way on at least a couple of occasions, and that moreover his delivery had been as slow as a hearse backing out of a crematorium. Doodle said nothing. He was by nature inclined to see the other person's point of view, and a little voice in his head advised that Daphne, while doubtless overstating the case, might be right. He had perhaps dragged out the thing too much.

Now that he was sitting at his desk, with a cup of tea brewed by his secretary Dora in front of him, he could at last relax. He reached for his copy of *Rural Retreats* and began to turn its glossy pages. This, after his businesslike perusal of the newspapers during the forty-five-minute drive from Wimbledon, was the high point of his day before a series of tiresome meetings began.

As usual, Doodle passed over the articles about badgers and farm subsidies, though he would be happy to read them when he had finished studying each of the many advertisements for country houses which filled the first quarter of *Rural Retreats*. To this task he brought all the love and care of a medieval monk examining an illuminated manuscript.

As well as the magazine Doodle had a tattered map of England in front of him, which he would frequently consult, sometimes ringing a village with his pencil, or inserting a thin arrow, or making some other mark intelligible only to him. His iron rule was to exclude the counties of south-eastern England on grounds of cost and their likely proximity to large conurbations. Other counties he also vetoed for reasons that might seem skittish to some. He did not regard Cornwall as fully English. Norfolk was too flat. Derbyshire he associated with his great-aunt Daisy with whom he had spent several unforgettably awful holidays as a child. In fact, when a whole range of considerations had been taken into account there remained only nine or ten counties in which buying a country house seemed feasible.

Doodle accepted that it was in one sense a highly theoretical exercise. Daphne did not want to move from their commodious villa. She was happy to tolerate her husband's late-developed love of shooting because it took him out of the house at weekends. But she hated the countryside. Crops gave her hay fever. The stench of pig manure particularly vexed her. In the course of their thirty-year marriage she had never ventured into the country with her husband, except on that disastrous weekend when they had been invited to the Entwistles' estate in Shropshire – disastrous because Daphne had suffered an allergic reaction to a nettle sting, so serious that she had to be driven at high speeds by Sir Edwin's not entirely sober butler to the Royal Shrewsbury Hospital.

So Doodle's rational mind understood that he was essentially engaged in a game and that, at any rate for as long as he remained in conjugal union with Daphne, which almost certainly would be until one of them died, there was not the remotest possibility of their decamping to the countryside. Nonetheless, he persisted in his researches, and delighted in them.

On this morning his eye had been caught by a Georgian rectory in Lincolnshire. Surrounded by twenty acres of its own pasture, it had an asking price appreciably less than the likely proceeds of 2 Common View. The house's beautifully proportioned windows made his heart ache. A stream ran through the garden below a small ha-ha. Doodle imagined himself in his library, perching on a wooden ladder and reaching down a dusty leather edition of Dryden or Pope. He knew Sir Cumming Brewster's estate lay somewhere in the Lincolnshire Wolds, and he imagined the telephone ringing as he turned the pages of *The Rape of the Lock*. How good to hear from you, Brewster. A day's shooting? Just a few close friends? I should love to come. Been wanting to try out my new gun.

'Eric?'

Doodle looked up from the pages of *Rural Retreats*, his

eyes still swimming with dreams, to see the pretty figure of
Dora standing in front of his enormous desk.

'Eric?' she repeated.

'Yes? What is it?'

'There's someone to see you.'

Doodle had left the Lincolnshire Wolds behind him.
He pushed a piece of paper over the magazine to conceal it.

'Who is it?'

'A trainee journalist.'

Doodle felt irritated. His life was too busy for him to be
worrying about trainee journalists. He had a meeting with
the Prime Minister that very afternoon.

'Ask Yapp to talk to him, would you, Dora? You know
I'm busy.'

Dora was not easily deflected. 'The thing is, Eric, you
apparently asked him to come and see you when he arrived.
Or that's what you told his father.'

'His father?' Suddenly it all came back to him. For a
moment he was back in his imaginary library talking to Sir
Cumming.

'What's this boy's name?'

'Benedict, Eric. Benedict Brewster.'

'Better show him in.'

Benedict had been hovering uneasily in the outer office.
Now Dora opened the door, beckoned him in, and closed it
as she left.

He saw an elderly balding man with heavy spectacles
writing at his desk. Benedict was reminded of the family
solicitor who made occasional visits to his parents' house
from his offices in Lincoln. For at least ten seconds the editor
did not look up, and when he did so he had a preoccupied

air, as though he had been involved in great matters which the young trainee could not be expected to understand.

'My dear boy.' Doodle thought this a correct way of addressing someone of Benedict's background, and could imagine Sir Cumming using the phrase. 'Do come and sit down.'

Doodle noticed that Benedict was not wearing a tie, a serious dress-code infringement in the offices of the *Daily Bugle*: only a handful of incorrigible employees, among them Sam Blunt, were granted an exemption. However, now was probably not the moment to mention such a thing. Better leave it to Yapp.

'Well, my boy, good to have you on board. Anything you need?'

'Er, no, I don't think so,' replied Benedict. In truth he felt in need of almost everything.

'Good. Now we'd better get you started. I'll ask Dora to introduce you to Trevor Yapp. He runs the news side, and he'll be your point man.'

'Thank you,' replied Benedict. It was not often that people expressed gratitude on being told that they would be introduced to Trevor Yapp.

Doodle was furrowing his brow. It was apparent to Benedict that a new idea was forcing its way into his mind.

'It might be a good idea if our chief reporter took you under his wing for a day or two. Nice enough fellow, though a bit of a rough diamond. Good journalist. I'll ask him to take you out for a drink and show you the ropes.'

'Thank you.'

Doodle added that it might be sensible for him to try his hand at a 'colour story', a journalistic phrase for a descriptive and evocative piece. Benedict, who had no idea what a colour story was, nodded gratefully.

When he had gone, Doodle pressed a button and asked Dora to get hold of Sam Blunt.

For once the chief reporter of the *Daily Bugle* was all alone in his bed, sleeping off the effects of the party in his tiny flat in Barons Court. At the best of times he did not arrive at Pepper House until about eleven o'clock, and on this day did not have any plans to get there much before one.

He was dreaming of an exotic garden such as might have been conceived by Gauguin. There were gourdes and coconuts and lush tropical vegetation, though for some reason there weren't any bare-breasted young women in grass skirts. Perhaps they would appear on the scene in due course. He noticed a colourful parrot balancing on a branch which was making an odd croaking noise that was rather irritating. In fact, very irritating. He wanted to throttle the parrot. It was then that he realised that his phone was vibrating a couple of inches from his right ear.

'Sam?'

He recognised Dora's voice.

'Sam, are you there, or are you making love to some unfortunate lady?'

Dora, who was fond of Sam, had occupied the time while he was listening to the parrot in his tropical garden by reading an article in the *Bugle* about the perils of drinking too much bottled water.

'I'm here, my lovely. What is it?'

'Your editor wants a word with you.'

Sam sat up. This was unusual. Doodle almost never telephoned him. The thought flashed across his mind that he had behaved badly last night, and was about to be reprimanded for some forgotten misdemeanour.

'Better put him on.'

'Sam?'

'Yes.' Sam could not bring himself to address his editor as either Mr Doodle or Eric.

'All well, I trust?'

'Yes, thank you. Just working on a story.'

'Good. Good. I'd like you to do me a small favour.'

'Of course.'

'We've got a new trainee on the paper. Nice young chap. Bit wet behind the ears, no doubt. Looks clever, though. Answers to the name of Benedict Brewster.' Doodle paused.

'I see.'

'Could you keep a friendly eye on the young fellow? Give him a drink – even a light lunch in a pub? I'd be grateful if you'd show him where all the pulleys and levers are.'

In normal circumstances Sam might have been rather affronted to be asked to undertake so menial a task. He was, after all, chief reporter, even if his duties nowadays mainly consisted of rewriting agency copy of foreign stories involving Britons, the *Bugle* being reluctant in these straitened times to pay the travel and hotel costs of sending him abroad. But he was relieved not to be in any sort of trouble, as well as reassured by Doodle's friendly voice, and readily agreed that he would indeed show Benedict where all the pulleys and levers were.

After the call had ended Sam lit a cigarette and set about making some coffee. He would deal with Benedict Brewster later. The most pressing issue in his life was Caroline Entwistle.

It was a long time since a beautiful woman had made such an approach to him, and he was flattered as well as staggered that Caroline should have done so. Of course he fancied her. Who wouldn't? Presumably she was keen on sex. So much the better. Sir Edwin Entwistle certainly didn't seem much of a proposition on that front. Sam imagined himself dining with her before repairing to their hotel suite.

But then a warning voice piped up. Caroline was the wife of the proprietor of his newspaper. Was he bonkers? asked the voice. He'd surely learnt by this time that adulterous affairs were always discovered in the end. He knew it as a journalist – look at the Lady Evelyn Wherewill case – and he knew it from personal experience, having been finally booted out by his ex-wife after she had discovered his umpteenth infidelity. For pity's sake, said this insistent voice, get a grip. Anyone but Caroline Entwistle. The moment Sir Edwin found out, he would hang him from a gibbet and distribute his entrails around London. No one would employ him again, not even the *Chronicle*.

Sam was not a fool. He was persuaded. She might be beautiful and sex-mad but she would finish him off.

He delved into the pockets of his trousers, which lay in a tangled heap on the floor, and extracted the note Caroline had given him the previous night. He noticed the numbers had been roughly written, suggesting she might have been drunk. She had probably already forgotten all about it.

Sam gently brushed his lips over the piece of paper, remembering that it had been in her delicate hand, screwed it up, and dropped it into the wastepaper basket.

Chapter Five

Benedict returned to the tiny desk that had been assigned to him in the corner of the newsroom and awaited developments. He did not have the faintest idea what anyone there was doing. There were clusters of desks as far as his eye could see, forming weird patterns like lily pads in a pond. Some were populated with busy-looking people, others with journalists who seemed to have very little to do, while others were completely deserted. He decided the best course of action would be to give an impression of industry, and peered into his computer screen, assuming what he hoped was a look of preoccupied intelligence. He was examining the barely dressed buxom women featured on the *Bugle*'s website.

During the morning someone called Sam Blunt rang him and suggested that the two of them might have lunch at the Saraceno, an Italian restaurant close to the office, the following day.

Benedict was later summoned to Trevor Yapp's office. The deputy editor had been unaware of his existence, and was annoyed that the young trainee had already met the editor.

Yapp assumed Doodle had been up to his old tricks again. On at least two occasions the editor had given jobs to wholly unqualified young people. Yapp had reason to believe that the father of one of them, a girl with no journalistic aptitude, owned the large yacht on which Eric had spent two weeks in the Greek islands. (Daphne, who did not like foreign climes any more than the English countryside, had stayed at home.)

'What journalistic experience have you got?' Yapp asked, tapping a pen on his desk, and turning it over in his hand as he did so.

'Er – a bit at university,' fibbed Benedict.

'Where did you go?'

'Oxford. I read Anthropology,' Benedict replied. 'I got a First,' he added unnecessarily.

Yapp scowled. He had achieved a lower second in chemistry at a polytechnic that had since become a university.

'Let's see what you're made of,' he said. 'I'll tell you what I want you to do.'

Trevor Yapp had spent several minutes during a busy day dreaming up what would have been a challenge for the most resourceful young journalist. The President of Kangala was paying an official visit to Great Britain. The *Daily Bugle* did not have the slightest interest in this gentleman, who had seized power in an almost bloodless coup twenty years earlier. His small country was poor and sparsely populated. He did not even have the distinction of having killed very many of his countrymen, and the number of Britons living in Kangala could be numbered on the fingers of two hands. There was not the remotest possibility of the *Bugle* mentioning that His Incomparable Excellency Moses Ovambo had set foot on British soil.

Splash!

Yapp explained to Benedict that the news desk would secure accreditation for him when the President went to the Banqueting House in Whitehall in two days' time. He should come back to the office, and file a thousand words by six o'clock.

'One more thing,' snapped Yapp, as Benedict was leaving. 'You're not wearing a tie.'

Benedict put a hand up to his bare neck.

'No.'

'Go and buy one.'

'Now?'

'Yes.'

When Benedict arrived at Pepper House at ten o'clock the following morning, his tie was neatly in place. He had stopped off at the Western Library on the way to work, where he had had a membership for several years paid for by his father. Benedict had looked for a book about Kangala, and had found a thin volume called *Desert Paradise*, which, though thirty years old, and therefore pre-dating His Incomparable Excellency Moses Ovambo's seizure of power, might be of some use.

Dragging his eyes from the screen which displayed that day's crop of Bugle Online 'Lovelies', Benedict began to read. He learnt about irrigation schemes, poaching in the Wali desert, game conservation and residual tribal differences. After a time he began to wonder how these researches were likely to benefit his colour story the following day. But from an early age the younger son of Sir Cumming Brewster had had an insatiable appetite for acquiring knowledge, and quite soon he was gripped by the undeniably serious challenges facing the desert paradise that went under the name of Kangala.

It was lunchtime. As Benedict was about to put down his book, Sam was sitting in the Half Moon, an uncharming pub approximately equidistant between Pepper House and the Saraceno. He had briefly popped into the office to advertise his presence, and to pick up his post and a couple of newspapers. Among the usual readers' letters, which he dropped unread into the bin, there was a handwritten note that caused his heart to jump.

Taking a slurp from his second double gin and tonic, Sam looked at the letter again in the hope he might be able to tease out some extra meaning from its few words. It was unsigned but there was no doubting its authorship. The note read: *Why haven't you rung me?*

Sam refolded the letter, and drained his glass. The woman was obviously mad. Only three days had passed since she had pressed her number into his hand. This was how the rich behaved, he reflected. They couldn't understand not instantly getting their own way.

He ordered another gin and tonic and tried to think. The internal voice that had prudently advised him the previous morning had taken leave of absence to be replaced by an altogether less responsible colleague accustomed to receiving a fair hearing after the third drink. What in heaven's name was he up to? Caroline Entwistle was a woman in a million. She had evidently developed a passion for him. Yes, she might be a shade loopy – better watch out a bit further down the track – but it would be idiotic to look a gift horse in the mouth.

The sheer rashness of this advice brought the first voice back from its slumbers. What was he thinking of? Hadn't he been warned of the dreadful retaliation that would be unleashed on him by Sir Edwin Entwistle when he inevitably found out?

Former carpet billionaires do not usually take kindly to being cuckolded, especially by their employees. The retribution would be dreadful. Besides – and at this point the first voice became almost exultant – *you can't ring Caroline Entwistle because you haven't got her number.*

Sam started. It was true. His cleaning woman had been yesterday afternoon. She would have emptied the wastepaper basket. He couldn't telephone Caroline even if he wanted to. Her mobile number would be known to only a few people, and ace reporter though he was he couldn't get it without arousing suspicions. Nor could he ring her at her house without risking talking to Sir Edwin. The realisation that he had no way of safely contacting her induced in him a feeling partly of sweet regret, and partly of relief.

He looked at his watch. Christ! It was half past one. The trainee would have been waiting at the Saraceno for half an hour.

Benedict, who had eaten six breadsticks and two bread rolls, drunk a bottle of water and read the menu from top to bottom three times, saw an inquisitive-looking man with tousled hair who was wearing a brown corduroy jacket approach his table. Though he felt slightly resentful at being kept waiting for thirty-five minutes, he struggled to his feet, sending a wine glass flying, and put out a hand.

'Benedict Brewster,' he announced, rightly thinking that Sam might have forgotten his name.

Sam looked at the long extended limb for a few seconds before clasping Benedict's hand.

'Sorry I'm late,' he said. He turned to the maître d' who had ushered him in. 'Marco, give us a bottle of your finest red. We'll order straightaway.'

The *Bugle*'s once legendary chief reporter had given no thought whatsoever to this lunch. He did not like the idea of trainee journalists. He had only exceeded Doodle's suggestion of a light lunch in a pub because talking to such a person over a sandwich and a pint of beer would have been more irksome than doing so over a bottle or two of Barolo, and Marco's famous saltimbocca.

Sam looked at the trainee and to his surprise felt a pang of compassion. Benedict was a handsome boy, with a long pale face and crinkly black hair. He was fiddling nervously with his breadsticks, making a mess on his side of the table-cloth while looking downwards, as though shy of meeting Sam's eyes. Sam could see at once that Benedict was a public school type. It didn't worry him. He took people as they came.

They ordered, and he sloshed some wine into Benedict's glass, and some into his own.

'So how's the *Bugle* treating you, Ben?'

'Fine, thank you, Mr Blunt.'

'Call me Sam. Met Doodle?'

'Yes.'

'And Yapp?'

'Yes.'

'Take my advice. Treat him as you would a Staffordshire bull terrier with a short fuse. He's lethal. Good journalist, though.'

'He did seem rather acerbic,' agreed Benedict.

Sam poured some more wine into his glass and Benedict's.

'Has he asked you to do anything?'

'A colour story about the visit of the President of Kangala.'

'You don't say?' Sam did not seem very interested.

'Yes. I've been reading up about the country. It seems to be an extraordinary place.'

'Is that really necessary? You're writing an article, not a book.'

Benedict rightly took this as a rebuke and said nothing. The food arrived, and Sam attacked his saltimbocca as though he hadn't eaten for twenty-four hours, which he hadn't. For the best part of ten minutes he said nothing to Benedict as he munched away, though he replenished both their glasses whenever the wine fell below the halfway mark, and ordered another bottle of Barolo from Marco.

'That was good,' declared Sam when he had finished wiping his plate with a bread roll.

He felt much better disposed towards the world than he had in the Half Moon. For the moment the problem of Caroline Entwistle had receded. The gin and tonics and more than half a bottle of wine had suffused him with a feeling that life was not so bad after all. He observed the young man opposite him with something like fondness. He didn't seem a bad sort.

'I suppose you went to Eton,' said Sam.

'I did, as a matter of fact.'

'There's a strange thing about old Etonians,' said Sam, taking another gulp of wine. 'I've learnt never to trust one of them who doesn't have any money.'

'Really?'

'Yes. I reckon the poorer ones spend their lives trying to grab what they've seen the rich ones have.'

'Maybe,' said Benedict. This was a novel train of thought. His mind felt fuzzy after the wine. 'What about George Orwell?'

'There are always one or two exceptions,' conceded Sam, who was not a great expert on the writer. 'But I stick by my point. Look at that MP Terence Glasswell. He went to Eton. Dazzled by wealth. Always trying to hobnob with the aristocracy. Get his hands on what he hasn't got.'

Benedict mumbled that he thought his father knew Glasswell slightly.

'Would you say you were a poor or a rich Etonian?' asked Sam.

The young man was not offended by the question. He pondered it carefully. It was true his father was the owner of a Regency country house and five thousand acres of fine Lincolnshire land. That presumably made him rich. On the other hand, he himself lived in a one-room rented studio flat in Hackney. That surely made him poor.

'I don't know,' he replied. 'I suppose I could be both.'

Sam gave a little laugh, as though to convey that he thought Benedict was ducking the question, and poured himself another glass of wine.

'You haven't asked me about my own educational background.'

'No,' agreed Benedict.

'Willesden Comprehensive. Left school at sixteen. One O level in religious studies.'

'Ah,' said Benedict, who was quite a churchy young man, having been brought up as an Anglo-Catholic. His mother was very religious.

'Then I became a messenger on the *Ealing Times*. Made tea and delivered the post. Before you'd know it, I was covering cases in the local magistrates' court.'

'That must have been interesting.'

Benedict glanced surreptitiously at his watch. It was quarter past three. He was happy to stay here all afternoon – Sam seemed a very pleasant man – but he was worried about what Trevor Yapp would say. He also felt the pull of *Desert Paradise*.

'Mr Blunt, I think I should be going. Could you tell me how much I owe you?'

'Owe me?' Sam squinted at Benedict. 'Don't be daft. Doodle's paying.'

Benedict, who had no idea about expenses, said that was very generous of him.

'Not actually Doodle. Sir Edwin Entwistle, in fact. I'll describe you as a "top political contact" as I've somewhat exceeded my brief.'

'But—' Benedict was about to say that he would rather pay his half than involve Sam in any kind of deception, but thought better of it.

With repeated thanks he left Sam to settle the bill and finish the second bottle of Barolo, knocking a couple of spoons off the table as he left.

The chief reporter of the *Daily Bugle* did not have a great many responsibilities that afternoon. Later he would pop into Pepper House to do a three-hundred-word rewrite of an agency story about the results of the Portuguese election, which would almost certainly not make the paper even in an abbreviated form.

Sam ordered another glass of wine from Marco, and began to read Steve Rutt's Celebrity Diary in the *Daily Dazzle*. It did not engage his mind. He found himself thinking of Caroline Entwistle and, for some reason, Trevor Yapp. Then the rather sweet face of Benedict floated into his mind. Nice boy. Too nice. Perhaps he should have offered him a word of advice about that colour story. One thing was crystal clear, though. Benedict Brewster would never make a journalist.

Chapter Six

Trevor Yapp threw down two pieces of paper on Eric Doodle's desk with a look of triumph.

'Read that,' he suggested.

'What is it?' asked Doodle.

'It's Benedict Brewster's colour piece. He's got a screw loose.'

'I see.'

The editor of the *Daily Bugle* did not like to hear the younger son of Sir Cumming Brewster described in such a way but he was increasingly wary of Yapp. He had received good intelligence that he had recently been spotted lunching at the Fig Leaf with Sir Edwin Entwistle. Of course there was not necessarily any harm in that, but Sir Edwin's failure to notify him that he had been hobnobbing with his deputy had set alarm bells ringing.

Doodle began to read Benedict's article as Yapp stood in front of his desk.

Surely the most colourful event of the diplomatic year took place in London yesterday. His Incomparable Excellency Moses Ovambo, President of Kangala, paid an official visit to the capital. As he was driven in his carriage down Birdcage Walk, it was noticeable that his three-piece suit was in a shade redolent of the apricot sands of his native Kangala. By his side was his wife, Her Magnificence Stella Ovambo, arrayed in a dress of peacock blue decorated with white swirls. The procession made its way into Parliament Square, sweeping imperiously through the black, white and orange request of a zebra crossing. It passed a modest crowd in which there were a surprising number of red hats – every sort of red from brick to scarlet to cherry. As the cavalcade moved into Whitehall towards the white-grey Portland stone of the Banqueting House, there was a kerfuffle. An angry knot of protesters (waving the green and ochre banners belonging to the Movement to Free Kangala from Oppression) stepped into the road. But they were quickly intercepted by police, who took some of them away in a white van with blue and orange markings.

His Incomparable Excellency Moses then delivered a speech at the Banqueting House to which journalists unfortunately were not invited. The ceiling of the hall is possibly the most beautiful in the country, featuring paintings by Peter Paul Rubens. As he spoke, it is not unlikely that the President stole an upward glance at James I in a vermilion robe being crowned by a number of pink-cheeked blond cherubs amid the pale cerulean heavens. Perhaps he also considered the gloomy steps of Charles I (believed by some historians to have been wearing a blue knitted silk waistcoat) as he was led from the Banqueting House sporting a silver-grey beard, on his way to his untimely execution . . .

Splash!

The editor of the *Daily Bugle* was forced to suppress a smile as he felt Yapp's eyes boring into him.

'I see what you mean. The silly boy has obviously got the wrong end of the stick.'

'Wrong end of the stick!' sneered Yapp. 'He should be locked up. He's a halfwit!'

'That's going a bit far. He's young, after all. I don't suppose anyone bothered to explain to him what a colour story is?'

'I can't have idiots like this in my newsroom. I can't believe you gave him a job.'

Yapp had placed the fingers of his right hand on Doodle's desk, and was leaning over it menacingly.

'What do you suggest?' asked Doodle.

'Get rid of him!'

'Oh, I don't think we should do that.' Doodle could see Sir Cumming's disappointed face, and imagine the inevitable withdrawal of invitations to countless shooting weekends.

'Think what would happen if the *Chronicle*'s diarist got hold of this! We'd be a fucking laughing stock!'

Doodle conceded that might be the case.

'And imagine if Sir Edwin found out,' Yapp continued. 'Of course, I'd never tell him, but there are people in the newsroom who know, and I can't stop them blabbing.'

'That's true,' Doodle replied.

Yapp had a point. It wouldn't look good if it were discovered that he had offered a job – well, a paid internship – to the wholly unqualified son of Sir Cumming Brewster in the hope of having favours returned. It might be better to be rid of him now before there was further trouble.

And yet Eric Doodle was not a bad person and he did not think solely of protecting his own skin. He could not bring himself to cast out this pleasing and innocent young man after only a few days. It would be an offence against natural justice.

Even Daphne Doodle, though an unflagging critic of most aspects of her husband's behaviour, would concede that he had a quick and nimble mind. An idea entered it now that was weighed, sifted and approved in a matter of seconds.

It was not ideal, of course. In normal circumstances he would not have wanted to send the younger son of Sir Cumming Brewster to the dungeon – the airless basement of Pepper House where young men and women toiled ceaselessly to produce the online version of the *Daily Bugle*, presided over by the Mephistophelean figure of Trevor Yapp, who in these subterranean climes reigned unchallenged. It was not what he wished for Benedict – or anyone, come to that – but it was also perfectly true that most of the 'galley slaves', as they were light-heartedly described in the newsroom, also had Firsts from one of the top universities, and some of them eventually emerged into the light of day to live normal lives.

'What about the dungeon, Trevor?' asked Doodle in his sweetest tones.

Yapp hesitated. It went without saying that Benedict was wholly unsuited to the dungeon. On the other hand, he had taken an immediate dislike to the young man, and could see the advantages of making his life there as miserable as possible.

'I'm not sure,' said Yapp. 'He's not remotely qualified.'

'That may be true,' countered Doodle, in a firmer voice now that he thought he might be getting his way. 'But I think anyone deserves a second chance.'

Splash!

'All right,' said Yapp. 'I'll tell him.'

'No, let me,' said Doodle. 'Better that way, I think. I know the boy.'

Benedict was admiring the contours of one of the half-naked C-list celebrities who dominated the *Bugle*'s website, while simultaneously wondering what had happened to his colour piece about the President of Kangala, when the phone rang. It was Dora. She was a kind girl, and she knew that Trevor Yapp's visit had signified bad news for some unfortunate soul.

'The editor would like to see you,' she informed him gently.

Doodle had tried to escape from the unpleasantness of his encounter with Trevor Yapp by snatching a few precious moments with the latest weekly edition of *Rural Retreats*. He had found a very pretty half-timbered Elizabethan manor house with ten acres. The trouble was that it was in Somerset. That county was not on his official blacklist but nor was it one of the nine or ten wholly approved counties. Doodle would have freely admitted that his reasons for entertaining reservations about Somerset were questionable. He knew its countryside was renowned for its beauty but he had a prejudice against the county as a result of five unhappy years spent there at prep school under a sadistic headmaster. He sighed. How much easier life would be if one were not beset by disagreeable memories.

'Eric?'

Doodle looked up and saw Dora with Benedict by her side, towering above her.

'Ah, thank you, Dora dear. Sit down, my boy. Do sit down.'

Benedict sat down.

'Now – that colour piece. Very entertaining in its way, even quite well done, but a bit of a mess-up, to be frank.'

Benedict looked mystified.

'You see, "colour piece" doesn't mean what you seem to think it does. It's about being descriptive, summoning up the moment, not referring to every colour in the rainbow.'

'Oh,' said Benedict.

'An understandable mistake, in its way, I suppose, though undeniably a bit unusual. Trevor Yapp is a bit upset about the whole affair.'

'I'm sorry. How stupid of me.'

'No need for sackcloth and ashes, but he runs news these days, and I have to listen to what he says.'

'So I'm sacked?'

'Good God, no! No, but he thinks – and I think – that there's no point in leaving you to flounder in the newsroom even if Sam Blunt is supposed to be keeping an eye on you. Have you met him, by the way?'

'Yes, I have. He's a nice man.'

'I wouldn't say that precisely, though he may have a good enough heart. Anyway, Trevor and I think you might benefit from a spell on Bugle Online.'

'Oh, I should like that.' Benedict had warm feelings towards the website having become a convert to its curvaceous celebrities.

'Splendid. It may be a bit hot and crowded down there, I should warn you, but you'll find plenty of agreeable and clever young people, I'm sure. Online is the future, after all.'

In fact, Doodle privately abhorred Bugle Online, though he seldom looked at it, because of its obsession with the sexual antics of meretricious celebrities. It reminded him of the worst aspects of the *Daily Dazzle*. The thought that what it represented might be the future of popular journalism depressed him. But he dared not share his misgivings with Sir Edwin Entwistle or Trevor Yapp.

Half an hour later Dora escorted Benedict to the dungeon. As soon she opened the door Benedict felt a gust of warm air which carried a powerful scent of human bodies. He saw a huge room down which ran rows of desks. Numberless people, all of them apparently young, were crammed along each row, peering into computers. He fancied he could hear the distant sound of bells.

Well disposed though he was in principle to Bugle Online, Benedict gulped. He glanced at Dora. The look on her face – half apologetic, half apprehensive – reminded him of his darling mother when she had dropped him off, aged eight, on his first day at boarding school.

'I'd better find you a seat,' said Dora.

She led him halfway down one of the rows where there was an empty space. Benedict noticed a young man to his left and a young woman to his right. Neither of them looked up. He was sure now that he could hear the sound of ringing bells.

'Sit down,' advised Dora. 'I expect Trevor Yapp will be here in a moment. Or Andy Dodd.'

'Who's he?'

Dora pulled a face. 'He's the news editor of Bugle Online.'

As Benedict sat down, Dora gave him a sympathetic look which conveyed that he was now on his own, and left.

He sat there for several minutes wondering what to do. His computer screen was turned off and, although he pressed several buttons, it remained stubbornly dead. Benedict considered for a moment whether he should get out his copy of *Desert Paradise* from the plastic bag he had with him. He still had the last two chapters to finish, and although less kindly disposed towards Kangala than he had been before his idiotic mistake, he felt he should complete what he had started. But an inner voice warned him that the dungeon was not a place for reading books.

Benedict looked over a little partition at the young woman on his right. Her head was no more than three feet from his, although because her eyes were fixed on the computer screen in front of her he could not see her face. She had long thick auburn hair that fell in ringlets on to her shoulders.

As he was looking at her, the woman turned to him, and he saw her face. She had pale green eyes. Her beautiful lips moved. It was the doomed, calm smile of a pre-Raphaelite heroine about to be devoured by dragons. It stirred in Benedict's soul deep feelings of chivalry and protectiveness.

'Welcome to Hell,' she said.

Chapter Seven

The precise whereabouts of Lady Evelyn Wherewill's house has long been a matter of some dispute. Lady Evelyn herself firmly maintains that her simple abode lies comfortably within the boundaries of Chelsea, and argues that it was only the intransigence of a narrow-minded bureaucrat that deprived her of the right to a Kensington and Chelsea parking permit. Other knowledgeable authorities, including her friend Caroline Entwistle, contend privately that the house is firmly situated in Fulham. They point out that to get there one has to travel what seems like several miles down the King's Road before veering off in the direction of the river.

It is a matter that will probably never be definitively settled because those like Caroline who know that Lady Evelyn lives in Fulham are unprepared to resort to scientific proof. They indulge Lady Evelyn's fantasy, while sometimes in their own much grander homes making fun of her. There is a general feeling that she should be allowed to believe she is a denizen of Chelsea. Her relative penury and the tight-fistedness of her brother the earl are well known. It would be a piece of unkindness to destroy her illusions.

Whether Lady Evelyn's two-storey terraced house is in Chelsea or Fulham, there is no doubting that its proximity to the capital's great artery has not been without its drawbacks. Guests at her lunch parties have occasionally noticed a whiff of sewage as they arrive. What they do not know, and have certainly never been told, is that when the sewers become too full human detritus is sometimes pumped into the Thames, yards from where Lady Evelyn Wherewill lives. On one never-to-be-forgotten occasion after torrential rain, when some functionary failed to pull a lever, or pulled one too soon, sewage intended for the river banked up and finally burst through the floor of Lady Evelyn's dining room.

It was in this same small room that the hostess was now putting the finishing touches to her *placement*. She always gave much thought to such matters. Proper *placement* was the essence of a successful salon, and Lady Evelyn liked to think that her regular lunches, though never distinguished by fine wine or sumptuous fare, had conferred on her the status of London's leading society hostess.

She had been an acknowledged beauty in her youth. Experts could not agree about her age. Some said she was not yet sixty, others that she had already passed that landmark. All parties accepted she was still a striking woman. Lady Evelyn paid proper attention to her appearance, repairing and stitching old clothes, and judiciously buying new ones. Today she wore a black suit edged with crimson ribbon which proclaimed that it came from Forrestière. She had bought it for a song at a second-hand clothes shop in the country, and sewn on the ribbon herself.

There were six guests. She would put herself at one end of the oblong Sheraton table, and the Home Secretary at the other. The Bishop of Middlesex should go on her right. That was only fitting in view of his media notoriety and his position as the Church of England's leading evangelical, which, according to rumour, might soon be consolidated by an Archbishopric.

Her brow furrowed as she tried to work out where her other guests should sit. Madame Po could go on the Home Secretary's left and on the bishop's right. Though not a worshipper at Middlesex Cathedral, she had given generously to charitable causes championed by Bishop Bob. Unfortunately that meant Lady Evelyn would have Adam Pride on her left. The thought of the pompous columnist deepened the lines on her forehead. In an ideal world she would have invited clever Timothy Brown of the more upmarket *Chronicle*, but at a previous lunch he had demonstrated a disagreeable habit of picking his ears and then absentmindedly popping the findings in his mouth. Pride at least knew the rudiments of good behaviour.

That left Caroline and Sam Blunt. When Caroline had telephoned her a week ago to ask whether Sam might be invited to the lunch, she had at first put up some resistance. It wasn't that she bore a grudge against him as a result of his revelations about her unfortunate liaison with Terence Glasswell. She realised he was only doing his job, and in any case preferred to be on good terms with her enemies. Her reasoning was that she had already invited one *Bugle* journalist in the shape of Adam Pride and it would be an offence against the conventions of a properly run salon to invite two.

But Caroline had persisted, saying she had a piece of intelligence from Sir Edwin which she wished to transmit to the *Bugle*'s chief reporter, and this could be most delicately done at lunch. This made no sense to Lady Evelyn, who wondered why the newspaper proprietor could not simply summon Sam Blunt and pass on the information himself, but she finally acquiesced, not wishing to offend her rich and powerful friend. The lunch would doubtless be ruined but there was nothing that could be done about it. Caroline's true motives she did not suspect. She knew her friend had intermittent affairs, and assumed Sir Edwin did not supply all that might have been hoped for in that department, but it did not occur to her that anyone could find an impecunious tabloid reporter attractive.

The question now was whether to put this creature between Caroline and Adam Pride, which would make a nasty cluster of *Bugle* people but enable the wife of the proprietor to confide in him, or have Sam sit between the Bishop of Middlesex and Madame Po, which would disrupt a natural pairing. She wondered what they would make of such a man. What a stew Caroline had landed her in.

As Lady Evelyn was straightening knives and grappling with these difficulties, Adam Pride was heaving himself into a waiting taxi outside Pepper House. Madame Po, who was never late, was already sitting back in her padded limousine as it swept her from her great mansion in Kensington. Caroline was applying some final touches to her make-up in her boudoir in Eaton Place. The Home Secretary was delivering some parting words to his special adviser in his surgically clean office. Bishop Bob was sitting on the upper deck of a number eleven bus, which had ground to a halt in a traffic jam on the King's Road. The dapper bishop was wearing a collar and tie and suit that offered no hint of his episcopal rank. He had been putting the world straight by tweeting his latest reflections about the Middle East peace process, and was now reading an article by Timothy Brown in the *Chronicle* which weighed the merits of the various contenders for the Archbishopric of Canterbury.

Sam was finishing his third double gin and tonic at the Half Moon. He was no longer preoccupied with the problem of Caroline. He had not thought about her for a week. A new, and far more disturbing, worry had just been introduced by Trevor Yapp.

That morning Yapp had summoned him to tell him that his services were no longer required at the *Daily Bugle*.

'There's another round of cuts. We're going to have to get rid of you.'

'Why me? I've been here twenty years.'

'You're paid twice as much as the young reporters, who don't get pissed on the job. And you've had fewer words published in the paper than anyone else over the past six months.'

This was not a point Sam could deny.

'We'll expect you to work out your three months' notice. Do me a favour and fucking pull your finger out before you go.'

Sam never pleaded. He could have said that this was no way for the *Bugle* to treat a reporter who had risked his life in the course of duty – being shot at on several occasions, and once being lowered from a helicopter into a crocodile-infested swamp. No less dangerously, he had interviewed the gang leader 'Nipper' Richards in his Malaga house on the subject of the unaccountable disappearance of his business associate 'Shifty' Perkins, whose partner, glamour model Suzy Wattle, Nipper had subsequently married.

Sam might have asked to speak to a higher authority, namely Eric Doodle. He should have questioned Yapp about the redundancy terms.

As it was, he simply got up and walked out. It was only when he was almost out of Yapp's office that he turned around and spoke.

'Oh, Trevor, I've been meaning to say this for a while now,' he said. 'You're a complete and utter cunt.'

With that encomium he departed.

Sam did not regret these words. Nor was he sorry he hadn't tried to argue Yapp around. You can't work for cunts who don't want you.

But as he sat in the Half Moon nursing his fourth gin and tonic there was no denying he was in a pickle. He had an interest-only mortgage covering about 95 per cent of the value of his flat in Barons Court. When he had divorced his wife three years earlier he had given her everything and started again. Since then, being by nature extravagant with his own money as well as with Sir Edwin Entwistle's, he had saved nothing, and was to all intents and purposes broke.

What could he do? He couldn't imagine being offered a job on the *Daily Dazzle*, and the thought of working on the prim, sanctimonious *Chronicle*, even if they would have him, was not alluring. Perhaps, God forbid, he'd be forced to seek a job in PR, working for someone like Ambrose Treadle. At least he had three months' notice, which would give him time to ask around while still employed.

Sam had forgotten about the lunch at Lady Evelyn's. When he had received a handwritten note from her a week previously, he had puzzled over it. He had never been asked to a society lunch before, and it was baffling that the invitation should have come from a woman whom he had so memorably 'turned over'. Sam had stuffed the letter in a pocket and put it out of his mind.

For almost half an hour the guests sat with knees hunched in Lady Evelyn's tiny sitting room waiting for Sam. Adam Pride was unceasing in his speculations that the chief reporter of the *Bugle*, being notoriously unreliable, was probably propping up the bar of a hostelry. The columnist's rich, fruity voice suggested that his vocal cords had been marinated in a superior make of furniture polish. Lady Evelyn was reluctant to accept his declamations. It was only when Madame Po's stomach began to rumble and the Home Secretary squinted at his watch, that London's foremost hostess decided that decamping to the dining room could no longer be respectably delayed.

Caroline, however, was unwilling to see her stratagems undone. As the other guests were queuing to get into the next room, she suggested *sotto voce* to Lady Evelyn that she might ring the *Bugle* to remind Sam of his missed lunch.

Lady Evelyn was shocked. She had never in her life chased a guest who had not turned up, believing it would be an affront to good manners to do so. Not for the first time, she reflected negatively upon her friend's social origins.

Nonetheless, Caroline persisted. Realising that persuading Lady Evelyn might be a protracted business, she seized the fleshy arm of Adam Pride as he was about to follow Bishop Bob into the dining room, and whispered into a large ear.

'Adam, Lady Evelyn would like you to ring the *Bugle* and get a message to Sam Blunt in case he has forgotten.'

The columnist found himself in a quandary. At the best of times he did not like assuming a servile role, and it was

galling to be asked to do so where Sam Blunt was concerned.
On the other hand, he could hardly deny Lady Evelyn's wish,
whose importance had been amplified by being transmitted
by the wife of the proprietor of his newspaper.

Caroline divined his feelings and capitalised on his hesi-
tation.

'Better use your mobile outside,' she suggested, demon-
strating surprising strength as she gave Pride a shove that
propelled him several feet in the direction of the front door.

So it was that, as Sam was beginning his eighth gin and
tonic in the Half Moon, his mobile rang. In answering it, he
managed to spill the entire contents of his glass on his crotch.
He heard Dora's welcome voice.

'Sam, what are you up to?'

'Wishing I was lying in bed with my arms around you.'

Dora giggled. 'You're meant to be having lunch at Lady
Evelyn Wherewill's.'

'Oh, shit.' Sam looked at his watch. It was quarter to two.
'Bit late now, isn't it?'

'No, Sam, it isn't. Adam Pride says everyone is waiting for
you. Including the Home Secretary.'

'Adam Pride?' Sam's head began to spin. 'What the hell is
he doing there?'

'He just is. Don't ask questions. Jump into a cab.'

An empty place at an otherwise full dining table inevitably
has a disconcerting effect. Adam Pride had told a flummoxed
Lady Evelyn that he had spoken to the editor's secretary.
In the circumstances she thought it best to leave things as
they were.

Though no one other than Caroline was remotely disconcerted by Sam's absence, a sense of gloom had overcome

the guests sitting around the slightly bowed table, a cast-off of Lady Evelyn's brother, and only reproduction Sheraton notwithstanding his assurances. Bishop Bob was especially uncommunicative. No one realised his spirits had been cast down by the article in the *Chronicle*, which rated his chances of being elevated to Canterbury below those of the Bishops of Bournemouth and Halifax. Timothy Brown suggested that even in the modern Church of England the most senior primate should have some spiritual qualities. It was not calling out for a sleek media bishop devoted to writing his blog and showering the world with his Twitter effusions.

Adam Pride interrogated the Home Secretary about the latest prison riot in the lofty tones of an eighteenth-century aristocrat cross-examining a farm labourer. The Home Secretary was anxious to blame the prison warders' union for what had happened.

Madame Po was asked by Lady Evelyn where her industrious husband was at that moment. She replied that he was attending to some business interests in Africa.

Caroline Entwistle ventured the opinion that, with unemployment still high, it was a pity the Government did not consider applying tax relief to employing domestic servants, since that would be one way of helping to get people off the dole. Reliable servants, she could attest, were increasingly hard to come by. There were no strong takers for her point of view.

Lady Evelyn remarked to Madame Po that when she had recently stayed with her brother the earl at Hastings Hall she had noticed a simply divine Qing vase which one of her ancestors had picked up out East, delicately omitting to mention that this particular gentleman, father of the 1st Earl, had plundered and rogered his way around China during the Second Opium War, helping himself to whatever he pleased. She expressed the hope that Madame Po might give her opinion on the vase if ever she and Mr Po were able to visit Hastings Hall.

Madame Po, who understood perfectly well that she was being invited to buy the vase for an enormous sum of money, replied that she would be happy to offer her inexpert view.

Then the front door bell rang. Lady Evelyn was in the throes of distributing pudding – cheese flans that had every appearance of having emanated from Patisserie Balzac though they hailed from Wedderburn's supermarket – and looked imploringly at the bishop. Though judged unsuitable for the See of Canterbury by the *Chronicle*, he was ready to do his Christian duty.

The distance to the front door and back was no more than thirty feet, but the great ecclesiastic took unaccountably long. After a while the sound of voices could be heard in the sitting room, and Lady Evelyn thought she could make out the soothing tones of the bishop and the more agitated sounds of a stranger. She wondered in alarm whether a tramp had somehow gained entrance, and was holding the prelate captive.

But before she had time to go and investigate, the door opened and the bishop walked in, wearing a self-satisfied expression that would have been familiar to worshippers at Middlesex Cathedral. The figure of Sam swayed behind him, and the bishop stepped to one side, as though inviting the company to take a good look at a sinner. Lady Evelyn turned her head so as to get a complete view of him. Sam was plainly in an advanced state of drunkenness.

Splash!

Lady Evelyn's expression was oddly enigmatic. Outrage was written all over Adam Pride's features, incredulity on those of the Home Secretary. Not a muscle moved in Madame Po's face. Caroline regarded Sam with horror, touched by something like compassion.

Sam tottered, and put his hand on Lady Evelyn's table to steady himself, knocking over a wine glass.

'Sorry I'm a bit late,' he announced. 'Been working. That arsehole Yapp only went and sacked me.'

The assembled company could not fail to notice a large wet patch on the front of Sam's trousers. Adam Pride was in no doubt as to its cause. The columnist rose furiously to his feet.

'This is too much,' he boomed. 'You're a disgrace to the *Daily Bugle*. I must ask you to leave Lady Wherewill's house immediately.'

Sam narrowed his eyes and peered at Pride as though struggling to recognise him.

'Why, if it isn't old Pompous Pants! I bet you've been boring these nice ladies and gentlemen.'

Sam looked down at the table, and saw a plate of cheese flans which Lady Evelyn had been in the process of serving to her guests. He picked one up as though to examine it. Madame Po wondered for a moment if he was about to take a bite out of it, but instead he drew back his arm and hurled the cheese flan in the direction of Adam Pride.

If Sam had been even half sober he could not have missed so large a target at such close range. Pride was not a nimble man, and made no attempt to duck when he saw the flan flying across the table. Fortunately for him, Sam's aim was very wide. The missile flew a full yard to his left, and struck the sitting figure of the Home Secretary smack on the face. Cheese began to trickle down the ministerial chin.

The effect of this act of hooliganism was to galvanise Pride. He lunged forward as though to grab the miscreant, in the process squashing Caroline against the wall. Sam had not noticed that his admirer was present.

Bishop Bob, still standing close to Sam, was also energised by the Home Secretary's misfortune. He believed the time had come to effect a citizen's arrest. Sam sensed his plan, and picked up a second cheese flan with the thought of deploying it in some way to ward off the interfering prelate.

'Stop it!'

Caroline's instruction carried authority. Adam Pride ceased in his attempts to squeeze his body between the reproduction Sheraton table and the proprietor's wife in order to put his hands around Sam's neck. Bishop Bob became rooted to the spot. The room fell silent.

'Leave this to me. I'll see he gets home,' Caroline announced.

Chapter Eight

Within half an hour of Sam's spectacular entrance into Lady
Evelyn's dining room, the entire newsroom of the *Bugle* was
aware of what had happened, and a slightly bowdlerised
account had even reached the dungeon. Adam Pride had
wasted no time in telling Trevor Yapp who in turn informed
Eric Doodle. Censure and sorrow struggled in the editor's
mind. He never liked to hear of his journalists misbehaving,
but on the other hand he had a certain guarded fondness for
Sam, and drew no joy from his humiliation. Only sorrow
took hold of Dora.

Pride had a field day. He regaled members at his club that
evening, offering his audience an impersonation of the
Home Secretary's look of astonishment in the millisecond
before the cheese flan hit him in the face. His own role in
the affair was made to sound more heroic than it was.
In Pride's version he had the drunken reporter in an armlock.

Sam was in his way a well-known journalist, more feared
than liked, and it was not long before the story was being
relayed by a dozen voices, gaining ornamentation as it spread
through the capital, before ending up in the diary of an

57

exultant *Chronicle*. Some ungenerous souls were disposed to opine that it offered proof that Lady Evelyn Wherewill's salon had seen finer days.

Sir Edwin Entwistle enjoyed a cuttings service arranged for him by his PR adviser, Ambrose Treadle. Sitting in his Mayfair offices, the tycoon read the item from the *Chronicle*, which some minion of Treadle's had ringed with a red pen to attract his attention. Sir Edwin immediately picked up the telephone to speak to Eric Doodle.

The editor's spirits happened to be unusually low. Doodle had just received a cheery call from Sir Cumming Brewster, who was naturally eager to hear about the progress of Benedict, from whom he had not heard for several weeks. The editor had been unable to bring himself to tell the baronet that his younger son had been banished to the dungeon on a charge of half-wittedness. He reasoned that there was no point in disconcerting the father, though he had to concede to himself that he was partly swayed by self-interest. The longed-for shooting invitation might vanish if Sir Cumming believed his boy had been harshly treated. Doodle had left the big-hearted landowner with the impression that all was as well as it could be. When he had put down the phone he felt a stab of guilt, which he attempted to neutralise by picking up the latest issue of *Rural Retreats*.

Doodle was imagining himself in the billiard room of a Victorian mansion in Northamptonshire when he heard Dora's voice informing him that Sir Edwin Entwistle was waiting on the line.

'Eric?'

Perhaps he would have a stag's head above the fireplace. Did he even like stags' heads?

Splash!

'Are you there, Eric?'

'Yes, Sir Edwin. I'm here.'

'What's this I hear about your chief reporter Sam Blunt?'

'Ah. I imagine you're referring to that unfortunate incident.'

'You can say that again. Pissed all over himself in front of the Home Secretary and Madame Po Chun.'

'Not precisely, Sir Edwin. I'm told he had an accident in the pub, and spilt his drink over his trousers.'

'That's not what Adam Pride says.'

'I fear Adam is mistaken. I have spoken with Sam, and I believe his account.'

'It makes no difference either way. The *Daily Bugle* is a laughing stock. For God's sake, it's a fucking family newspaper. What are our readers supposed to think? You'll have to get rid of him.'

'Well, the fact is that he had already been given his notice by Trevor Yapp. That may have been responsible for his unusual behaviour. I think it might be better, in the circumstances, to let him serve out his time. He has been working for this newspaper for twenty years, after all. '

'You always were too bloody soft. I want him out now.'

Doodle looked at the open copy of *Rural Retreats* lying in front of him. Six acres. Two loose boxes. A small cottage in the grounds. The insane thought entered his mind that Daphne might prefer to live in the cottage by herself, leaving the big house for him.

'If you say so, Sir Edwin. I'll speak to him.'

'And I don't want him getting any money. Throwing pies at the Home Secretary is a sackable offence.'

'I think he may have statutory rights.'

'Bugger that,' declared the proprietor of the *Daily Bugle*. 'Just get rid of him.'

When Sir Edwin Entwistle arrived home at Eaton Place that evening he went straight up to the huge gilded bedroom he shared with Caroline. The *Chronicle*'s diarist had listed Lady Evelyn's other guests – including his wife. He was anxious to hear her account of what had happened. The puzzle was that she had not told him she had been present at so scandalous a lunch.

Caroline was lying naked on the vast acreage of their bed with a slice of cucumber on each eye and a wax plug in each ear. The cucumber had been recommended by her beautician as a way of reducing incipient puffiness around her eyes; the wax plugs were intended to keep out the distant murmur of traffic in the King's Road. Without eyes to see or ears to hear, Caroline was unaware of the approach of her husband, who gave her right nipple a playful tweak. She screamed.

Sir Edwin instructed her to be calm, and sat down on the bed as Caroline removed her earplugs. He produced his copy of the *Chronicle*, and invited her to read an item in its diary.

'I didn't realise you'd been at Lady Evelyn's. Why didn't you tell me?'

Though she was still recovering from the shock of the rude intrusion, Caroline kept her wits.

'I must have thought it too boring. He is such a seedy journalist. I didn't think you'd be interested.'

'Not interested? He only happens to work for me.'

'Perhaps I should have mentioned it.' Caroline gave her husband's left forearm an affectionate rub, and smiled at him. 'I imagined you had more important things on your plate.'

Sir Edwin was slightly mollified. 'Well, I've sacked him anyhow.'

'Sacked him?'

'Yes. I can't have my employees behaving like that in front of bishops and Cabinet ministers. I don't expect your friend Evelyn was over the moon about it all. And what do you suppose Madame Po told her husband? The man's no longer even a functioning journalist. He's finished.'

Caroline bit her lip. This was not the moment to mount a defence of the man with whom she intended to have an affair. It might make her husband suspicious. She gave his arm another rub.

When he had left she lay down again, and put back the cucumber slices over her eyes. She thought of Sam, of his sweetness when he was drunk, and of his touching gratitude when she had left him at his flat.

After she left her friend's house with Sam she had wondered whether her haste in helping him might have given her away. But who could have guessed that her heart was touched by this unhappy journalist? They would have thought, Evelyn included, that she was discharging her seigniorial duties as the wife of the proprietor of the *Daily Bugle*.

Sam had gone to sleep in her car. When they got to Barons Court he gave Caroline and her driver mumbled directions which they could barely follow. Eventually they found his basement flat in a dank late-Victorian mansion block.

As soon as they got inside Sam collapsed on the bed in his horrid little bedroom. He would doubtless have slept for many hours if left alone but Caroline was not going to let him. First she yanked off his trousers and then, with some small cooperation from him, took off his jacket and shirt.

Soon he was lying on his bed wearing nothing but his underpants. Caroline observed his slender body with some approval. For someone with a drink problem he was in surprisingly good condition.

Drunk as he still was, Sam could sense Caroline eyeing his underpants. In normal circumstances he would have been very happy for her to have removed them but he felt he would lose dignity if she did so now. He managed to heave himself off the bed, and staggered wordlessly into the bathroom. Caroline heard the sound of running water.

She gathered most of his clothes, went into the kitchen, and put them in the washing machine. Then she returned to the bedroom. The floor was covered with old newspapers, empty bottles of wine, grimy glasses, dirty plates and an ashtray overflowing with cigarette butts. She began to restore some order.

Sam re-emerged, washed and clean in a dressing gown, walking like a trapeze artist terrified of toppling over. He gave her a sheepish grin.

'Sorry about this. It's good of you to help.'

'That's all right,' said Caroline.

They looked at each other and smiled. Sam was thinking that if he weren't so drunk and hadn't made such a fool of himself he would like to go to bed with her.

He lay down on the bed and within seconds was asleep. Caroline looked at him tenderly. Then she bent over, kissed him gently on his forehead, and left.

She relived those moments as her head rested on the rolling uplands of Sir Edwin Entwistle's stomach some hours after his return. A sexual encounter of a sort had taken place. Her naked husband lay like some beached sea monster, his stomach heaving as gales of air pumped through his lungs.

Splash!

'Edwin?'

'Mmmm?'

'Darling, I was thinking earlier about that journalist you've sacked. I can't help feeling sorry for him.'

'Why, my sweetie?'

'He's worked for the *Bugle* for a very long time – even before you bought it from Lord Pepper. They say he's been a very brave reporter. It seems sad to throw him on the scrapheap.'

Sir Edwin stirred. He could feel the feather-like brush of his wife's hands between his sturdy thighs.

The proprietor of the *Daily Bugle* was not a stupid man. He had not moved from carpets into newspapers and then international hotels by taking what people said to him at face value. He suspected his wife had some secret motive. She was a compassionate creature, insisting he give money to starving Africans whenever there was a famine on that unfortunate continent, but her generous nature could not really explain her wish to help this pitiful man. There must be other reasons. And yet the idea that his beautiful and glamorous wife might be attracted to the ex-chief reporter of the *Daily Bugle* did not enter Sir Edwin Entwistle's mind.

He felt Caroline's hand move up to regions where it had lately been, and he emitted a low noise, like a distant foghorn on a lonely winter night.

'I'll do what Yapp originally offered,' he ruled. 'Sam Blunt can have three months.'

Chapter Nine

One of Sir Edwin Entwistle's gifts is his ability to keep unconnected thoughts in his mind at the same time. He did not care a fig for Sam Blunt or his future. Nonetheless, he had undertaken to revoke his immediate dismissal and, despite having many more pressing issues to think about, rang Trevor Yapp to inform him of Sam's stay of execution as soon as he arrived at the worldwide headquarters of Entwistle Enterprises in Grosvenor Square.

Sir Edwin could now turn his thoughts to an infinitely more important matter. He was going to sell the *Daily Bugle*. It had not been an easy decision. Owning the paper conferred power and prestige. It made him a figure to be reckoned with. But Sir Edwin was above all a businessman, and he could see the newspaper would not be in profit for much longer.

Its circulation, already less than a quarter of what it had been in its heyday fifty years before, continued to decline month by month. The readership of Bugle Online was increasing sharply but the website was attracting only modest advertising revenues – and no subscription revenue at all since it was free. Sir Edwin had calculated that the financial worth to his company of one new Bugle Online reader was about one fortieth of one old reader of the *Daily Bugle* who had given up the paper, or died. He doubted whether the website would ever generate substantial income, though he wouldn't share his misgivings with prospective buyers.

He had to concede that this group was not a large one. Rival publishers were aware of the *Bugle*'s difficulties, and in most cases were struggling to keep their own titles afloat. The *Daily Dazzle* was the only newspaper making significant money. The *Chronicle* was losing vast amounts. The *Financial Gazette* was barely treading water. What Sir Edwin needed was a fantastically rich man who could take on the prospective losses of the *Daily Bugle* without noticing. He believed he had found such a person in Mr Po.

The Chinese tycoon had built up huge businesses in Chengdu and Hong Kong before taking up residence in London with Madame Po. Sir Edwin, whose own fortune was not quite as great as was widely thought, had estimated that Mr Po was a billionaire ten times over. He could cheerfully absorb the losses of twenty failing newspapers. The current proprietor of the *Daily Bugle* suspected Mr Po sought the influence that ownership of the title would bring. His challenge lay in beguiling him into paying more than the *Bugle* was worth.

Sir Edwin knew that a salesman with several eager buyers is in an ideal position. He had only one. Lacking the means to create a lively market, he had attempted to fire up Mr Po's interest by presenting himself as a reluctant seller who might decide to hang on to his precious newspaper after all. He realised that while Mr Po would see through this ruse he couldn't be sure it did not contain an element of truth.

During several conversations in which he had striven to appear tantalisingly circuitous, Sir Edwin had gained the impression that the enigmatic Chinese was becoming more enthusiastic.

The moment had not arrived to force the matter to a head. Yet rather as the seller of a second-hand car knows when to polish its bumpers and touch up its paintwork, so Sir Edwin sensed the time had come to put his newspaper in order. For that reason he had made up his mind to sack Eric Doodle and replace him with Trevor Yapp.

He had not arrived at this decision lightly. Doodle was in his way a significant figure, taken seriously in some quarters. He was the only newspaper editor in whom the Prime Minister confided his anxieties. It was well known that once every fortnight or so Doodle would be invited to Number Ten, where he would listen to the Prime Minister's tribulations, and pat his trembling hand. This doubtless reflected well on Doodle's good nature. It also invested him with a kind of significance. Sir Edwin imagined him as a sleepy but sizeable beast grazing the savannah who could not easily be brought down. His sacking would be less traumatic if it were accompanied by the granting of a knighthood. Sir Edwin was hopeful he could prevail on the Prime Minister, whose outpourings Doodle had so patiently endured, to confer this honour.

Yapp was a rough and abrasive figure who Sir Edwin felt certain would appeal far more to Mr Po than Doodle ever could. He was also younger, and radiated vigour. Unlike Doodle he understood the world of Bugle Online, whose fabulous future would be unveiled to the Chinese billionaire. Though Sir Edwin hesitated to put an actual value on Yapp, he had no doubt that his appointment would enhance the package in the eyes of Mr Po.

The newspaper proprietor inspected his telephone, the instrument with which he kept in touch with his far-flung empire. He would not tell Doodle immediately why he was being cleared out. There was no point in providing unnecessary information. He would arrange a meeting – either lunch here in his private dining room at the headquarters of Entwistle Enterprises or at the Fig Leaf – and tell him the time had come to make way for a younger man. Doodle must be sixty if he was a day, and Yapp couldn't be much more than forty. The handover should be smooth. Doodle would step down in a month or two. That would give Sir Edwin time to persuade the Prime Minister that an adequate gong should be tossed in the direction of the departing editor. So far as his own life peerage was concerned, he had reason to believe it was now assured.

While Sir Edwin was sitting in his airy office preparing to telephone Eric Doodle, Benedict sat perspiring in the dungeon of Pepper House, unaware that he might soon lose his patron. He had survived nearly three weeks. The time had been mostly spent rewriting stories filched from other websites. Whenever he finished a piece he would click an icon on his computer which rang a bell that alerted Andy Dodd, the news editor, or his deputy. Then an instruction was sent to his screen to start another story. When he had finished that, he pressed the icon once more, and the process began all over again.

At one end of the dungeon there was a huge screen which recorded how many stories had been generated during the past twelve hours, and the number of people who had viewed each of them. When this figure reached one hundred thousand for a single article, a constellation of lights above the screen flashed and the first few bars of Beethoven's 'Ode to Joy' were blasted out. This happened often.

Benedict had never been so bored in his life, or so tired. From nine o'clock in the morning to six in the evening he sat peering into his computer. At lunchtime he was allowed half an hour off, which was barely enough time to get to the sandwich shop next to the Half Moon and back, and breathe the summer air.

Knowing nothing about newspapers, Benedict was unaware that young journalists had once been encouraged to venture into the outside world. He had observed Sam Blunt, of course, but could not relate to the easy-going life of the chief reporter, about whose recent humiliations he had heard. As far as he was concerned, journalism was the most pointless and tedious occupation imaginable. He would far rather have spent the day sitting in a tractor spraying crops on his father's estate.

There was, however, one bonus which made his life not only endurable but endowed with purpose and hope – Sophia, the pre-Raphaelite beauty. Although none of the galley slaves had a fixed desk, Benedict tried whenever possible to sit near her. They were all discouraged from speaking to one another while working. He and Sophia were in any case too preoccupied with the words and images flitting across their screens to exchange more than the briefest of civilities, and she usually disappeared as soon as her shift had finished.

So they had hardly spoken. And yet he thought about her almost every waking hour. He went to sleep with her on his mind, met her often in his dreams, and woke up to a vision of her long solemn face and flowing auburn hair. Well-brought-up Anglican though he was, he had covered her body with kisses in his imagination. He realised, of course, that Sophia didn't appear to feel about him as he did about her. Once, at the end of a shift, he had overheard her talking on her mobile to someone to whom she seemed to be close. No endearments were offered by her, but arrangements with another party, presumably male, were entered into, though without much animation, and with her natural hauteur only slightly abating.

While Benedict sometimes wanted to kill this unknown admirer, his most murderous thoughts were reserved for Trevor Yapp. The hourly grind of overseeing the galley slaves was entrusted to Andy Dodd, a stooping rat-faced man, but Yapp would make occasional tours around the dungeon, looking over shoulders and making derogatory comments. Benedict might be cobbling together a story about a sneezing squirrel or a chimpanzee that could read Serbo-Croat. Sophia, fractionally further up Bugle Online's food chain, would be writing words to go with pictures of half-naked C-list celebrities, a task Benedict certainly envied. Having invariably said something disobliging to Benedict, Yapp would linger by Sophia's chair, leering at pictures of Bugle Lovelies on her screen, and mocking her for her insufficiently prurient write-ups. Sophia bore his taunts stoically. Benedict was forced to grip the edge of his desk for fear of assaulting the deputy editor.

That morning Yapp had stood behind Sophia's chair for longer than was usual.

'I see Suzy Wattle's up to her old tricks,' he observed, gesticulating at Sophia's screen.

'Yes, she's just put up a hundred more pictures on social media of herself having a shower,' replied Sophia. 'As her husband has just been arrested, Andy thought we might as well use a few of them.'

'She's getting on a bit, but her breasts still look OK,' opined Trevor Yapp.

'Yes, I suppose so.'

'Must be her second or third boob job. How much do you reckon it cost?'

'I've no idea.'

'Ever thought of following her example?'

Yapp moved on without waiting for an answer, and Benedict swore to himself that one day he would spring to Sophia's defence, and hit him.

Two floors above, Eric Doodle sat perusing the latest edition of *Rural Retreats*. He had presided over a most unsatisfactory morning editorial conference, feeling more than usually detached from the proceedings. The news editor's list had featured two critical stories concerning the Prime Minister about which he would have rather not heard. The foreign editor had offered little of interest beyond the news that Nipper Richards had been arrested by Spanish police on a drugs charge.

'What's brewing on the books front?' Doodle had asked the literary editor in a distracted voice.

He could have sworn he had heard a subversive chuckle, possibly emanating from the City editor.

'Not a great deal,' admitted the literary editor, before proceeding to list the books that were being rewarded with brief reviews in the *Bugle*'s weekly books spread.

After the departmental editors shuffled out, Doodle

settled down with his magazine. He stroked the glossy front cover lovingly. It carried a picture of gun dogs. Postponing for once the delights of the property section, he turned to an article about the relative merits of working cockers. Did Sir Cumming Brewster use these spaniels, described in the piece as the most obedient and malleable of dogs? Or was he a Labrador man? Doodle realised these were matters about which he knew little or nothing. He imagined Sir Cumming asking him whether he preferred working with cockers or Labradors or even setters, and felt a chill pass over him.

Before flicking to the house advertisements, he got out his map from a drawer and began to study it. Any disinterested observer would have been impressed, as well as bewildered, by the array of neat marks with which he had covered many of the counties of England. A few of them – those which for one reason or another Doodle had vetoed as places to spend his declining years – had been left untouched. On borderline cases such as Somerset he had drawn a criss-crossed pattern with obscure hieroglyphics. On the nine or ten preferred counties he had written in tiny script a huge number of marks and figures – an intricate rating system to do with house prices, the beauty of the countryside and distance from London.

He could not deny that under this system Herefordshire did particularly well. It scored four out of five on price, meaning that it was cheaper than most counties, though not so cheap as Northumberland and Cumbria, to which he had given straight fives. As regards beauty he had had no compunction about giving Herefordshire five out of five, remembering a camping holiday he had spent among its woods and hills with a male friend at university. As to distance, he had awarded the county four out of five, signifying that it was neither too close to the capital nor too far from it. This made thirteen marks, the same as Shropshire, to which it was, however, preferred because the Entwistles had a country house in that county, and one more than Lincolnshire, which should arguably be given a special extra mark as the cradle of Sir Cumming Brewster's rolling acres in the Wolds.

The editor of the *Daily Bugle* sighed. If only Daphne were not so hostile to the countryside. For Doodle, England was its countryside – the copses and ploughed fields, the ditches running with lapping water, the crack of guns on a wintry day, the white, rose-covered cottages and, of course, the great grey mansions looming out of the mist . . . How could Daphne not love all this?

He turned a page of *Rural Retreats* and there, as though by divine providence, saw a picture of a perfectly proportioned Queen Anne former rectory, thirteen miles from the Cathedral City of Hereford. There was a kitchen garden, enclosed by a wall of soft red brick, in which he could grow sweet peas and runner beans and gooseberries. He realised with surprise that he had always wanted to grow gooseberries.

The telephone rang, jolting Eric Doodle out of his reveries. It was Dora, telling him that a restless Sir Edwin Entwistle was on the line.

Chapter Ten

Sam had left Caroline in the hotel room in Notting Hill. It was a balmy evening, and he decided to walk the first part of the journey back to Barons Court. He crossed Notting Hill Gate by the underground station, and cut down to Kensington High Street via leafy Billionaires' Row.

He felt happy. Caroline was a sexpot and a sport, though their first tryst a few days earlier in the same hotel had not started well.

She had disappeared into the bathroom and come out wearing very little. Her teeth were startlingly white as she gave an encouraging smile. Her body was perfect. Sam, who was lying on the bed, did not feel as aroused as he should have done when she lay down alongside him. What his Uncle Walter had described to him as 'old Percy' when he was a little boy remained intransigently limp. Caroline peered at it as though looking at an unexpected specimen in a jar. Then she began to knead it, good-humouredly at first, but with signs of impatience as she made no progress.

'You drink too much, Sam,' she observed.

'That's true. But that's not the reason. It hasn't ever bothered me before.'

'What's wrong, then? Don't you fancy me?'

'Of course I do. Anyone would.'

'What is it?' She had stopped pulverising Percy.

Sam sat up in bed. 'You frighten me.'

'Me? Frighten Sam Blunt? The famous Lothario? The derring-do reporter?'

'Yes, you do. I'm not used to posh women.'

'I'm not posh.'

'Filthy-rich ones then.'

'I see.'

She began to rummage in her handbag, and produced a pill which she had removed from a small box in Sir Edwin's sock drawer, the contents of which were apparently intended for use with the lady to whose residence in Earls Court, Caroline knew, her husband paid clandestine weekly visits.

'Take this,' she ordered.

Though he had always deprecated the idea of any pharmaceutical assistance in the bedroom, Sam obliged, and after a while Percy began to behave as they had both hoped he would.

When they had met again that evening in the same hotel, Caroline had offered him another pill. Sam refused, and proceeded to make love with enthusiasm.

Now that he was walking past the monstrous late-Victorian and Edwardian palaces that lined Billionaires' Row, he felt like doing a little skip and a jump. The uncomfortable awareness that he would be unemployed in a little less than three months had momentarily deserted him. He asked himself whether he wanted to stop off at a pub for a bracing gin and tonic and was surprised by the answer that he didn't. Caroline was a peach. He loved her glossiness, the sense she gave of being newly minted.

Sam looked up and noticed a man walking in the same direction about twenty yards ahead. He lowered his eyes and starting thinking about the smoothness of Caroline's body. Then he felt the stirrings of recognition. He only had the back of the man to go on, but he was a practised observer, and there was something familiar about the gait and the light-coloured hair, which curled over his collar. He recognised Terence Glasswell, the married Old Etonian MP whose affair with Lady Evelyn Wherewill he had exposed in the *Daily Bugle* three years previously.

His natural instinct was to presume that what might appear innocent to others wasn't. Nine times out of ten his suspicions would turn out to be unfounded, but it was the tenth case that made him a good journalist.

What was Terence Glasswell doing here at this time in the evening? Sam hung back so as not to be noticed. The MP walked in the direction of Kensington High Street before suddenly crossing the broad avenue and veering off to the right. He passed through the iron gates of a particularly grotesque and oversized mansion, and bounded up its steps in a way that suggested to Sam a familiar routine. He pressed a bell and was quickly let in.

Sam loitered behind a tree on the other side of the avenue and waited. After about half an hour the door opened and Glasswell re-emerged. Once through the gates, he looked to his right and left as though quickly scanning the street, and then turned back towards Notting Hill, walking more briskly than before.

Sam had no idea who lived in the house where Glasswell had been. Because there were several embassies in Billionaires' Row there was a police box at each end to keep a watch on interlopers. When he reached the box by Kensington High Street he stopped and smiled at a burly policeman bristling with automatic weapons.

'Nice evening,' he said.

The policeman agreed that it was.

'Tell me, that house halfway up on the left – number forty-two, I think it is – am I right it's the Russian ambassador's residence?'

'Why do you want to know?' asked the officer suspiciously.

Sam got out his Press card and flashed it in front of him. 'I'm doing a piece about ambassadorial residences. Slightly lost my bearings.'

'You're a bit off beam, then. Number forty-two? If that's the one that looks like a wedding cake, it's a private house occupied by a Chinese bloke.'

'Do you remember his name?' asked Sam lightly.

'Can't say I do. They say he's a billionaire. Bo something?'

'Mr Po Chun?'

'Could be,' the policeman agreed.

As soon as he got to Kensington High Street Sam hailed a taxi and asked for Barons Court. He sat back and thought. If it was Mr Po's house, what was Terence Glasswell doing? There weren't any other visitors so it couldn't have been a party. Maybe he was friends with Po. But prominent MPs can't just be friends with Chinese billionaires. Sam suspected Glasswell had expensive tastes and lived beyond his means. He was a famous shagger, too – Lady Evelyn Wherewill had been the tip of an iceberg. Might he be having a dalliance with Mrs Po? Half an hour would be just about right for a chap like Glasswell. Then he remembered a photograph in a gossip column of a large Chinese lady called Madame Po. He vaguely remembered her being present during that ridiculous business at Lady Evelyn Wherewill's lunch party. Hardly Glasswell's type, he would have thought, but he might do anything if there were money to be made. Sam relegated the idea without dismissing it, and returned his thoughts to the husband. What had the MP been doing in his house? The way he had run up those steps definitely suggested he'd been there before.

When Sam got back to his flat he went straight to his computer. Within half an hour he had found out quite a lot about Mr Po. The son of a hard-line senior Communist apparatchik, he was sixty-three and had been born in Chengdu. He'd been married to Madame Po for forty years. Mr Po had made the first slice of his fortune building flats in his rapidly developing home city. After a time he had diversified into commercial real estate in Hong Kong. There was a suggestion he had not always seen eye to eye with some senior officials of the Chinese Communist Party, though many of his interests were still in China. His business empire now included construction, banking and mining. According to an American business magazine, he was the forty-ninth richest man in the world, and one of the three wealthiest Chinese. He had moved his main residence to London from Hong Kong three years ago.

Sam then turned to *Famous People* to remind himself of the major events in Terence Glasswell's life. Son of a colonel who won an MC in Burma during the war. Aged fifty-five. Joined the Life Guards after Eton and Sandhurst but left after three years. A job at a small investment bank. Married Cynthia, the daughter of a baronet. One son, one daughter. Elected MP for a rural Yorkshire constituency. Member of the Foreign Affairs Committee. Chairman of – this was new to Sam – the Anglo-Chinese Inter-Parliamentary Group. Presumably they swapped ideas about democracy.

He closed the book. Somehow Glasswell was dipping his fingers into the honeypot of the booming Chinese economy. Hardly surprising. He plainly wasn't canvassing Madame Po's support for a new charity to help widows and orphans. What *was* he doing? Sam realised he was far from having any dirt on Terence Glasswell.

He was a seasoned journalist. He knew there were bad things going on all over the place – in politics, the civil service, the NHS, business and the City. Only a fraction of these ever emerged into the light of day and were published by newspapers. The difficulty always lay in getting the evidence. It was going to take a lot of luck and bluster to corner the MP. But he suddenly felt the thrill of the hunt. He was certain Glasswell was up to something he ought not to have been.

Sam longed to restore his own reputation. If he skewered this scoundrel, Sir Edwin Entwistle and Eric Doodle and Trevor Yapp would crawl before him and beg him to stay. He'd show them.

The next morning, as Sam arrived at Pepper House shortly before nine o'clock, he got tangled up with Benedict Brewster in the revolving automatic door. Benedict had misjudged its speed of rotation and they both ended up jostled together in the same section. When they had extricated themselves Sam recognised his former charge, though he couldn't remember his name.

'Hello,' he said.

'Good morning, Mr Blunt,' said Ben.

'I heard you'd been transferred to Bugle Online.'

Benedict's sunny faced darkened slightly. 'Yes, Mr Blunt.'

'Not working out?'

Benedict looked around to check there was no one close enough to overhear him. 'A bit boring, actually. And terribly hard work.'

'I'm sorry,' said Sam, patting his shoulder.

Benedict gave him a grateful look, and turned in the direction of the stairs that led down from the foyer into the dungeon. When he had gone about three yards, Sam remembered his name.

'Ben?'

The younger son of Sir Cumming Brewster swivelled around, nearly upending a fellow galley slave rushing to meet the nine o'clock deadline in the dungeon.

'Are you free this evening?'

'Yes, Mr Blunt.'

'Sam.'

'Yes, Sam.'

'Meet me at half past six in the Half Moon. I've got a project that might interest you.'

Chapter Eleven

While Benedict laboured miserably in the dungeon, Sam sat rapt in front of his computer in the newsroom. Journalists arriving at ten o'clock expressed amazement that the former chief reporter of the *Bugle* (he had been stripped of his old title by Yapp while he served out his notice) should be at work so early. They were even more astonished that he did not once leave his desk for a cigarette outside Pepper House. The sight of Dora bringing him a sandwich and a cup of coffee at lunchtime induced even greater disbelief. He ignored every comment and snigger. When Adam Pride coasted past him on his way to lunch at his club, protesting in an audible voice that he couldn't believe the evidence of his own eyes, Sam did not bother to look up.

His object was to discover everything interesting that had ever been written about Terence Glasswell. He knew he would have to unearth the really important stuff from the MP's colleagues, former lovers and anyone else he might have done down. What he wanted to discover now was 'background' that might provide leads. He searched for parliamentary questions Glasswell had asked in the past year, speeches he had made in the Commons and elsewhere, his register of interests, the parties he had attended and his foreign visits.

By five o'clock he had completed his researches. As he had expected, there was nothing obviously suspect, but there were some interesting revelations, as well as reminders of Glasswell's old tricks. After Sam had broken the news of his affair with Lady Evelyn Wherewill, the MP had arranged to be photographed with his wife Cynthia and their two teenage children outside his house. The only clue that things were not as happy as Glasswell maintained was the sadness in Cynthia's eyes. He had given an interview to the *Chronicle* in which he inveighed against the 'relentless nihilism' of the 'feral' Press, and wondered whether anyone would want to enter Parliament if MPs were to be persecuted for wearing the wrong colour socks.

Of Glasswell's interest in Chinese affairs there could be no doubt. He had declared two visits to China during the past twelve months, once as a member of a parliamentary delegation, and once as a guest of the Shenzu Corporation, which Sam discovered was a company controlled by Mr Po. He had made a speech in the Commons about the Chinese regime, arguing that while its human rights record was not perfect, it was better to try to exert influence from the inside rather than criticise from the outside. Glasswell had attended a party with Cynthia at the Pos' Kensington mansion at which Sir Edwin and Lady Entwistle, the Bishop of Middlesex, Ambrose Treadle, Sir Archibald Merrick, Lady Evelyn Wherewill and Boris Vrodsky had also been present. He and Cynthia had been invited, as had Mr and Madame Po, to an official dinner to mark the recent visit to London by His Incomparable Excellency Moses Ovambo, President of Kangala, and his wife Stella. That was not unusual in view of Terence Glasswell's membership of the Foreign Affairs Committee.

No single fact was discreditable, though the visit to Beijing as a guest of Mr Po's company was certainly interesting. Yet Sam was certain in his bones that Glasswell had been receiving money from Mr Po in exchange for favours or information. But for what? Making one sympathetic speech in the Commons? It hardly seemed worth bankrolling him for that. There had to be something more significant.

When Benedict arrived at the Half Moon just after half past six, Sam was already there, consulting his smartphone. Sam bought him half a pint of bitter. He began to describe his sighting of Terence Glasswell, and to outline his discoveries.

'If Glasswell is on the take, why would he go to Mr Po's house and risk being seen?' Benedict asked Sam when he had finished.

'He'd think it a very small risk of being spotted by hacks, most of whom are pretty dozy anyway. Certainly a much smaller risk than having money paid into an account that might one day be traced. Cash is always best. And it's preferable to talk in person. Telephone conversations can be listened to. Emails and texts intercepted, and kept.'

'I suppose so,' said Benedict. 'I told you my father knows Glasswell. They were at Eton together.'

'Are they friends?'

'Hardly. When Glasswell was caught having an affair my dad said it served him right to be exposed by some greasy reptile. Evelyn Wherewill is a sort of cousin of ours.'

'That reptile was me.'

'Oh. I'm sorry.'

'Your dad was probably right.'

Sam used Benedict's embarrassment to fetch him another half pint. He had barely touched his own drink.

When he returned, Benedict was looking ruminative.

'I did have one thought, Mr Blunt.'

'Sam.'

'Sorry. It's just what you said about the official dinner for President Ovambo. Is it odd that the Pos and Terence Glasswell should have been there? Probably a coincidence.'

'Or?'

'I was thinking of what you said about Mr Po having moved into mining. I know a bit about Kangala, having covered Ovambo's recent visit.' Ben reddened at the recollection. 'There are zinc mines in the Wali desert. Everyone knows the Chinese are moving into Africa.'

Sam looked at Benedict with a new respect. 'It's worth looking into. We should check whether Glasswell has shown any interest in mining. Or Kangala, come to that.'

'I could try to find out,' said Benedict, who did not have the faintest idea of how he might set about it.

'All right.' Sam sounded a bit doubtful. 'Tell me how you get on.'

'What else would you like me to do?'

Sam might not think Benedict had any future as a journalist, but he had a pair of eyes and apparently a decent brain. He liked the boy and wanted to help him.

He explained his hunch that if Glasswell had visited the Po mansion he probably would do so again. He might turn out to be a regular visitor. Or maybe he was an intermittent one. Just conceivably, Sam admitted, his visit might have been a one-off. The only way to find out was to mount a regular watch in Billionaires' Row. It was possible the MP called once a week around the time Sam had seen him. We all of us like routines.

Benedict would have liked to be accorded a more central role in the affair, but even standing watch sounded more fun than rewriting other websites' copy in the dungeon.

'I can do that,' he said. 'But I'm working on Bugle Online all day.'

'I'll keep an eye on the house in the daytime,' replied Sam vaguely. 'In any case, I have a feeling that if he comes back it'll be in the evening. It's when both of them have more time. And bad things tend to happen in the evening.'

Sam looked at his watch. It was nearly half past seven. He was almost due to meet Caroline at the hotel in Notting Hill.

'So are we in business?' he asked Benedict.

'Yes, Mr Blunt − I mean, Sam. I can start tomorrow evening.' He looked uncertain. 'What happens if I do see Terence Glasswell?'

'Oh, that's easy,' replied Sam breezily. 'You just slip a tiny microphone into his pocket.'

They left the Half Moon together. Sam took a taxi to Notting Hill, Benedict the tube to Hackney.

When he got back to his dingy studio flat he went straight to the fridge, took out a bottle of wine and poured himself a large glass. He felt nervous and excited. Putting a microphone into someone's pocket! This, at last, seemed like real journalism. Then he wondered whether it was ethical. What would his father say if he ever found out? Terence Glasswell might be a creep but he was also Sir Cumming Brewster's old school contemporary.

Though Benedict had been schooled in the doctrines of the Church, the possible wrongs of slipping a microphone into an MP's pocket began to seem less pressing as the wine took effect. He poured himself another glass. Then he thought it might be a good idea to practise the surreptitious art of microphone slipping, using a door as a stand-in for Glasswell.

At the best of times Benedict was not very nimble on his feet. While at Eton he had not shone at any sport apart from the Wall Game, where his strength and courage counted in his favour and his want of perfect coordination was no disadvantage. If you were looking for ideal candidates to slip microphones into the pockets of passing MPs, Benedict Brewster would not necessarily be top of your list.

Nonetheless, buoyed up by several glasses of wine, he persisted in his dress rehearsal. He smashed his shoulder against the side of the door with more force than could have been prudently applied to Terence Glasswell, and he grabbed the door handle, which served as a substitute pocket, with greater vigour than would have been recommended by an experienced slipper of microphones. In so doing he managed to lose his balance and ended up splayed on the floor, having crashed his head against the wall. The telephone rang.

Four weeks had passed since Sir Cumming Brewster had spoken to his younger son. He did not consider himself guilty of the same tendency towards over-protectiveness as his wife. Lady Celestine had, for example, insisted that Benedict have a landline (whose apparatus was now ringing a few inches from his ear) in order to be spared what she feared were the harmful effects of radiation emitted by mobile phones. Sir Cumming would not have concerned himself with such worries. He would have thought it unmanly on his part to do so, as well as liable to induce neurosis in his offspring. But four weeks is a long time for a loving father not to hear from a loving son and, although he had received a bulletin of sorts from Eric Doodle, he felt the time had come to take command.

Benedict was dazed by the blow to his head. It took him a while to decipher the sound of the phone ringing. For a time he fancied it was his alarm clock, and registered the customary dread at the thought of another day at Bugle Online. Eventually he picked up the receiver.

'Yeah?'

'Is that you, Ben?'

'It's me, Benedict.'

'This is your father.'

Benedict sat up. 'Hello, Dad.'

'Are you all right? You sound a bit odd.'

'No, I'm fine, thanks. Absolutely fine.'

'Your mother was a bit worried about you so I decided to give you a call.'

'Are you both well?'

'Yes, thank you, Ben. Nothing much going on. Mollie got a thorn in her paw and Mother had to take her to the vet. Old Mrs Parry died. Do you remember her?'

'Yes. No. I'm not sure.' Benedict had a thought. 'Dad, there was something I wanted to ask you. I'm trying to find out about your old school contemporary Terence Glasswell.'

'Why?' asked the baronet, for whom the process of investigating people's backgrounds was unfamiliar.

'Oh, something to do with the *Bugle*. I'm working with the chief reporter on a story. It's quite hush–hush, actually.'

Sir Cumming was impressed. He had never met a chief reporter.

'The thing is, Dad, could you find out a bit about Glasswell? Who he works for, where he gets his money – that sort of thing? I'm interested in whether he has any mining interests. Could you ask at the club?'

Sir Cumming was flattered. 'I'll see what I can find out. I'll ask a few fellows.'

'Thanks, Dad. I'd better be going.'

'Are you sure you're all right, Ben? Your voice sounds a bit slurry.'

'I'm fine. Just tired. Been working hard. Give my love to Mum.'

So it was that Sir Cumming Brewster, 7th Bart, owner of five thousand acres of Lincolnshire, deputy Lord Lieutenant of the county and a former Justice of the Peace, found himself supplying information to Sam Blunt, ex-chief reporter of the *Daily Bugle*, alumnus of Willesden Comprehensive and current lover of Caroline Entwistle.

Chapter Twelve

Sir Cumming Brewster's club, though not necessarily the grandest gentlemen's establishment in the capital, thinks well of itself. In the nineteenth century, and for some of the twentieth, Stride's had been the home of Tory squires and landowners who regarded neighbouring Tuffs Club, patronised by richer, Whiggish gentlemen, with suspicion. As time swept on, the backwoodsmen of Stride's dwindled in number, and the survivors came to realise that they would have to bring in unlanded new members if their club were to survive and prosper. Respectable bankers and wealthy businessmen would have to be admitted. Nonetheless, firm lines were still drawn. The 3rd Viscount Pepper had escaped a black ball but it is very doubtful whether Sir Edwin Entwistle would have done had he not preferred the charms of a louche Mayfair dining club where Russian oligarchs, such as his friend Boris Vrodsky, and their peroxide-blonde ladies liked to mingle.

Though times had changed, the committee of Stride's had agreed that journalists were unacceptable in any circumstances. This prohibition included editors, as Edward

Sneed of the *Chronicle* had learnt to his cost when a new member, inexperienced in these matters, had incautiously proposed him. Without bothering even to convene a meeting, the chairman of the committee had taken the greenhorn aside and asked him whether he would mind withdrawing Mr Sneed's candidature.

In this way England continued to be England without being quite the England it had been. Sir Cumming's grandfather and great-grandfather would have recognised the Stride's Club they had loved, while perhaps deprecating innovations such as the coffee machine in the small library, and looking askance at one or two of the gentlemen in their double-breasted Savile Row suits who were driven up from their great offices in the Square Mile.

Sir Cumming had no such qualms. He had arrived at the club with the express hope of bumping into Sir Archibald Merrick, a City magnifico of great wealth who was chairman of a large German-owned investment bank and a vice-chairman of the governing party. He had known Sir Archibald at Eton, and the two of them had intermittently crossed paths at various shoots over the years. They would sometimes drink a glass or two of port together at Stride's after the chocolate pudding had been demolished. Sir Archibald was reputed to know everything about anyone of importance. Sir Cumming felt sure he was the man to dish whatever dirt there might be on Glasswell.

He first had lunch with a landowning chum from Norfolk who had diversified into tulips. After his friend had left, he repaired to the small library and poured himself a generous glass of port.

On entering the library Sir Archibald did the same. He

spotted his old acquaintance flicking through a back copy of
Rural Retreats, and came over to join him.

'Afternoon, Cumming.'

'Afternoon, Archibald.'

'Mind if I join you?'

'Not at all.'

Archibald flopped back into a capacious armchair, nearly
losing hold of his glass of port in the process.

'In London for long?' he asked.

'Just the day.'

'Rather warm,' observed Sir Archibald.

'Yes, it is,' agreed Sir Cumming.

The two men fell into a comfortable silence such as can
exist between English male acquaintances of any class when
they are drinking. Sir Archibald swilled his port around his
glass, looking wise and thoughtful. Sir Cumming pretended
to read his magazine. After a few minutes had passed he
judged the time had come to make a start.

'Archie, do you remember that shit Terence Glasswell
from school?'

Sir Archibald nodded.

'I'd rather not say why just now, but a friend of mine
wants to know what he's been up to.'

Sir Archibald pursed his lips. He leant slightly forward
and across in his chair so as to be closer to Sir Cumming
sitting in a parallel chair. 'Are we talking about his private or
his public life?'

'Mainly the latter.'

'It's no secret he still plays around. Can't imagine what
they see in him. Cynthia's a nice girl, too.'

'I'm sure she is.'

'Don't know who he's having it off with now, though there's been talk of a certain lady.'

'Don't worry about that,' said Sir Cumming, dismissing a line of enquiry that would have interested Sam greatly. 'What about the business side of things?'

Sir Archibald drained his port and assumed the omniscient look he liked to adopt at Board meetings.

'I'm told he was on his uppers after being sacked by a small hedge fund.'

Sir Cumming, who had only a hazy idea what a hedge fund was, nodded sagely.

'And absolutely between the two of us' – Sir Archibald leant further forward so his red face was very close to the baronet's, over whose handsome features he exhaled port fumes infused with a whiff of chocolate pudding – 'I gather he's working for Mr Po.'

Sir Cumming had never heard of Mr Po. He felt he should intervene this time for fear of losing the thread.

'You haven't heard of Mr Po?' Sir Archibald looked shocked, as he settled back into his armchair. 'Chinese. Colossally rich. Interesting figure. Seems to be his own man but is close to the Chinese government.'

'Ah,' said Sir Cumming. 'And how do we know Glasswell's working for the Chinese?'

'A good question,' conceded Sir Archibald, who was being much more confiding with this innocent backwoods baronet than he would have been with a business associate in the City or a politician. 'I'm told he does some work for a Chinese bank that's owned by Po.' The City magnifico leant forward again. 'Between you and me, the PM's a bit worried.'

'Why?'

'Don't you see? Glasswell is a prominent party MP and a member of the Foreign Affairs Committee. Think what the newspapers would make of it if they found out he's practically working for the Chinese!'

'Why doesn't the Prime Minister tell Glasswell to behave himself?'

Sir Archibald gave a little snort. 'Because he's frightened of Glasswell for some reason. And I suppose he also thinks it's a good idea to keep the Chinese onside.'

'I see,' said Sir Cumming. In truth, he thought it was a rum do. If one of his tenant farmers started burning tyres or cutting down estate trees, he would have it out with him. Much better to be open about these things. But perhaps politics was different.

'Tell me, Archie, do we know whether Glasswell has any mining interests – in Africa or elsewhere?'

Sir Archibald looked at the baronet keenly. 'None that I know of.'

Sir Cumming thought over what he had been told, and wondered whether it was enough for Benedict. It seemed to him it probably was. By all accounts, Glasswell was misbehaving on a considerable scale. My God, he was virtually spying for a foreign power. And the Prime Minister was concerned! It made Sir Cumming's blood boil to think about it. What a bounder the man must be.

'All very interesting,' he said laconically. 'You don't happen to remember the name of the bank Glasswell works for?'

That evening Benedict rang Sam in an excited state. It was not perfect timing because he was at that moment making love to Caroline in the hotel in Notting Hill where he had been spending an increasing amount of time.

Splash!

Benedict blurted out that Terence Glasswell was working for the Chinese and the Prime Minister was very worried about it. Sam asked him how he had come by this information.

'From my father.'

'From your father?' This did not sound promising.

'He spoke to someone at his club.'

'I see.'

They agreed to meet in a café near Pepper House at 8.30 the following morning.

When a slightly bleary Sam had heard Benedict's full account over croissants and coffee, he had to admit to himself that the boy had done astonishingly well. Sir Archibald Merrick was a copper-bottomed source who would have had no reason to mislead Sir Cumming Brewster. He obviously couldn't be identified in any story but he had named the bank owned by Mr Po as Anglo-Chinese Investments, and Benedict had discovered that it had offices in Park Lane. What Sir Archibald had said to Sir Cumming about the Prime Minister's concerns could be attributed to 'top party sources'. Sam was well aware that journalistic textbooks demanded two direct sources on important stories whereas he only had one indirect one, but it was nonetheless unimprovable. He thought he was close to being able to write a front-page splash with what he knew. The headline would read: PM'S ALLY PAID BY BEIJING. The strapline would refer to Terence Glasswell's 'secret visits to controversial billionaire's mansion in Kensington'.

And yet he knew he still hadn't got the knock-out blow he needed. Not declaring an association with Anglo-Chinese Investments in the Register of Members' Financial Interests was a serious, but probably not fatal, matter. The visits were not in themselves evidence of a disreputable relationship. There was no proof that cash was changing hands.

'I don't suppose your dad asked Sir Archibald about Glasswell's possible mining interests?' he asked.

'I think he did but Sir Archibald said he didn't know,' replied Benedict.

'Pity.' Sam saw Benedict's face drop. 'But he did fantastically well. And so did you, Ben, in thinking about his club. He must think the world of you to have done such a thing.'

Benedict looked at his watch. It was five minutes to nine. He could not afford to be late for the dungeon.

'I'd better be off,' he said.

'OK. We'll talk. I think we should go ahead with the microphone – with a slight variation.'

'What's that?'

'Well, there's no point, if you think about it, in waiting for Glasswell to come back to Billionaires' Row, God knows when. He's probably up to no good in that bank. Or Parliament, come to that. Much better to slip it in when he's leaving home.'

'Maybe,' said Benedict cautiously.

He wasn't sure he liked the idea of placing a microphone on the MP which would be on his person while he was in the Palace of Westminster. It smacked of treason.

'Which of us would do it?' he asked. Despite the proud history of the Brewsters there was a tremor in his voice.

'Oh,' said Sam, 'the thing is that he knows me, so I can't very well do it. It'll have to be you, Ben.'

Chapter Thirteen

Eric Doodle had been shocked to learn from his proprietor that he was being sacked. Sir Edwin did not beat about the bush.

'You've had a good run, Eric. It's time to let a younger man have a go. I mean Trevor Yapp.'

'But why now? And so soon after we celebrated our centenary. You told me I was doing a good job.'

'So you were – a proper decent job. You've been a credit to the company and yourself. I make no bones about it.'

'I like to think I've been a loyal servant to this newspaper.'

'You bloody well have been. But the world's changing, Eric, and so is journalism. You know what Bugle Online is like – all those little tarts tweeting pictures of themselves with barely a duster to hide their bits and pieces. I'm sometimes taken aback myself, but it's the future, and Yapp understands it better than me or you.'

Doodle could not dispute this point. Sir Edwin was right. Bugle Online did not represent what he understood by journalism.

Daphne was even less pleased than her husband to learn

about his dismissal. Nor did she believe the theory planted in Eric's brain by Sir Edwin Entwistle that his demise would be accompanied by the award of the long-awaited knighthood. She reasoned to herself, and informed Eric, that prime ministers are selfish, forgetful creatures, and if the present incumbent of Number Ten had not felt it necessary to hand out a gong while her husband had power, he was hardly likely to do so after he had relinquished it. Eric Doodle had replied that even in politics there is a code of honour, a system of rewarding old friends and remembering past favours, and he remained confident the Prime Minister would not let him down. Daphne, who had long coveted the title 'Lady Doodle', called her husband a credulous old booby. There the matter had rested.

Her ill-humour was also stirred up by the thought that after his retirement Eric would often be found at 2 Common View, where he would doubtless disrupt her life. As editor of the *Bugle* for ten years, and deputy editor for as long a period before that, he had habitually left home at a quarter past eight in the morning and returned late in the evening. During the week she had never had to worry about his lunch, and usually not about his supper either, since Eric might dine out at Sir Edwin Entwistle's expense with friends or politicians, or stop off at his club for a solitary meal. With her book and bridge club meetings and evening classes, as well as lunches in the company of other Wimbledon ladies, Daphne had carved out a life of her own. The thought that this might be affected by her husband's unexpected retirement deepened her gloom.

Eric Doodle could not help dwelling on his wife's recent sourness as he was driven by his chauffeur Ted Daws to

Number Ten for what might be his last meeting with the Prime Minister. He wished she would be more understanding. The news delivered by Sir Edwin over lunch at Entwistle Enterprises two days earlier had been almost as much of a shock to him as to her. He had caught wind of rumours but had assumed they were no more than the usual heartless gossip endemic in all newspapers. In Doodle's experience there was no subject which journalists relished discussing more than the likely timing of the defenestration of their editor, however successful or popular he or she might be. He'd been no better himself as a young journalist, chattering with colleagues about the prospects of poor old Sir William Enstone, despite his being the editor who had given him his first job. What ingratitude he had shown! And yet, as Sir William himself had once observed to him, you couldn't expect journalists to behave as though they were in the Brigade of Guards.

Arriving at Number Ten, Doodle was ushered up to the Prime Minister's flat above Number Eleven. He was greeted by a slight, untidy man who looked more like a junior clerk than the leader of a great nation.

The PM's mood was even more tetchy than usual. He forgot to ask Doodle whether he would like a drink.

'You know, Eric, I sometimes wonder why I bother to do this job.'

Doodle did not venture to suggest that there were many in the country who shared this view.

'I spend my time dealing with fractious backbench MPs and civil servants who delight in telling me what I'm not supposed to do for this or that reason. Why do I do it?'

'For your party and your country, Prime Minister.'

'I know, I know. And then there's the Press.' He pointed to a copy of the *Chronicle* that was lying on the table in front of him. 'Have you read this rubbish?'

'I am obliged to read all the newspapers.'

'They say I'm weak, Eric. That I should stand up to my backbenchers and be more European-minded.'

'I know, Prime Minister.'

'As for the *Daily Dazzle*!' He now brandished a copy of this outspoken publication. 'They call me indecisive, too! But in this case I am supposed to be *too* nice to the Europeans. It seems I can't win.'

'I suppose it is in the nature of a democracy that you will get opposing views.'

The Prime Minister appeared not to absorb Doodle's little dictum. He had picked up a copy of the *Daily Bugle*, and was flicking furiously through its pages. Seemingly unfamiliar with its topography, he spent some time rifling through the sports pages before he finally found what he wanted.

'Here it is. Your Adam Pride turns his guns on me, describing me as "arguably vacillating". It's a bit much, Eric, when the only friends you thought you could count on let you down!'

'Those are Pride's views, Prime Minister, not the *Bugle*'s.'

'Can't you control him?'

'Unfortunately not, Prime Minister.' The editor suddenly felt brave. 'Any more than you can always control the Home Secretary.'

The Prime Minister looked at him sharply. 'So you think he's plotting against me?'

'Everyone seems to believe he is.'

'Even though he swears undying loyalty to me and says he never wants to be Prime Minister?'

Doodle nodded.

'You're right, of course. What a snake he is! I've half a mind to sack him, but the chief whip wouldn't let me. He's got too much support on the backbenches.'

They continued to talk about potentially mutinous ministers and difficult MPs until Doodle felt he should steer the conversation towards his own affairs.

'Prime Minister, there's something I should tell you. This may be the last time I come here as editor of the *Daily Bugle*.'

'Why?'

'I've decided to retire.'

'Is that good timing? We've an election coming up, and we will need to count on the *Bugle*'s support.'

Doodle could have sworn that a childish pout was fighting for supremacy on the prime ministerial face.

'Rest assured, that will continue under my successor, Trevor Yapp. He's a very capable man.'

'Well, I suppose Sir Edwin can always be relied on. I don't know this Yapp fellow. I must say that I shall miss your support, Eric.'

The editor of the *Daily Bugle* knew the moment had come. Daphne had told him that he must on no account leave without raising the issue of his knighthood. She said there were a dozen different ways of doing this without actually mentioning the thing itself. Her parting words rang in his head. 'Just tell the old fraud it has been a pleasure to have offered such help as you have been able, and if your name were ever to be put in front of the honours committee you would feel inexpressibly grateful.'

And yet when the moment came Doodle was unable to

say anything. He realised his failure would provoke bitter criticism from Daphne. But that, after all, was the unending pattern of his life. It was not fear but pride that held him back. Despite all the compromises that had littered his career, despite his prolonged indulgence of this self-pitying Prime Minister, there remained a small residue of that journalistic idealism that had once driven the young Eric Doodle as he set out on his path. He would be damned if at the end of it all he would kowtow to a politician.

As Doodle was driven away from Number Ten, Ted asked him whether he wanted to return to the office. He looked at his watch. It was quarter past seven. He should go back to the paper, and in normal circumstances would have done so. But with his own departure looming he felt rebellious. Yapp could manage. He always saw off the front page in any case.

'Take me to Bright's, would you, Ted?'

Doodle reflected how much happier he would have been if he could have said to Ted 'Take me to Stride's'. Though Bright's occupied a finer and more commodious building, Doodle had come to see it as a club of no particular distinction, as its relatively short waiting list attested. From his researches in *Joyce's Baronetage* he had discovered that Stride's was Sir Cumming Brewster's London club. He was well aware of its horror of journalists, including even long-standing editors who knew how to handle a gun. Yet how he yearned to be admitted to that shining citadel.

Bright's was not one of those clubs where solitary members sit together on a long table. Doodle repaired to his usual corner table to dine alone, nodding at the familiar figure of Terence Glasswell, one of a party of four, as he passed. He gave his order – potted shrimps, lamb chops and half a bottle of club claret — and began to relive the last part of his encounter with the Prime Minister.

About an hour later, while Eric Doodle was thoughtfully spooning chocolate pudding into his mouth — the two clubs, though differing in many ways, shared a remarkably similar menu — Trevor Yapp was standing in the doorway of the office of the editor of the *Daily Bugle*. Dora had long departed. Yapp knew Doodle would not be back.

For a moment he eyed the empty room in the declining light, as a wolf might its prey, watchful and without pity. Then he moved behind the desk, and stood by the chair where the editor sat. He knew this formidable Victorian desk and its heavy ornate chair had once dominated Arthur Pepper's office in the original Pepper House in Fleet Street. Along with the newspaper's title, and some small portion of Arthur's dream, they were all that survived from those distant days.

Presumptuous though he was, Yapp dared not sit down in this chair. Even he was held back by superstitious fear from planting the hollow crown on his head. Doodle might be idiotic and risible, and his reign nearly at its end, but he was still editor of the *Daily Bugle*. Yapp, expecting soon to take over, felt awe for the office. It was imbued with a kind of absolute power. If the editor of a newspaper told the picture editor in a moment of whimsy that he had an aversion to yellow, the minion would never again show him a photograph with the colour. An opinion delivered from the editor's chair that no column or news story should ever begin with the indefinite article — a ludicrous contention if uttered at a dinner party — would be reverentially received by departmental editors, and uncritically observed. Even an assertion that Manchester is north of Newcastle would be humoured and, if repeated enough times, finally accepted as geographical fact. Trevor Yapp thought Doodle's great weakness was that he so seldom insisted what was untrue was true. And yet even when filled by a feeble man like him, the office retained a sacred significance for Yapp. He could not yet place his bottom on Eric's chair.

He leant across it now and eased open the central drawer. There was still enough light for him to identify its contents: a hairbrush, a crumpled handkerchief, a copy of *Rural Retreats* and a tube of suncream; fragments of Doodle's life that did not touch Yapp's heart. He also noticed a map of England which he opened, to find it covered with what looked like hieroglyphics and unfathomable patterning.

How bizarre, he thought. Doodle was always an odd one. He closed the drawer, folded the map, slipped it into his jacket pocket, and left.

Chapter Fourteen

Would he go to bed with her? Sam examined his watch. He had only two minutes left. Should he choose her? She had large breasts and full lips. A bit overweight perhaps, but there was something sensuous about her. He wouldn't do much better. He tried to imagine himself with her. He glanced at his watch again. One and a half minutes. Better a bird in the hand, surely. He strained his eyes to see who was coming down the street. A figure in the distance might be a transvestite for all he knew. OK, this one. He could do a lot worse.

Sam was smoking a cigarette at a pavement table outside the Half Moon waiting for Benedict, playing a game he sometimes used to occupy the time when bored. The rule was he had only ten minutes. During that time he had to choose a woman he could imagine going to bed with. The challenge lay in not plumping for anyone too early. If he picked the first half-presentable specimen that came along, a blonde beauty might pass by two minutes later and be out of the running. On the other hand, if he rejected a number of perfectly serviceable candidates he might find himself thrown into the arms of a turkey. It was a game of chance, obviously, but also of skill and judgement. Sam never cheated. Once he had made his choice he always stuck with it.

'Sam.'

Benedict was standing on the pavement looking unhappy. Sam had been so preoccupied with his game that he had not seen him approach.

'Sit down, Ben. I'll get you a drink. You look depressed.'

Benedict had spent the last nine hours labouring in the dungeon which, because of the warm weather, was exceptionally hot and airless. But he could have cheerfully endured all that were it not for Sophia. Over the past week she had deigned to pass her pale green eyes over him a couple of times. Once she had agreed to walk with him to the sandwich shop, and twice had used his Christian name. These small gifts, nothing to her, had induced in him a spirit of ecstasy. He was in love. And yet his happiness had been destroyed only ten minutes earlier by Trevor Yapp.

He had noticed that the editor-elect of the *Daily Bugle* had got into the habit of lingering longer by Sophia's chair, and that his remarks to her, previously astringent and even cruel, had taken on a joshing quality that might be interpreted as flirtatious. Having previously ignored Yapp, Sophia began to engage with him, at first haughtily but then amiably and, in recent days, almost teasingly. Her behaviour had worried Benedict but he argued to himself that it was probably just a survival strategy for dealing with Yapp. And then, just before his shift was about to end, he had seen her flash a smile at the saturnine monster which contained – he could not convince himself otherwise – an unmistakeably sexual element.

'I'm all right,' said Ben.

Sam went off in search of a pint of beer for him and a tonic water for himself. When he returned he leant towards the young man so as not to be overheard.

'I've got the mike, and the receiver.'

'Good.' Benedict's thoughts at this moment were a long way from Terence Glasswell.

'Cost a packet, I'm afraid. Put it on expenses.'

'I see.' Benedict was surprised. 'Did you lose the last one?'

'What do you mean? This is the only one I've ever had.'

'Haven't you used a microphone before?'

'No. This is the first time.'

'I'm sorry – I got the impression you'd done this sort of thing loads of times before.'

'Not exactly.' Sam put a hand on Benedict's forearm to reassure him. 'But I've done similar things. I once bugged Nipper Richards' telephone in Malaga. Bribed a Spanish telephone engineer. It's all much of a muchness.'

'Maybe.' Benedict felt uncertain. He had qualms about slipping a microphone into Terence Glasswell's pocket. Somehow the exercise seemed less intimidating if sanctioned by practice and experience. The thought that he was going to do something which even the ex-chief reporter of the *Daily Bugle* had never attempted – and which had perhaps never been undertaken by any journalist – cast a chill over him.

'Don't worry, Ben. It'll be a piece of cake.'

Leaning closer, Sam began to unveil the plan. Benedict would position himself near Glasswell's house in Victoria at about eight o'clock in the morning. He mustn't look conspicuous. Best not loiter. Move around. Try to look natural.

When the MP emerged, he should follow him and, as soon as there were plenty of people around, brush against him and slip the tiny microphone into his breast pocket. It was no bigger than a twenty-pence piece.

'Just like that?'

'Just like that. We can practise if you like.'

'Thanks,' said Benedict. He was wondering what his father would say if he were caught red-handed. Or, even worse, his poor darling mother.

But it was not for nothing that the Brewsters had laid claim to a sizeable portion of Lincolnshire for a couple of hundred years. A younger son had been killed and mutilated in the Indian Mutiny. A great-uncle had perished in the fields of Flanders. A distant aunt had disappeared over a precipice during a walking holiday in the Swiss Alps. One way and another, the Brewsters had done their bit. Benedict was not going to let the side down now by admitting that the prospect of planting a microphone on Terence Glasswell, MP, terrified the living daylights out of him.

'When do I do it?' he asked Sam Blunt.

'No time like the present. What about tomorrow morning? If Glasswell takes his time coming out – I expect he's a lazy sod – you'll have to be late for work.'

Ben imagined Trevor Yapp's face. For once it was not particularly scary.

'All right,' said Benedict.

'Let's go and practise in the park.'

Six weeks earlier, when the young man had walked across St James's Park to take his first look at Pepper House, the whole world had seemed to lie before him, full of promise and hope. The park had then been green and fresh; now it was dry and parched. In those far-off days he had not known about the dungeon, or imagined that a man such as Trevor Yapp could exist. Nor had he met Sam Blunt.

The two of them now practised the art of slipping a microphone into the breast pocket of a jacket, with Sam playing the part of Terence Glasswell, Benedict playing himself and a twenty-pence piece doubling up as a microphone.

On the first attempt Benedict bumped into Sam so savagely that he sent him flying. The second time he missed him altogether and landed flat on his back. On the third occasion he got a side pocket instead of the breast pocket. Sam begun to wonder whether his lanky protégé could ever pull it off. Then, at the seventh try, Benedict dropped the coin into its intended home, albeit slightly ham-fistedly. After a couple of final practice runs Sam assured him he couldn't feel a thing.

'Where will you be tomorrow morning?' Benedict asked when they had finished.

'I'll see you by the taxi rank outside Victoria Station at seven forty-five and give you the mike. Then I'll go to the office. Ring me when it's over. We'll meet in the Half Moon for a debrief.'

When Benedict had gone, Sam sat down on a park bench and lit a cigarette. He liked the boy's gutsiness. He was obviously unused to behaving illicitly. Sam had spent his whole life on the wrong side of authority. It was what had drawn him into journalism. He remembered his sense of joy when his first editor on the *Ealing Times* – a short fat man who looked like a bank manager – had told him: 'Mark this, my boy, and never forget it. Journalists are always the wrong side of the barricades.'

What a beautiful evening it was. The sinking sun warmed his face. Sam lit another cigarette. He knew he should have been at the hotel in Notting Hill with Caroline half an hour earlier but couldn't stir himself. He suddenly didn't want to be there on an evening like this. He'd send her a text saying he wasn't coming after all. She was a big-hearted girl though her enthusiasm for sex sometimes tired even him. He felt cooped up in that little room. They did everything there as well as make love – eating, drinking champagne (though Caroline never drank much) and watching the news – because Caroline said she couldn't risk being seen with him in a restaurant or anywhere else. What if a journalist from the *Daily Dazzle* were to spot them together? It hadn't occurred to Sam that what he was doing was morally indistinguishable from the shenanigans of Terence Glasswell and Lady Evelyn Wherewill. He reasoned that he was a journalist and no one cared what he did. But he could see Caroline had a reputation to defend, and he certainly didn't want Sir Edwin to find out.

As Caroline read Sam's text in the Metropolitan Hotel, disappointment and irritation competing on her face, Benedict sat alone in his tiny flat in Hackney. He had poured a glass of wine which lay untouched. The young man was deep in thought. He was overcome by a sense of the enormity of what he was about to do. Much as he liked Sam, he couldn't suppress a feeling that the journalist ought not to have set him so perilous an assignment on his first outing – second, if the debacle over the colour story were included. Was his excuse that he might be recognised by Glasswell a good one? Couldn't he have slipped the damn thing into his pocket himself without being seen?

Splash!

Like many a hero on the eve of battle, Benedict felt uneasy. And then he thought of his loving father. Sir Cumming, who was generous and forgiving, had called Terence Glasswell a bounder. He had expressed astonishment that the MP should be working covertly for Mr Po and the Chinese. He had not used the word, but he clearly thought Glasswell was a traitor.

Weren't any methods allowable with such a man? Weren't he and Sam on the side of truth and justice? He was doing what his father would want, and more than anything he yearned for his father to be proud of him.

Chapter Fifteen

Sam's suggestion that Terence Glasswell might take his time leaving his mews house was not wide of the mark. The MP liked a full and leisurely breakfast, which was prepared for him by Cynthia. He sat at the kitchen table in his silk dressing gown reading the *Chronicle* as his wife bustled around him. Glasswell was pleased to see the Prime Minister was again under attack. If there were a leadership battle, and the Home Secretary emerged victorious, he might be rewarded with a junior ministerial post.

When he had breakfasted, Glasswell went upstairs, leaving Cynthia to clear away. He was in unusually high spirits, and not just because of the Prime Minister's tribulations. The day looked promising. He would stroll down to the Commons and get some paperwork done. Then he would have lunch at Stride's, to which he had been invited by Sir Archibald Merrick. The man was an old fool but Glasswell liked the club and had hopes of becoming a member. After lunch he would pop around to Anglo-Chinese Investments, where the highlight of the day might await him. His new secretary, whom he had chosen for her looks rather than her shorthand skills, had not demurred when he had placed a hand on her bottom the previous day. He intended to take matters further that afternoon.

Glasswell opened a cupboard and surveyed his many suits. He would need to look smart for Stride's. He reached down a chalk-stripe suit which he had had made when he was last in Hong Kong. He had never worn it and its jacket pockets were still stitched up. On reflection, he put it back. It was too heavy for such a warm day. He reached down an older and more lightweight creation whose pockets had been slit open long ago.

Half an hour later the front door opened and Terence Glasswell emerged into the bright street. He walked at an even pace up to Victoria Street, before turning right towards the House of Commons.

As a young man, he had had a short service commission in the Life Guards, where he had distinguished himself as a brave, even ruthless, officer. He had trained in jungle warfare and most of the skills he had learnt had not deserted him. He remained a fine shot. Dropped into the rainforest, he would still have known which leaves to eat and which to avoid, and trapped and strangled small furry animals without compunction. Terence Glasswell had also not forgotten the sensation of being tracked.

He had felt a presence almost as soon as he left home. There was no need to turn around. It would have been stupid to have done so. He couldn't hear any footsteps but he knew he was being followed. He sensed his stalker was gaining ground on him.

Glasswell crossed the road so that he could see his pursuer reflected in a shop window. He saw a tall gangly man no more than thirty feet behind him. Glasswell took a sharp turn into a side street, and darted into the doorway of a shop.

Benedict, who had no idea he had been noticed, was moving in for the kill. Putting his hand in his trouser pocket, he took out the tiny microphone, which he gripped between his right thumb and forefinger. The moment was coming. Glasswell's sudden diversion down a side street had surprised him, but he followed unsuspectingly. The next thing he knew, the MP had his hands around his throat.

'Why the fuck are you following me?'

This was not a question Benedict was able to answer even had he been minded to because of the extreme pressure of Glasswell's hands on his neck. He choked as he fought for breath. It seemed to him that the MP's grip was tightening.

Terence Glasswell was fit for a man of fifty-five; lovers such as Lady Evelyn Wherewill had admired his toned body. On the other hand, Benedict was six inches taller and less than half his age. Moreover, he had a pair of hands around his neck which seemed to be squeezing the life out of him. It was not a state of affairs that could be endured much longer. With a roar such as a brontosaurus might have uttered on seeing a cherished offspring being stolen away by a marauding predator, Benedict gave Glasswell such a blow to his ribs with his right elbow that his neck was freed. As the MP staggered, Benedict lashed out with his right fist and landed a blow on his adversary's face that sent him tottering. Unfortunately, in so doing he let go of the microphone, which spun through the air and disappeared.

He knew he had failed irrevocably. He also realised that nine times out of ten, if you are involved in a fight with a well-known MP, disinterested spectators will leap to the conclusion that you are at fault, a not wholly unsustainable point of view in this instance. A small crowd was building up, and he thought he heard someone cry, 'He started it!' With a quick glance at Glasswell, who was cursing as he rubbed his face, Benedict turned and ran as fast as he could.

Later he wondered whether it was dignified to retreat in such a way. At the time he simply ran as rapidly as his long though not particularly well-coordinated legs could carry him. He shot across Birdcage Walk, narrowly missing a motorcycle, and sped through St James's Park, crossed the Mall, and raced up St James's Street. Only when he reached Stride's did he stop running. In fact, no one had followed him for a single yard.

Heaving from his exertions, Benedict looked at the familiar portico, which seemed to belong to a lost era of calm and innocence in his life. A police siren could be heard wailing in the distance. Were they looking for him? He would be wanted for assaulting a Member of Parliament. He had also failed in the task Sam had set him. For a moment he wondered whether to throw himself at the mercy of Geoff, the club doorman, and pretend he was waiting for his father, but he decided to move on. He hailed a taxi and asked to be taken to Pepper House in Pimlico via Belgrave Square and Sloane Square so as to avoid Victoria.

Once in the taxi, Benedict phoned Sam, and told him in terms that wouldn't be understood by the driver that the mission had been aborted. Sam sounded as sympathetic as he could.

What neither of them could know is that when the microphone escaped Benedict's grasp, and spun wildly into the air, it ended its journey by falling into the turn-up of

Terence Glasswell's left trouser leg, where it remained snugly lodged.

The MP downplayed the significance of the incident when the police arrived, suggesting that his assailant was a common-or-garden mugger who had taken fright after meeting spirited resistance, though he didn't say he had nearly throttled him. There were several festering scandals in his life. He felt that as his pursuer could be linked to any of them it would be better if the police were kept in the dark. They seemed to accept he was the victim of a random attack, and hadn't caught a good look at his mugger. But Glasswell would never forget Benedict's face.

When the MP arrived at Stride's, Geoff Dobbs enquired kindly as to the cause of his bruised eye, but was brushed aside. Sir Archibald Merrick was also solicitous. For most of the lunch the financier's concerns seemed purely social. It was only when they were sitting in the small library nursing glasses of port – and occupying the very armchairs in which Sir Archibald himself and Sir Cumming Brewster had lately conversed about the MP – that the magnifico revealed his hand.

'Forgive me, Terence, for mentioning this, but the Prime Minister's a bit anxious that your close connections with Mr Po are being talked about.'

'Is he?'

'Just a bit. He's worried what would happen to us if the Press got wind of it. He thinks you could be a bit more discreet.'

'It's no secret I know China well, and there's no crime in doing some work for Mr Po.'

'Of course not. But you can see what the newspapers could make of it. You know how they twist things.'

'The last thing I would ever want to do is to embarrass the Prime Minister.'

'I am sure he's well aware of that.'

'And for the life of me I can't see how anyone could say that what I'm doing is wrong. Mr Po is one of China's richest men. China is a friendly country which happens to have the second biggest economy in the world, and will soon be the biggest. I'd have thought the PM would be happy that one of his loyal MPs has his finger on this particular pulse.'

'Of course he is, Terence. Your links are very important to the country and – er – the party. The Prime Minister is very grateful for everything you've done. It's purely a matter of perception. We need to be careful.'

'I shall be careful, Archibald, rest assured.'

The tycoon poured two more glasses of port and asked the MP what his plans were for the Glorious Twelfth. When he replied he had none, Sir Archibald mentioned vaguely that he had a couple of spare guns on his Scottish estate without quite extending an invitation.

Feeling that his host was now in a receptive mood, Glasswell raised the subject of his possible membership of Stride's. Sir Archibald, who knew the members would rather commit mass hara-kiri than admit this man, undertook to have a quiet word with the club secretary.

All this might have been overheard by Sam if the ex-chief reporter of the *Daily Bugle* had known that a live microphone was hidden in Terence Glasswell's turn-up, relaying a conversation that could be picked up at a distance of a hundred yards.

And, if only they had known, Sam and Benedict could have eavesdropped on an equally illuminating exchange after the MP had arrived in the offices of Anglo-Chinese Investments in Park Lane. His new secretary was extremely concerned to see her employer's black eye. It was not long before she was applying with her little finger some balm she kept in her handbag for just such an eventuality. Had Sam and Benedict been parked outside Mr Po's bank, they could have overheard Terence Glasswell's moans as his soothing new assistant performed what the *Daily Dazzle* would have termed a sex act.

As it was, Benedict was being gently cooked in the dungeon, thinking himself the biggest chump in Christendom, and expecting to feel the hand of a policeman on his shoulder at any moment. Sam was sitting forlornly in the Half Moon, having returned from a fruitless mission searching for the lost microphone at the scene of the fight while trying not to attract attention. Against all his resolutions, he was downing his third gin and tonic.

But why should we blame them? Newspapers know only a minuscule fraction of the skulduggery, cheating and dishonesty of the very rich and powerful. They provide only fleeting snapshots in which many miscreants are invisible. Sam and Benedict had nearly got their story. Think of all the extraordinary things we are so far from ever knowing.

Chapter Sixteen

Lady Evelyn Wherewill had been pleased to receive Caroline's invitation to lunch at the Fig Leaf. The wife of the proprietor of the *Daily Bugle* normally proposed a less fashionable venue. Lady Evelyn suspected her friend was still trying to atone for inviting that ghastly reporter who had made such an exhibition of himself. She knew her detractors had enjoyed some fun at her expense, and feared that her reputation as one of London's leading hostesses had been punctured. Caroline owed her the Fig Leaf at the very least.

Caroline poked at a small mound of boiled seaweed, and drank some salty water which claimed to hail from a Norwegian fjord. Lady Evelyn made do with a little plankton soup, and a small glass of organic wine from Puglia. The bill when totted up would be roughly a hundred times the cost of the raw materials. But no one who went to the Fig Leaf was going to worry much about money, or question the fantastic creations of London's most brilliant chef, and the restaurant's moody proprietor, Emmanuele Botti. It was a place to observe and be observed.

Caroline had booked what was considered the best table in the house. From their vantage point on a raised platform the two ladies looked down on a lower tier of tables laid out on the Carrara marble floor, which was vigorously polished every morning on Emmanuele's express orders. There had been reports of casualties. Evelyn Wherewill knew for a fact that the German ambassador has been hospitalised for a bruised coccyx as a result of losing his footing. The actor Tray Nevada had cracked a front tooth and was said to be suing Botti.

The two ladies could see Adam Pride lunching with Terence Glasswell, whose black eye was easily visible. Caroline hoped the long-suffering Cynthia had finally clocked him. Madame Po, swathed in a red dress covered with gold stars, was enjoying a tête-à-tête with the Bishop of Middlesex. It was rumoured that he had made it on to the shortlist for the Archbishopric of Canterbury. Caroline noticed her husband closeted at a corner table with the loathsome Trevor Yapp. She had heard about his thuggish ways from Sam, and did not at all approve of her husband's decision to make him Doodle's successor. The PR king Ambrose Treadle was dispensing wisdom to the Russian oligarch Boris Vrodsky, who would be paying handsomely for the privilege. Lady Evelyn's brother the earl could be seen with an unknown gentleman of Middle Eastern appearance. Perhaps surprisingly, in view of his newspaper's annual losses of tens of millions of pounds, Edward Sneed of the *Chronicle* was entertaining the Home Secretary. Caroline spotted her friend Annette Bustome, who did interviews for that newspaper's Sunday edition that were famous for being hostile and packed with inaccuracies. Willing subjects queued up all the same to be destroyed by her. Sensing that she was being watched, Annette looked up at Caroline and blew her a kiss.

The two ladies did not dwell on the lunch at which Sam had disgraced himself. Caroline lightly mentioned that she was sorry she had ever suggested that he be invited. Lady Evelyn assured her friend she had long ago put the incident quite out of her mind. They had many other more agreeable matters about which to talk.

Contrary to what Lady Evelyn had supposed, Caroline had not chosen the Fig Leaf in any spirit of contrition. Nor did she believe in spoiling her friends unnecessarily. Her choice had been intended to set Lady Evelyn at ease so that she would be as helpful as possible when Caroline finally steered the conversation in the direction she desired. It didn't do any harm that the person about whom she wanted to talk, Terence Glasswell, was sitting only thirty feet from them, and so could be recruited as a topic of conversation in an artless way.

Caroline had been angry with Sam when he sent the text telling her he was unable to come to the Metropolitan Hotel. She had already suspected that he might be tiring of their affair. To her surprise she minded. It wasn't that her vanity was pricked. She did not want to lose him – not now, not so soon. She thought him dashing, and loved his air of unconcern.

On the day of the microphone imbroglio Sam had come to the hotel in the evening. After some listless lovemaking – so listless that Caroline had suggested she should delve into her handbag for a remedial pill, an offer that was spurned – she asked him what was wrong. Although he had been reluctant to confide in her, she had teased out the saga of Terence Glasswell. How Caroline had laughed at his account of Benedict's fight with the MP. Sam did not think it at all funny. He said he was close to having the story of his life that would nail one of the biggest rogues in the kingdom, but was short of one or two crucial pieces in the jigsaw.

'But darling, it's so simple!' she had cried. 'Don't you see?'

'What do you mean?'

'I'll ask Evelyn. She will have lots of dirt on Terence Glasswell.'

'Will she tell you?'

'She'll tell me everything. Just leave it to me.'

Now that they were sipping dandelion tea in the Fig Leaf, Caroline knew the moment had arrived.

'I wonder what Terence is doing with Adam Pride.'

Lady Evelyn inspected her former paramour. 'He's up to no good, whatever he's doing,' she suggested.

'Do you ever see him now?'

'We sometimes knock into each other. Whenever we do, I wonder what I ever saw in him.'

'He's quite attractive.'

'And doesn't he know it.'

Caroline realised it was time for a shift of gear. 'Evelyn, I am sorry to ask this, but you know I will do anything for Edwin.'

Lady Evelyn did not know this, but was happy to assent.

'Edwin is trying to find out all he can about Terence's background. Something to do with a deal.'

'What sort of things?'

'Anything, really. Bad things, I suppose. Particularly bad things to do with China.'

Lady Evelyn took another look at the man who had once, to her surprise, sodomised her. She did not bear him any ill will but equally she felt no loyalty to anyone in the world except herself and possibly her brother the earl, and would happily ship Terence if only she could remember. What had he told her? She tried to think back. There was a lot of stuff about Cynthia's mental breakdown and his other affairs but Sir Edwin wouldn't be interested in any of that. He had told her he had once shot dead an unarmed terrorist in Northern Ireland in cold blood but that was a long time ago and no one was likely to object. What had he said about China?

'There was one thing, now I think of it.'

'What was that?' asked Caroline eagerly.

'A couple of years ago he and Cynthia moved from Clapham to Victoria.'

'And?'

'They were short of a couple of hundred thousand pounds. Mr Po Chun lent him the money.'

'Lent?'

'Gave, I imagine. Is that very wrong?' Lady Evelyn had spent her entire life on the receiving end of other people's largesse.

'It is if he didn't declare it, which I bet he failed to do. Are you absolutely certain?'

'Of course I am. It wasn't long after he met Mr Po and started doing things for him. You know the Glasswells never had any money.'

'You're a darling. Edwin will be extremely grateful. We'll keep it to ourselves.'

Caroline could barely contain her excitement when Sam arrived in their room at the Metropolitan Hotel that evening half an hour late. To her dismay he smelt of drink, and did not look in much condition for lovemaking.

When she had finished her story, Sam asked her all kinds of questions about dates, house prices and addresses, none of which she was able to answer. He sat down on the bed and put his head in his hands as though in deep thought. Caroline felt that perhaps she had let him down and that, despite being the wife of the proprietor of the *Daily Bugle*, she didn't really know what a good story was.

'I think we've got him,' declared Sam at last.

He knew that neither Mr Po nor Glasswell would ever admit that two hundred thousand pounds had changed hands. He would put the allegation to the MP and the MP would not admit it. But there are allegations and allegations. This was a good one, supported by someone who could be fairly described as 'a close friend and former associate', which fitted into the pattern of facts and innuendo Sam had already amassed. Doodle and Yapp would calculate whether Glasswell would sue. Sam was sure he wouldn't because that would entail putting Mr Po in court. That was too great a risk. There was Cynthia, too, who presumably knew the source of the money, and could be easily broken down. Glasswell wouldn't dare put her in front of a pitiless QC. He would simply deny the allegation but the denial would seem unconvincing in the light of his provably close relations with the Chinese billionaire. The MP would have to resign, probably vowing to fight a court case that he would never pursue.

Sam would establish the facts about when the house in Clapham was sold and the one in Victoria bought, and for how much. That would show there was a gap that had to be bridged by someone. He would write the piece and then telephone Glasswell for his denial. Then he'd take the story to Yapp. He was certain he'd like it. Yapp was the biggest shit in the world but he was a fucking good journalist. He hated all politicians, prime ministers, Chinese billionaires and Old Etonians. There was everything in this story to appeal to his prejudices. He'd go ballistic. He'd splash it all over the front page and clear pages two to ten. Doodle would run a sonorous leader lamenting the decline in ethics among public figures. Even that pompous arse Adam Pride would be roped in to write some hand-wringing nonsense. The broadcasters and other newspapers would follow it up, and Sam would keep enough back for a second barrel in the *Bugle* the next day. He'd be famous again. They'd give him back his title of chief reporter. And Ben – yes, Ben! – he'd find some way of getting the poor boy out of the dungeon and into the newsroom, where he could learn his trade.

'Darling?'

Sam looked up and saw Caroline smiling at him from the other side of the room. He registered for the first time that she was wearing very few clothes. Had she been like that when he came in? What a good sport she was! What an amazing woman! How beautiful, how ridiculously sexy. Sam was gripped by a desire to rip off her remaining underwear and ravish her. The piece could wait. For God's sake, it was already written in his head. It was as good as done and dusted. First of all he was going to make love to this incredible, brilliant woman.

Chapter Seventeen

Sam hated ringing his victims before publication to put the facts to them. He thought it went against nature to alert people in this way. Of course, there was no requirement with known criminals to give prior notice or to invite a factual rebuttal. He hadn't notified Nipper Richards before writing a story which effectively accused him of being responsible for the disappearance of Shifty Perkins. Apart from anything else, thanks to a friendly Spanish engineer he had a transcript of several telephone conversations between Nipper and Suzy Wattle which established that neither of them wished Shifty very well. You couldn't easily traduce a criminal. But different standards obtained where Members of Parliament were concerned. When Sam discovered Glasswell's affair with Lady Evelyn Wherewill, Yapp had insisted that he ring the MP to put the allegations to him, though there was no doubting their veracity.

Sam had not wanted to telephone Glasswell from the *Bugle*'s newsroom, where he might be overheard by the flapeared Adam Pride, or even a prowling Yapp. It was not yet six o'clock in the evening, and he found a quiet corner in the nearly deserted bar of the Half Moon, where Benedict was due to join him later.

The inevitable tirade of abuse that lay in store did not concern him. A man who has been shot at by drunken soldiers in Africa is unlikely to be frightened of an irate MP. He had been called worse things in his life than Terence Glasswell could possibly come up with. His only fear was that, once apprised of the story, the MP would rush off to chambers to seek an injunction killing it. On balance Sam thought that even the most half-witted judge would be unlikely to indulge Glasswell because the facts spoke for themselves, and publication was so obviously in the public interest. But you could never be sure.

Sam got out his notebook. He was proud of his shorthand – it was a pity younger reporters relied on their smartphones as tape recorders these days – and would write down every word of the exchange. He dialled the MP's number.

Terence Glasswell was a few yards from his front door when his mobile rang. If he were the kind of man to hum a tune, he would have been humming one now. Matters had been advancing most satisfactorily with his new secretary, Finula, that afternoon in his office at Anglo-Chinese Investments in Park Lane. The girl really was most obliging.

'Hello?'

'Is that Terence Glasswell?'

'Who is this?'

'It's Sam Blunt of the *Daily Bugle*.'

There was a pause. He could hear Glasswell breathing into his phone.

'What do you want?'

'We're planning to run a story, and I am ringing to give you a chance to confirm our facts.'

'What kind of story?'

'We believe you've failed to declare a loan of two hundred thousand pounds from Mr Po Chun, which you used to buy a house in Victoria.'

Glasswell was now standing on the doorstep of the very same house. Through the basement window he could see Cynthia by the stove in the process of preparing his supper.

'You're the little worm who wrote about me before, aren't you? I won't waste my time on you. Do you have the faintest idea what effect that piece had on my wife and family? Or the difficulties you caused me?'

Sam did not reply to these questions.

'You can do what you like with your pack of lies, but if you go ahead and publish them you'll be hearing from my lawyer.'

'You don't deny that you received a loan from Mr Po?'

'I have nothing to say to you except that everything I've done has been open and legal.'

'Why didn't you declare the loan – or was it a gift?'

This was too much for Glasswell, who lost his temper.

'You can go and fuck yourself, Blunt. I've no more to say. But let me warn you. We've had enough of the intrusiveness of the Press. What gives you the right to go around poking your noses into people's private affairs?'

'Do you deny that you work for Anglo-Chinese Investments?'

'I do some occasional work for them. That isn't a crime.'

'Not in itself, no. As long as it's properly declared.'

'What an insufferably hypocritical lot you are. I don't suppose you'd be overjoyed if your expenses were published.'

Sam did not respond to this observation. Glasswell was warming to his theme.

'Do you have the faintest idea how important China is to Britain? You've never created any wealth in your life. You simply want to bring down those of us who do. We're a small island on the edge of Europe. No one owes us a living. We're losing ground all the time. But if anyone tries to increase business and trade with the country that is going to be the richest in the world in a few years' time, all they get is cynicism and false accusations. Do you lot ever look at yourselves? You're a worthless excuse for a human being. And you can stuff your story up Entwistle's fat arse!'

Glasswell was shouting so loudly now that Cynthia had left her stove and was peering anxiously out of the basement window.

'Thank you, Mr Glasswell. I've made a careful note of our conversation, and I'll make sure that all your comments are included in my article, with the possible exception of that last bit.'

'Just bugger off, won't you, Blunt?' With this, the MP ended the call.

Sam felt the exchange had gone as well as might have been hoped. Glasswell's failure to deny the existence of the loan would rubber stamp his story. Readers would naturally assume that a man who has not been lent or given two hundred thousand pounds is usually eager to say so.

Sam did not recognise Benedict when he sat down beside him in the Half Moon. The young man had put on a woolly hat that covered his ears and was wearing a pair of sunglasses.

'Is that you, Ben?'

Benedict nodded.

'Still on the run from the boys in blue?'

Ben nodded again.

'I expect they've probably lost interest by this time. Let me get you a drink.'

Every time someone walked into the Half Moon Benedict jumped, thinking that a police officer had come to arrest him. He thought of his poor mother visiting him in prison. What would she say? And Sophia. Would she even notice he had gone? Perhaps she would read about his arrest on Bugle Online.

A well-dressed man carrying a briefcase came into the pub. Benedict was sure he was a plain-clothes policeman. Maybe Special Branch. It was obvious the briefcase contained handcuffs and possibly more formidable means of restraint. The man went to the bar, ordered himself a drink, and sat down on one of the Half Moon's stained red velour benches. He took out a copy of the *Chronicle* and began doing the difficult crossword. Perhaps he wasn't a cop after all. He certainly didn't seem very interested in the other customers. Benedict relaxed a little.

'I've spoken to Glasswell, and he more or less admitted the whole story,' announced Sam.

'That's very good news.'

'I think we're there. I couldn't have done it without you, Ben. Your information about Anglo-Chinese was crucial. Your old man was pretty useful too.'

'Thanks.' The drink was helping him. He had taken off the sunglasses. Perhaps the police really had lost interest.

'Journalism can be fun, you know,' Sam went on. 'It's not all about rewriting other people's copy.'

'I suppose not.'

'Maybe after this we can get you out of the dungeon. Do some proper stories.'

Benedict brightened. Then he reflected that he would be leaving Sophia behind. Or could Sam save her too?

'That would be nice,' he said.

Sam was in expansive mood. It was a long time since he had felt like this about a story. This was one of the best he had ever done – not perhaps the equal of his piece about the headless torso in the Thames, because it lacked the human element of that lurid tale, and arguably inferior to his exposé of Nipper Richards. But it was a cracking good yarn all the same. He thought of the *Bugle* in the old days, of forays to Africa covering good old-fashioned military coups. That was when the newspaper still cared about foreign news.

'How many foreign correspondents do you suppose the *Bugle* had twenty years ago?' he asked Benedict.

Benedict said he didn't have the slightest idea.

'Ten. And twenty years before that, when it was still selling over four million copies a day, it had twenty-five.'

'My God. What happened?'

'Mostly money, I suppose – or lack of.'

'You'd have thought that with the global village people would have wanted more foreign news, not less,' ventured Benedict.

'I agree,' said Sam. 'It's a bit of a mystery. The trouble with foreign news is that you can't control it in the same way you can home news. It doesn't fit so neatly into little boxes. Editors don't like that. They don't like their prejudices being challenged. Maybe modern readers don't either.'

Benedict looked at a small grey-haired man who had just come into the Half Moon and was ordering a drink at the bar. He was casting furtive looks all around him. Benedict leant forward to recover his sunglasses off the table, and was about to put them back on.

'Don't worry,' said Sam. 'He's one of us. A sub on the sports desk.'

The young man smiled at his partner. He was moved by the thought that, despite their differences of age and background and experience, he and Sam and the unknown man were part of the same fraternity.

'Thanks for all your help, Sam.'

'That's OK, Ben. This is our story.'

Chapter Eighteen

The editor of the *Daily Bugle* was distraught. His first thought on discovering that his precious map had disappeared was that Dora might have hidden it for some odd reason. His secretary quickly convinced him that she hadn't. She was, of course, aware of the map's existence, and she knew that, out of longings she didn't really understand, Eric spent uncounted hours turning the pages of *Rural Retreats*. But she had no reason to move it from his drawer.

Doodle's suspicions then turned to the illegal immigrants from Kangala who ran a duster around his room every night. One of their number, who was known as 'the Doctor', was summoned. He persuaded the editor in oddly formal English that he and his colleagues lacked cause or motive to steal his handiwork. After an exhaustive search had failed to establish its whereabouts, Doodle sank into a paranoid gloom.

His despair was even greater after a telephone conversation with his proprietor. Sir Edwin described a most unsatisfactory encounter with the Prime Minister. Sir Edwin had gone to Number Ten to suggest that the retiring editor of the *Daily Bugle* should be rewarded with a knighthood. This idea had not been enthusiastically received. The Prime Minister had swept the conversation on. When Sir Edwin returned to the subject he grew tetchy and petulant. Honours, he insisted, were a matter for the Honours Committee, in this instance the members of the media sub-committee. He could not say what Mr Doodle's prospects might be since they had to consider many petitions. A CBE was perhaps more realistic. He would ask his private secretary to have a word with the relevant chairman but really was unable to promise anything. The days when prime ministers could dole out knighthoods to their friends in the Press were long gone.

Sir Edwin knew this was a lie. Though not normally given to sympathising with his fellow human beings, he thought the Prime Minister was ungrateful and disloyal to treat his long-suffering confidant in such a way. Nonetheless, he did not attempt to exert pressure by reminding the PM of the *Bugle*'s consistent support.

Doodle hadn't hidden his disappointment when Sir Edwin gave him an account of the meeting. He would have liked to have been a knight. He could even imagine some gamekeepers and beaters – oh, joy! – mistaking him for a baronet. But far more burdensome than his own sense of having been let down was the thought of Daphne's reaction. Almost every day his wife had asked him whether there was any news.

For the forty-eight hours after his talk with Sir Edwin he lived in a state of terror. Inexplicably her mind had temporarily moved on to other things. Then, just as he was beginning to wonder whether she had lost interest, she asked him at breakfast whether he had heard from Number Ten.

'Yes, dear, there are some developments.'

'What are they?'

'I gather from Sir Edwin that a knighthood is not very likely. Possibly a CBE.'

'A CBE! Why didn't you tell me?'

'I didn't want to upset you, dear.'

'It's about time you learnt to come clean. I still can't understand why you didn't raise the matter with him the last time you saw the old fool.'

'I don't see it would have made much difference if I had.'

'Why on earth not? He'd have been too embarrassed to fob you off if you'd summoned the courage to open your mouth. You're practically his only friend in the world.'

'I fear he has already made up his mind.'

Daphne expressed her conviction that her husband had behaved like a halfwit, and advised him not to hurry back that evening because she had a book club meeting in the house at which they were discussing *Anna Karenina*.

More momentous even than the bad news about the knighthood was the bombshell Sir Edwin had delivered at the end of their telephone conversation. He was planning to sell the *Daily Bugle*, very possibly to Mr Po.

Doodle was flabbergasted. When the centenary celebration had taken place only weeks previously, Sir Edwin's commitment to the paper had seemed as solid as the great Viscount Pepper's. He asked his proprietor why he was planning a sale. Sir Edwin cited falling circulation and the formidable challenges of making money out of the internet. Mr Po was hugely rich. He was also devoted to the principles of a free Press. The paper would be safe in his hands. Of course, the deal was not yet in the bag, but he had felt he should keep his editor in the loop before the handover to Trevor Yapp took place, which should probably now be sooner than had been envisaged.

What he did not add was that Mr Po seemed appreciably keener on the idea of owning the paper with Yapp at the helm than with Doodle. The billionaire had not had the pleasure of meeting either man, but felt that the sooner there was someone in charge who understood the internet, the better it would be.

Sir Edwin finished the conversation by swearing Doodle to secrecy. He was to tell no one in the world about Mr Po's interest, not even Daphne.

The editor still had ten minutes before morning conference. He took out the most recent edition of *Rural Retreats* and began to flick through its pages in a desultory way. All the enjoyment had gone out of the ritual since the disappearance of his map. He felt like a scholar who had lost his life's work. Irreplaceable research had vanished into thin air. It would be futile to buy another map and start again.

Disenchanted though he was, Doodle's eye was caught by an advertisement for a pretty gold-stoned manor house in Oxfordshire. It was not a county he knew well, though he had spent three years reading geography at an unfashionable college in the university. On summer evenings he would occasionally drive out into the countryside near Charlbury in the car of a friend from the same male-only college. He remembered the thick trees and the scent of flowers he could never identify and the feeling that something thrilling, the very breath of youth, was about to be revealed. The house only had four bedrooms, but its drawing room looked out to woods and fields, to the England Eric Doodle loved and yet would never be fully part of.

'Eric?'

He looked up and saw his successor standing above him, a suspicious and knowing smile on his face.

'What is it, Trevor?'

'We've got a fantastic story. Sam Blunt's pulled a fucking rabbit out of the hat.'

Because Doodle did not often use a computer, Yapp had printed out Sam's piece, which he now threw down on the desk in front of the editor. Doodle read an undeniably gripping story about the financial relationship between a prominent MP and a Chinese billionaire, an undeclared gift of two hundred thousand pounds, and the Prime Minister's indulgence of a corrupt relationship that possibly involved a foreign power. The article left dangling at the end the suggestion that the PM himself might be implicated in the rotten state of affairs over which he had presided.

When he had finished reading the story, Doodle placed it reverently on his desk as though it were a crucial piece of evidence that must not be mislaid.

'Exciting stuff, I agree, though he's obviously beaten it up a good bit.'

'Possibly,' conceded Yapp. 'It might need toning down a little. I'll get it lawyered. Glasswell hasn't sought an injunction – he must know his position is hopeless. It'll finish him off, and torpedo the PM and this Po villain. It's just what the paper needs.'

'No doubt it is,' replied Doodle. 'If we were able to use it.'

If he had heard that Benedict Brewster had won a Pulitzer Prize for journalism, Trevor Yapp could not have looked more astonished. 'What the hell do you mean?'

'We can't print it. It's as simple as that.'

'Why not?'

'I'm not at liberty to say,' said Doodle. 'Rest assured the proprietor will back me up. I know I can say with total confidence that I am speaking in his name.'

Yapp was not so easily persuaded. He leant across Doodle's desk as he had when remonstrating over Benedict's colour piece, and jabbed his fingers towards the editor's face.

'It's because your fucking friend the Prime Minister's involved, isn't it?'

Eric Doodle, who had no reason at that moment to feel beholden to his fucking friend the Prime Minister, assured his deputy that he was mistaken.

'I don't believe you,' cried Yapp, who was pacing to and fro in front of the desk from Arthur Pepper's old office in such a menacing way that Doodle half wondered whether he was going to hit him. 'You're just protecting your mate. I'm going to ring Sir Edwin Entwistle now.'

'Go ahead,' replied Doodle. Then his self-respect as a journalist got the better of his enjoyment of baiting Trevor Yapp. 'It's a great piece. I'd like to use it, but I can't. Maybe Sir Edwin will tell you why.'

The morning editorial conference was cancelled as telephone conversations took place between Trevor Yapp and Sir Edwin Entwistle and then between Sir Edwin and Eric Doodle.

The proprietor informed an agitated Yapp that the editor had made the right decision because he was in discussions with Mr Po about selling him the paper. If Trevor Yapp ever mentioned to another soul that talks were going on, or the reason for killing off the story, he would be out of the door of Pepper House within five minutes, and could kiss goodbye to any notion of ever becoming editor of the *Daily Bugle*, or for that matter one farthing of compensation. This threat quietened Yapp, though it did not make him gracious.

The editor-elect ended his side of the conversation abruptly. 'All right, then. I'll tell Sam Blunt. He won't be happy.'

'Believe me, Trevor, I don't give a damn for the state of mind of Sam Blunt.' With that, Sir Edwin put down the phone.

Journalists! They never had any idea about commercial realities. They thought all that mattered were truth and justice, and that they had a God-given right to print whatever they deemed was in the public interest. Well, he, Sir Edwin Entwistle, knew otherwise. He knew about money. He understood that truth and justice never came free, that there were necessary trade-offs and compromises along the way. He picked up the telephone to thank Eric Doodle for holding the line. Thank God that with a bit of luck, if old Po played ball, he would be out of all this quite soon. As he heard the editor's pleasant and reasonable voice, he couldn't help feeling that he was a lot easier to deal with than Trevor Yapp.

Chapter Nineteen

Sam was dumbfounded when an uncharacteristically crest-fallen Trevor Yapp told him his scoop had been spiked. His amazement turned to anger when the deputy editor refused to offer any sort of explanation.

In view of his previous enthusiasm, Yapp could hardly pretend the piece had been canned because it wasn't good enough. But despite some aggressive questioning by Sam, he had no intention of risking his future by flouting Sir Edwin's injunction. He simply repeated that, for reasons he didn't agree with, it had been decided not to run the story. Sam should take up the matter with Eric Doodle. When the reporter suggested that the real reason for the outrage was the editor's closeness to the Prime Minister, Trevor Yapp did not demur.

Eric Doodle was stealing another look at the golden Oxfordshire manor house when he heard a commotion in his outer office. Dora was telling Sam as sweetly as she could that it was customary to make an appointment to see the editor, and Mr Doodle happened to be occupied at that precise moment. Sam was informing Dora that this was a newspaper office rather than a doctor's surgery and he couldn't be expected to hang about all day. The dispute was settled by Sam simply walking past Dora and opening the door into the editor's office.

Doodle did not appreciate angry journalists barging into his room. But he sympathised with Sam. When long ago he had been a writer he would have been astounded to be treated in this fashion. He was also quite fond of the louche reporter, who had joined the paper shortly after he had been made deputy editor twenty years ago.

'Can you tell me what's going on?' Even in this moment of drama Sam could not bring himself to address the editor as either Eric or Mr Doodle.

'I'm sorry, Sam. It's beyond my control.'

'Don't I deserve a better explanation than that?'

'You do, but I'm afraid I can't give you one.'

'I think you're trying to protect the Prime Minister.'

'I give you my word that is not the case.'

Sam looked at his editor, and despite his anger was inclined to believe him. 'Why, then?'

Doodle was tempted to tell Sam the truth, but he knew that even if he were sworn to silence he would be unable to keep quiet. He sensed that in the power struggle between him and Yapp the advantage had for the first time swung fractionally in his favour. He wasn't going to jeopardise this unexpected bonus by confiding in Sam and incurring Sir Edwin's wrath.

'All I can say is that it's company policy. I'm as unhappy as you are about it, but we both have to accept what has happened.'

Sam could see that he was getting nowhere. He swung

around and marched out of Doodle's office, not forgetting to blow Dora a kiss as he passed.

The inexplicable spiking of Sam's story engendered much speculation in the newsroom. Although sentiment was mostly on his side, there was a lively faction led by Glasswell's recent lunching companion Adam Pride which held that the real reason the piece had been killed was that it was full of inaccuracies and downright lies. This theory was authoritatively adumbrated by Pride at his club that evening before, during and after dinner.

Sam retreated to the Half Moon, where he began to develop a plan. He would give the story to the *Chronicle*. There was no way of disguising his role in an act that would be regarded by many of his colleagues as a shameful betrayal. He would be immediately dismissed, but if this was the price he must pay for ensuring that Glasswell received his just deserts, so be it. Besides, there were only two months of his three months' notice at the *Bugle* remaining. With a bit of luck he would be represented as a heroic figure in some quarters, and walk into a job on another newspaper.

The only person he knew well on the *Chronicle* was the columnist Timothy Brown, whose habit of consuming his own ear wax at lunch had so appalled Lady Evelyn Wherewill. Years ago, when Brown was a young reporter, and the *Bugle* still interested in foreign stories, the two men had worked together in Africa. On one occasion, Sam had hired a helicopter to get into the capital of a former British colony where soldiers were butchering civilians after a coup. Sam had offered a ride to Brown, who would otherwise have been left marooned in a neighbouring country and missed the story. He had done this knowing that a reporter on the cash-strapped *Chronicle* would never be able to put his share of the cost of the helicopter on expenses. A sense of journalistic solidarity that went deeper than newspaper rivalry had impelled him. Timothy Brown had not forgotten this act of kindness.

Sam had given up trying to work out why his story had been spiked. A couple of miles away, in his house in Eaton Place, Sir Edwin Entwistle was about to provide his wife with the explanation. Though he knew she could be trusted with confidences, he worked on the principle that there was nothing to be gained in life from telling people secrets they did not need to know. For this reason he hadn't informed Caroline about his discussions with Mr Po. Circumstances had now changed, as he had decided to ask Mr and Madame Po for a weekend at his Shropshire estate. There, among signs of bucolic charm that might soften Mr Po's heart, he would attempt to ease him over the line, or at any rate close to it. This couldn't be accomplished without Caroline knowing what was going on.

Sir Edwin had not foreseen the strength of her opposition. He had proceeded as though it was for him alone to determine what should be done with the *Bugle*. Insofar as he had taken his wife's feelings into account, he had assumed she would be pleased by an unexpected windfall of tens of millions of pounds. He was wrong. Caroline relished being the wife of a newspaper proprietor. She was much less enamoured by the prospect of being married to an ex-newspaper proprietor.

'But why, Edwin? Why sell the *Bugle*? And so soon after the centenary celebrations!'

'It's not making any money, my sweet, and before long it

will be losing it – not that we shall dwell on that particular fact with Mr Po.'

'Can't you sack a few more people?'

'You can't go on sacking people for ever.'

'And what about the life peerage? Won't that be threatened?'

'I dare say I'll still be able to convince the Prime Minister that I remain a force to be reckoned with. If necessary, I can always make a donation to the party.'

Caroline knew that once her husband had set his mind on a particular course of action he could seldom be dissuaded. Her brain was clicking into gear. She realised that if Mr Po was being lined up to buy the *Bugle*, there would be no prospect of it running Sam's story about Glasswell's links to him.

As soon as Sam walked into their room at the Metropolitan Hotel that evening, she told him about her discovery that her husband intended to sell his newspaper to Mr Po. When Sam explained how Doodle had spiked his story, and divulged his plan to give it to the *Chronicle*, Caroline saw that fate had given them a perfect opportunity to scupper her husband's deal.

Sam's piece would be twice as deadly with her new information. It would not merely discredit and ruin Glasswell. It would also ensure that Mr Po never got hold of the *Daily Bugle* – and that she remained married to a newspaper proprietor. She had no doubt she could brazen it out should Edwin suspect her of breaking his confidence.

If things did not turn out exactly as they calculated, that was because she and Sam did not have a perfect insight into the petty and rancorous mind of Edward Sneed, editor of the *Chronicle*.

Splash!

The next day Sam arranged to meet Timothy Brown. The columnist knew he was no longer the apple of Sneed's eye. He had received second-hand reports that his pieces were considered predictable and lacking in edge. As a result, Brown's already impressive alcohol intake had risen. So too had his nervous consumption of his own ear wax, which was almost as disgusting to his colleagues and his wife as it had been to Lady Evelyn Wherewill. His columns had also got worse.

Brown was consequently very grateful to Sam to be handed a scoop such as he could never have written himself. He spoke to Sneed who in turn consulted the *Chronicle*'s political editor. There were numerous meetings and pow-wows. Gradually a consensus emerged that Sam's revelations about Glasswell were not all he had cracked them up to be. The political editor, who knew Glasswell and quite liked him, questioned the strength of Sam's sources. All this was music to Sneed's ears. He saw a way of damaging the *Bugle*, and was much less interested in damaging Terence Glasswell.

The headline of the *Chronicle*'s front-page splash when it appeared three days later was: *DAILY BUGLE* SUPRESSES SCANDAL ABOUT PROSPECTIVE BUYER. The story stated that Sir Edwin Entwistle, the newspaper's owner, had intervened to kill an article about the allegedly nefarious business dealings of Mr Po Chun, a prospective purchaser of the title. Only those with the stamina to read to the end of a rather convoluted piece learnt that these unspecified dealings had to do with Terence Glasswell, a prominent MP and member of the Foreign Affairs Committee. In descending order, the villains of the piece were Sir Edwin Entwistle, Mr Po Chun and Terence Glasswell.

In one sense the story achieved everything Caroline had hoped for. Within an hour of its publication Mr Po had dispatched a handwritten note to Sir Edwin Entwistle at his Mayfair offices. He was no longer interested in talking about possibly acquiring the *Daily Bugle*, and had been shocked to read references in the *Chronicle* to business meetings between them that were supposed to have been private. Their association was at an end.

But the piece did not achieve the outcome on which Sam had set his heart. Glasswell had escaped with a very few minor nicks on his armour. Television and radio bulletins throughout the day dwelt on the perfidy of Sir Edwin Entwistle, who had championed Press freedom but was happy to act as censor where his own business interests were concerned. Neither Sir Edwin nor Eric Doodle – nor anyone else from the *Bugle* – came forward to defend the newspaper's actions, for the simple reason that they were indefensible.

Sam was sitting in the Half Moon rueing what had happened and nursing a gin and tonic. He had been rung by Timothy Brown, who apologised if the story had not turned out exactly as they might have hoped. Then his mobile rang again. It was Trevor Yapp. He heard the deputy editor of the *Daily Bugle* spit out some not entirely unexpected words. 'You're fired.'

Chapter Twenty

Newspaper proprietors are not always infallible creatures. Sir Edwin Entwistle soon convinced himself that it was Trevor Yapp who had passed the information about his negotiations with Mr Po to the *Chronicle*. It did not occur to him for a second that Caroline was responsible. What motive could she possibly have had? As for Doodle, Sir Edwin had known his editor long enough to be sure he did as he was told. But Yapp was different. There was something truculent and untamed about the man. He hadn't bothered to conceal his anger when the piece was spiked.

Sir Edwin rang Doodle to share his suspicions about Yapp. Doodle hadn't the faintest idea who had told the *Chronicle* but he was pretty sure it wasn't his deputy. The man was too ambitious to risk his future for a principle. But the editor was not a saint. He couldn't help agreeing with Sir Edwin that he might have a point, and that it wasn't easy to imagine who had spilled the beans other than Trevor Yapp. He observed that journalists in the newsroom hadn't known about Mr Po's interest in buying the *Daily Bugle*, and couldn't be responsible for the leak.

By the time Sir Edwin telephoned Yapp he was practically certain the editor-elect was the guilty party.

'Trevor, I was proper pissed off to read that piece in the *Chronicle*.'

'So was I, Sir Edwin.'

'It's bloody wrecked the deal, of course.'

'I'm sorry to hear that.'

'Are you, Trevor? There are people saying it was you that did it.'

'I can't believe you think that.'

'I'd like not to, but for the life of me I can't see who else it could have been.'

'I categorically deny it was me.'

'I find that hard to believe.'

'I don't deny I was upset when the piece was killed, but I respected your reasons. I am always loyal. As soon as I saw the *Chronicle* piece, I personally got rid of Sam Blunt.'

'There are different ways of looking at that. I think we'd better put your promotion on hold for the moment. Now Mr Po has dropped out, there's not so much sense of urgency.'

Yapp was shocked. 'I hope you will reconsider that decision, Sir Edwin.'

'I don't expect I shall.' The proprietor of the *Daily Bugle* put down the receiver.

Trevor Yapp went to close the door of his office, and returned to his chair. He ran his fingers through his thick black hair. The injustice of it was hard to bear. Was Sir Edwin implying he would never be made editor? Surely not. The old monster would soften after a while. He'd have to believe his denials in the end. You can't hang a man on a trumped-up charge. Or can you?

Splash!

Yapp opened the top drawer of his metal desk and carefully extracted Doodle's map. He had looked at it many times since stealing it, and still couldn't make head or tail of the thing. He sensed the map's deep significance. He knew that in some way it opened a window into Eric Doodle's soul. But what did it show? Once again he examined the hieroglyphics, the strange patterning, and the different numbers covering the counties of England, each of them neatly ringed in black pencil. It occurred to him they might indicate military installations. Was Doodle a spy, and, if so, for whom was he spying? He thought of the balding, ineffectual man sitting behind his huge desk in the editor's office, and doubted that there was a government in the world stupid enough to employ him.

He heard a knock on the door, and looked up. It was Sophia. The sight of her long pensive face and flowing auburn hair touched even his brittle heart.

'You suggested we might have lunch today,' Sophia reminded him.

Trevor Yapp never normally had time for lunch. Nor would he dream of conducting an affair with someone in the office. But both these rules he was prepared to bend in the case of this bewitching girl.

Down at the Half Moon Sam was talking with Sophia's more ardent and purer worshipper. Benedict had rung him that morning after hearing he had been sacked. Sam had been nearby as he had gone to pick up bits and pieces accumulated over twenty years. These had been stuffed haphazardly into a disintegrating cardboard box and dumped in the downstairs lobby of Pepper House. This tattered container had been handed by a commissionaire to Sam on the street because he was forbidden to set foot in the building ever again.

Although Sam had put away three double gin and tonics, he was still sober. Benedict was getting tipsy. He was sad because Sophia barely noticed him, and he was sorry their story had not been published in the *Daily Bugle* and that Sam had been sacked. In an unprecedented act of rebellion, he had already exceeded his allotted half-hour lunch break by twenty minutes.

'If you're going, I'm leaving too,' he declared.

'What do you mean?'

'I've had enough. I can't bear the dungeon any longer. I loathe Yapp.'

'Don't go. I may need you there.'

'Why?'

'Well, we're not finished yet, the old team.' Sam gave Benedict a friendly slap on a large shoulder. 'We've still got to get Glasswell.'

Getting Terence Glasswell did not rank very high in Benedict's priorities at that precise moment, but he had a strong feeling of solidarity with Sam.

'OK. I'll do whatever you want. I'll even stay with Yapp louring at me.'

'Thanks.' Sam gave Benedict another comradely slap.

The two men subsided into silence and continued to drink.

'What are you going to do now, Sam?'

'I don't know. I'd hoped to get another job on the back of that *Chronicle* piece but it pretty much damned everyone at the *Bugle*.'

'Shits,' said Benedict.

Sam looked at his watch. 'Shouldn't you be getting back, Ben?'

Benedict was unaware that Trevor Yapp was still lunching

at the Saraceno with Sophia, his right foot nudging one of her delicately shaped ankles. If he had known, he would have gone into the restaurant and punched the deputy editor of the *Bugle* on the nose. As it was, he expressed complete indifference as to what Yapp would say to him when he returned to the dungeon.

'I'd never thought of being a journalist,' Benedict reflected, 'but the old man had this idea. Odd, if you think about it. I mean, there haven't been any Brewsters in the newspaper business. Anyway, I wanted to give it a shot. My dad has been terribly good to me. But I can't tell you, Sam, how bloody awful it is being cooped up in that dungeon with Andy Dodd and Yapp yelling at you all day. They're much worse than the maddest beaks at Eton. I can't see the point of it.'

'Journalism wasn't always like this.'

'No, well, it is now.' Benedict fell silent again before his mind raced on. 'I've been thinking about newspapers and journalists and all that, but I can't get my head round it all.'

'I gave up trying long ago.'

'Take expenses. Of course I don't have any – no such luck. But you do – did. Adam Pride does. I've heard he takes his floozy out to dinner and writes something like "top political contact" on his expense form.'

'So what?' asked Sam.

'Well, if an MP did that, you'd have his guts for garters.'

'MPs are public servants paid for by the taxpayer. Journalists work for private companies.'

'I don't see the *moral* difference,' said Benedict. 'It's stealing either way.'

Sam looked at his watch again. 'Ben, old chap, I really think you should be getting back.'

'And there's another thing. Take Yapp. He's having it off with Sophia – or trying to. He's a married man, Sam! He even wears a wedding ring. And yet the *Bugle* is always banging on about the importance of family values. He's the bloody deputy editor!'

'That's true.'

'And you, Sam, you wrote a piece about Glasswell having an affair with my barmy cousin Evelyn. I'm not getting at you – you're not a married man, so the charge of hypocrisy doesn't really arise. But Yapp is, and he damn well published your story. I don't understand it.'

'I see what you mean,' said Sam uneasily. 'But we live in a fallen world, Ben. Where are all the saints who could run newspapers?'

'I'm just trying to understand your world.'

'Ben,' said Sam gently, 'maybe you're not cut out for my world. Maybe you should join the Church. Or the *Chronicle*. But I don't want you to get sacked now. I need you on the inside. If you're sacked, your father will summon you back to Lincolnshire. When we finish off Terence Glasswell, you'll think it all worthwhile.'

'Maybe,' conceded Benedict. 'I hope so.'

Trevor Yapp wasn't there when he got back to the dungeon, and there was no sign of Sophia. Andy Dodd had unaccountably gone absent.

Benedict tried to make sense of the undulating words on his screen. His next assigned task, which should have already been completed, was to cobble together a piece from published online accounts about the latest bogus shark sighting off the Cornish coast.

He stuck with it for about ten minutes, fighting off repeated waves of tiredness and repeatedly kicking his left shin to stay awake. He had managed to write about a hundred words in which various species of lethal and peace-loving sharks were hopelessly confused when he decided to take a quick peek at the most recent batch of Lovelies on Bugle Online.

This was a fatal step. The latest pictures of Suzy Wattle, who was disporting herself on the beach at Marbella during the prolonged interrogation of her husband Nipper Richards by Spanish police, were impossible to resist. Soon he was lying on the warm sand alongside Suzy's brown body. He buried his head in her artificially inflated bosom without registering any great twinges of conscience in respect of Sophia. Soon the gentle sound of snoring could be heard as Benedict did what no man or woman had ever dared to do before in the dungeon, or has done since. Sleep.

Chapter Twenty-One

When he was a boy Terence Glasswell had exasperated his mother with his untidiness. As with several of his other rather more important faults, she had been unable to make much headway. He continued to expect others to clear up after him. Cynthia took up where his mother had left off. Although Glasswell now allowed her to employ a Portuguese cleaner four hours a week for heavy-duty housework, Cynthia was left with many other tasks. One of them was tidying up her husband's clothes which he left lying around his bedroom.

She was standing there, shaking and smoothing a pair of suit trousers before putting it on its hanger, when she noticed a small object drop to the floor. Thinking it might be a coin worth retrieving, she bent down to inspect it, and found lying on the carpet the microphone that had flown out of Benedict's grip during his altercation with her husband.

Cynthia had no idea it was a microphone. At first sight it looked like a useless piece of plastic. She was on the point of throwing it into the wastepaper basket when she thought again. Whatever the object was, it looked as though someone had spent time and care making it. Long years of marriage to Glasswell had made her especially cautious. She popped the thing into a pocket, and later placed it on the mantelpiece in the sitting room so that she could show it to her husband when he returned.

Glasswell got back at ten thirty having popped into the Commons to vote on the way back from dinner at Bright's. He was in an especially good mood because relations with his new secretary had advanced to the point where the small sofa in his office scarcely seemed adequate for the tasks that were being asked of it. He poured himself a sizeable whisky, and sat down in front of the television.

'Darling?'

'What is it?'

'I found this.' Cynthia handed him the microphone.

Glasswell knew immediately what it was. 'Where did you find it?'

'It fell out of your trousers when I was putting them away.'

'Which ones?'

'The brown ones with turn-ups. You know, part of your lightweight suit.'

Glasswell's mind raced back. He generally had two or three suits on the go which he would rotate. He knew he hadn't worn the brown one for at least a week. When had he last done so? He cast his mind back and saw himself perusing his row of suits on the day of that lunch with Sir Archibald Merrick, and preferring the brown one to the chalk-stripe because it was a warm day. He had worn the suit then, and again perhaps a day or two later.

Suddenly the goofy face of his assailant swam into view. Of course! It was on that day. The gangly youth who had followed him must have planted the microphone. But where? Cynthia said it had fallen out when she was shaking his trousers. It couldn't have been in the side pockets as he'd have found it. The back pocket would have been buttoned up, and therefore inaccessible. Either by luck or by judgement – almost certainly luck, in view of the idiotic man's flailing arms – the microphone must have ended up in a turn-up.

Terence Glasswell put his whisky down with such a jolt that Cynthia jumped. He would have been miked up that afternoon when Finula gave him his first blow-job. Her energetic lips would have been no more than a couple of feet from the microphone. God knows what they would have made of her undeniably strange gulping sounds. And what on earth was he doing with her when he next wore the brown suit?

Glasswell thought there were three possible groups that could have been responsible for this outrage. One was the Chinese intelligence service, which might want to keep tabs on his relations with Mr Po. Another was MI5, which could have numerous reasons for wishing to bug either of them. But these theories were both fairly unlikely because of the amateurishness of the operation. Top-class outfits do not use half-witted youths to track you at a distance of thirty feet in broad daylight. No, it had to be some sort of half-cocked journalistic stunt. Glasswell was pretty certain that it was linked in some way to the telephone call he had received from that creep Blunt three or four days before that bizarre piece appeared in the *Chronicle*.

Splash!

The planting of the microphone *had* to be connected with him in some way. The *Chronicle* obviously couldn't be guilty of such an outrage. Blunt must have employed that ass. What were they up to? Was the *Bugle* biding its time before coming out with a sensational story which would make use of the material it had recorded with him and Finula? If that was their game, he would have to seize the initiative, and head off the reptiles before they got the chance to damage him.

'What are you thinking, darling?' asked Cynthia, who was about to go upstairs to her solitary bed.

'Oh, nothing much. As a matter of fact, I was just thinking of launching a national crusade to clean up the Press.'

He would hold a press conference to announce his campaign in a couple of days. Because he was a well-known MP, and could promise amazing revelations about newspaper surveillance, the event was bound to be attended by lots of journalists.

Toiling away in the dungeon, so far removed from the real world, Benedict Brewster was not one of them. He was on Andy Dodd's hate list for having fallen asleep at his desk. Dodd had discovered Benedict with a seraphic smile on his face. He was doing things with Suzy Wattle that a well-brought-up young man who went to church perhaps ought not to have done. Dodd gave him a sharp poke in the ribs, which his subconscious had difficulty in interpreting. Suzy, though a little vulgar, was a nice girl from whom a poke in the ribs was the last thing he would have expected.

Dodd had wanted to sack Benedict on the spot. There were plenty more competent and hard-working young people who would gladly take on his job. Sacking, however, was outside his remit. Normally he would have dispatched Benedict to Trevor Yapp for him to sign the death warrant, but the deputy editor was unaccountably absent that afternoon. It was the young man's good fortune that he was sent to see the editor.

Eric Doodle remembered far-off days when half the newsroom would have a snooze in the early afternoon, sleeping off the effects of a good lunch. The elephantine snoring of old Harry Frost, the education correspondent, had been as dependable a part of his young life as a reporter as the bells of St Bride's in Fleet Street. He had no intention of sacking any journalist for such an offence, far less the younger son of Sir Cumming Brewster. In order to placate Dodd, he delivered Benedict a little homily about the dangers of drinking too much at lunch, and the importance of hard work. Benedict thanked him for his helpful words, and promised never to fall asleep in the dungeon again.

For the past few days he had applied himself to his job diligently, avoiding drink as well as the lure of Suzy Wattle. His heart had leapt when Sophia once returned his smile. She seemed even more wan and preoccupied than usual.

On the evening of the day on which Terence Glasswell launched his Call to the Nation to root out the cancer in the modern Press, Benedict returned directly to his flat in Hackney. He cooked himself a microwave meal and drank a glass of orange juice. Then he took out a novel and began to read it. After a while, exhausted by his day, he fell asleep.

At about 10.30 the telephone awoke him. It was his father.

'Hi, Dad.'

'Are you all right, Ben? You sound sleepy.'

'I did drop off. How are you and Mum?'

'We're fine, thanks. Did you watch the news this evening?'

'No, I didn't,' admitted Benedict.

'There was an item about Terence Glasswell launching a crusade against newspapers. The damn fool is setting up some sort of task force. You didn't see it?'

'No.'

'He had a grim-looking Cynthia alongside him. Extraordinary behaviour.'

'What did he say?'

'He claimed a journalist had planted a microphone on him. Held it aloft. They interviewed a policeman who said it was one of a new type of high-tech microphones. Apparently they're hardly bigger than a twenty-pence piece. Incredible, really.'

If Sir Cumming Brewster had been able to see his son he would have known that he was wide awake and in a state of some agitation.

'Are you still there, Ben?'

'Yes, Dad.'

'Anyway, Glasswell gave an account of how he claims this journalist slipped the microphone into his trousers or something. There was a bit of an argy-bargy and the police were called, but the chap escaped.'

'Yes, Dad.'

'The thing is, Ben,' Sir Cumming lowered his voice, though Bassett Park was very far from the reach of Terence Glasswell, 'he said this man was young and, well, tall, and he would recognise him anywhere. He also said that he had a pretty good idea of which newspaper this person worked for.'

'Did he?'

'Yes. I haven't discussed this with your mother, Ben, because I don't want to worry her.' Sir Cumming had lowered his voice to little more than a whisper. 'But I couldn't help wondering, in view of what this bounder Glasswell said, and our previous conversations about him . . . I've naturally been asking myself whether the tall young man with a microphone might have been you.'

Benedict had not told his father a lie since he was twelve, when Sir Cumming, having come across a couple of cigarette butts in the kitchen garden, had asked his younger son whether they were his. His pretence that they weren't had weighed on his conscience for many years.

'It was me, Dad.'

Benedict heard an intake of breath the other end.

'I thought as much. I don't blame you, Ben – far from it. I'd probably have done the same myself. But there's no denying you're in a bit of a pickle. Glasswell will want his pound of flesh.'

'I expect he will.'

'I was wondering whether you would like to come back here. Lie low for a while.'

'How will that help if he's determined to get me?'

'It'd be more difficult to catch up with you here, I suppose. An Englishman's castle and all that.'

Benedict was thinking. He was remembering what Sam had said about still wanting to get Glasswell. He was a rogue and a menace. There had to be a way of fighting back. If Terence Glasswell was trying to destroy him, he would expose him for what he was.

'I think I'll stay here, Dad, if that's all right. I've got this friend Sam Blunt – he's the chief reporter I told you about.

He's a bit of a rogue in many ways but there's a sort of resolution about him, and also a strange kind of goodness, almost. He still thinks he can nail Glasswell.'

'I hope he can, but the man's got powerful friends.'

'I'm sure he has.'

'Be careful, Ben. Don't do anything that would worry your mother.'

'I won't.'

'Tell me if there's anything I can do. I'll put my own thinking cap on.'

'Thanks.'

'Goodnight, Ben.'

'Goodnight, Dad.'

Benedict lay on his bed. It was dark now, though the great engine of London would never cease. Who would have thought that he, Benedict Brewster, would have featured anonymously on national television news? He must be the subject of a police investigation.

He flicked on the television. There was a funny little man identified as the Right Reverend Bob Butcher, Bishop of Middlesex, who was being asked about media ethics on a late-night news programme. The bishop was of the opinion that the Press needed to examine itself if it was now going around planting microphones on MPs. He himself had had a shocking recent experience – it would be wrong to go into details – of the moral depths to which some journalists had sunk. He believed that the excessive alcohol intake of some reporters was likely to be a contributory problem to falling standards.

Benedict switched off the television and rang Sam.

The ex-chief reporter of the *Daily Bugle* was letting himself into his basement flat in Barons Court after returning from an exhausting tryst with Caroline at the Metropolitan Hotel.

'Sam?'

'Yes?'

'It's me, Benedict. Can we talk?'

Chapter Twenty-Two

The next morning's newspapers were full of Terence Glasswell's Call to the Nation with the exception of the *Financial Gazette*, which ignored the matter on its front page in favour of a piece about the latest European crisis. The *Daily Dazzle* dismissed the MP's remarks as a load of non-sense. The *Bugle* was less outspoken. Doodle had rightly sensed that the paper was in his sights more than any other, and was anxious not to appear too defensive.

He had also been struck by Glasswell's vivid description of the gangly youth he had beaten off. It sounded surprisingly like Benedict Brewster. Doodle comforted himself with the thought that his young protégé was the last person in the world to go around slipping microphones into the trousers of Members of Parliament.

The *Chronicle* gave over more space to Glasswell's crusade than any other newspaper, noting approvingly the broad make-up of the task force being assembled by the MP, which included such people of distinction as the Bishop of Middlesex and Sir Archibald Merrick. An editorial, which experts such as Eric Doodle and Trevor Yapp could recognise as Edward

Sneed's own work, recalled that Terence Glasswell had recently appeared in the paper's own pages in a story linking him to Mr Po Chun, the Chinese billionaire. Mr Glasswell was therefore not wholly untouched by controversy, though there was no suggestion that he had behaved in a discreditable way. For that reason it was a good thing that he would not himself sit on the commission which he had inspired. The *Chronicle* nonetheless welcomed his initiative. There was no doubt that some newspapers – this was perhaps not the moment to name them – had sailed too close to the wind. One title in particular had displayed an unhealthy interest in the private life of Mr Glasswell only a couple of years ago. Nine times out of ten the argument that the private lives of public figures were a matter of public concern was naked self-interest on the part of newspapers which merely wanted to sell more copies. It was too early to say whether or not the alleged planting of a microphone on Mr Glasswell was part of a further attempt to snoop into his personal affairs. All that could be stated with confidence was that the use of eaves-dropping devices by any newspaper would bring disgrace and ruin on the culprit, and shame on parts of the newspaper industry. With this flourish, Sneed signed off.

Trevor Yapp cast the paper aside. 'Bloody hypocrites,' he muttered to himself.

The deputy editor of the *Bugle* was not in a good mood. He didn't like being lectured to by Edward Sneed at the best of times. He knew for a fact that the star turn of the *Chronicle*'s Sunday edition, Annette Bustome, had once invented an entire interview with the film star Tray Nevada, full of verbatim quotes, after discovering when she returned home from their meeting that her tape recorder had run out of battery. Nevada, who had expected to be monstered, didn't complain when the predictably beastly piece was published, probably because he had been drunk during the encounter and had no memory of what he had said. Yapp thought it typical of the woman, who would be unable to provide a faithful account of a church fête. And then there was the paper's chief reviewer, Arthur Bagg, who once wrote and dispatched an excoriating review of a novel which the paper's literary editor had forgotten to send him.

On this particular morning the *Chronicle*'s lofty tone was more irksome to him than usual. Yapp felt his life's dream had been snatched away. For years he had put up with Doodle, first running the news pages, which the editor had been too idle to do, and then launching Bugle Online. Sir Edwin Entwistle, having at long last recognised his contribution and promised him the editorship, had withdrawn the prize for reasons which seemed as unjust as they were inexplicable. They had not spoken since the proprietor had delivered his bombshell. He had written him a wild letter, pleading for second thoughts and raising concerns about Eric Doodle's state of mind, which Mrs Yapp, on being shown the missive, had advised him not to send.

Yapp eased out the map again from his top drawer. Of course Doodle couldn't be a spy. It didn't make sense. But what could these markings signify? His eye was drawn to the neat lettering in a county south of Yorkshire which Yapp, London born and bred, conjectured might be Lincolnshire, if it wasn't Derbyshire. There was a tiny drawing of what looked like a large house, with turrets and a flagpole, by which the editor had written the minuscule letters 'SCB'. What could this mean?

Sometimes he felt like tearing up the map. At least he would be destroying something that had been cherished by the infuriating editor. But he remained confident that in some way this document was discreditable to Doodle, and might even have sinister implications. If he could only discover the key to understanding the thing, he would be able to show it to Sir Edwin Entwistle, and convince him that he was harbouring either a lunatic or a criminal.

Yapp placed the map back in the drawer, which he half closed; for some reason it did not run smoothly on its runners. He picked up his copy of the *Chronicle* again and studied the front-page picture of Glasswell. He was certain that Sam Blunt was behind this caper. Only Sam was reckless and desperate enough to think of planting a microphone on the MP. He felt a twinge of admiration combined with a desire to strangle the reporter. The Press was in enough trouble without stunts of this sort. Yapp was pretty sure from Glasswell's description that the bungling giant who had tried to plant the microphone was none other than Benedict Brewster. Unlike Eric Doodle, who quickly convinced himself that the younger son of Sir Cumming Brewster was incapable of such an act, Yapp thought that of all the certified clots in the world he was by far the most likely culprit.

The deputy editor of the *Daily Bugle* had not yet decided what he would do. Sam, having already been dismissed from the newspaper, probably lay beyond his powers of retribution. Benedict Brewster did not. The challenge lay in devising a punishment that inflicted the maximum amount of pain for the maximum length of time.

He must get on. It was time for a visit to the dungeon. The thought of his little empire put the ice-maiden Sophia in his mind. Trevor Yapp was not a romantic man but this haughty beauty had awakened longings in him that he had never previously experienced. Her apparent indifference to his strokings magnified his desire. He suspected she felt contempt for him. This insight served only to multiply her attractions, and deepen his fascination.

Sam and Benedict were sitting in the Half Moon, each sipping a non-alcoholic drink. Benedict was wearing sunglasses again. They had both forlornly digested the newspapers. There was no doubting Terence Glasswell had brilliantly seized the high ground. Instead of being pilloried in the Press for pocketing a large gift from a controversial Chinese billionaire, he was spearheading a crusade against tabloid newspapers.

Sam's downcast demeanour disconcerted Benedict. The irrepressible reporter had the stunned and beaten-down look of a chess player who, having been certain he was one move away from checkmating his opponent, suddenly discovers it is he who has been vanquished.

'What are we going to do?' asked Benedict.

'Stay shtum, that's for sure.'

'Do you suppose the police are still looking for me?'

'I doubt it. I dare say they don't take Glasswell entirely seriously.'

'How do we get him before he gets us?'

Sam looked pensive, stirring his drink with a straw. He had to admit to himself that he didn't have any particularly brilliant ideas. 'I suppose we could try planting another microphone on him.'

'No!'

'It would have worked. Just a pity he spotted you first.'

'I know.'

'You mustn't blame yourself.'

'I don't.'

Sam continued to appear reflective. 'We could try Cynthia. She must know enough to send Glasswell to the bottom of the sea.'

'But is she likely to talk?'

'Probably not,' admitted Sam. 'And if she didn't, she'd tell Glasswell, and he'd call another press conference, denouncing us for getting at his wife. That'd give his bloody task force something to chew over.'

'So what can we do?'

'Who knows more about Terence Glasswell's wrongdoing than any other person in the world?'

'Cynthia?'

'Apart from Cynthia?'

Benedict racked his brain. 'My cousin Evelyn?'

'Good guess. Try again.'

'Mr Po?'

'Exactly.'

'Is he likely to talk to us?'

'Not likely, perhaps, but he may have good reason to do so. Think about it. Old Po must be pretty sore at the moment. He had been planning to buy the *Daily Bugle* – an outrageous idea, by the way, which would have meant the paper was edited from Beijing, but that's another story. He's been made to look a fool by the *Chronicle*. Who does he blame? Entwistle, for sure, who Po must think blabbed to someone who blabbed to Sneed – which is actually more or less what happened. But he can't be feeling overjoyed with Glasswell either. The man's embarrassed him. His relations with him have been all over the public prints, and it's been implied they're not exactly wholesome.'

'So you think he wants to sack him?'

'Not just sack. Put as much distance as possible between him and Glasswell. Get out his side of the story. Portray himself in a favourable light.'

'And he could do that by talking to us?'

'Precisely.'

'And just how would we set about doing that?'

'That's a good question, Ben, and I don't have an answer to it right now. But let me work on it.'

Chapter Twenty-Three

Ambrose Treadle had begun his journalistic career on the *Financial Gazette*. In fact, he never worked on the paper itself but for a syndication service it supplied for rich clients. While more able contemporaries who worked on the newspaper advanced, Ambrose stayed near the bottom of a subsidiary ladder that led nowhere in particular. There he caught alluring glimpses of the multi-millionaires who paid handsomely for advice and insights they could have picked up for a thousandth of the price in the mainstream financial press – which was actually where they originated. He began to understand that wealthy businessmen will spend enormous amounts of their shareholders' money for guidance they could acquire vastly more cheaply elsewhere. So he came up with a plan to launch a financial PR company.

Though barely numerate, and not very knowledgeable about the media, Ambrose had one advantage in his new trade – gravitas. He brought a sense of seriousness to whatever he did. Often in meetings with clients he said very little. His studied silences, which frequently reflected an absence of ideas and occasionally a wholly vacant mind, were interpreted as evidence of a formidably active intellect forever weighing and sifting arguments before he made considered pronouncements. When uttered, the words themselves scarcely counted. Had they been written down on a piece of paper, some might have questioned whether they were worth tens of thousands of pounds. As it was, his authoritative delivery would have invested the recital of a bus timetable with significance.

Not long after the *Chronicle* ran its story about Mr Po, Sir Edwin Entwistle summoned Ambrose Treadle, much as a medieval monarch with a touch of ague would call for a favoured physician, who had occasioned a great deal of pain in the past, to bleed him. Sir Edwin knew his reputation had taken a knock. If he had sold the *Bugle* to Mr Po for several tens of millions of pounds he would doubtless have been criticised for putting a precious national asset in foreign hands. But at least the City would have been pleased that a potential drain on Entwistle Enterprises had been staunched. As events had unfurled, he was being attacked in the pages of the *Chronicle* and even on the floor of the House of Commons for unpatriotic behaviour without receiving any plaudits from investors for attempting to offload the paper.

Naturally he had replied to Mr Po's angry letter, pleading innocence and expressing the hope that he and Madame Po would still do him and Caroline the honour of coming to stay in Shropshire for what would be an entirely social weekend. He would welcome the opportunity of showing the Pos improvements he had made to his estate, in particular the erection on a hill he owned of an arc of wind turbines, each of which stood twice as high as Nelson's Column. To his mortification Mr Po did not deign to respond to this artless overture. Only when Caroline reported that she had been cut by Madame Po at the Bishop of Middlesex's charity auction did Sir Edwin finally accept the deal would never be resuscitated.

There was still his reputation to consider. Crude cynics might wonder why the proprietor of a national newspaper, who might be expected to know a thing or two about the workings of the media, should have turned to an unsuccessful former journalist turned PR man for illumination. These souls know nothing of the magnificence of Ambrose in his perfectly cut Savile Row suits. They have never seen his hand-made brogues or his high-collared shirts, or caught the flash of his 18-carat gold engraved cufflinks. Nor do they have any insights into the heart of a Press proprietor who has been disappointed in his hopes of selling a once great newspaper to a Chinese billionaire.

If not the genius some in the City proclaimed him to be, Ambrose was astute enough to realise that nothing much could be done. The news was out. Sir Edwin had been thwarted in a discreditable deal. The main cure lay, as it so often does, in the balm that passing time dispenses to its victims. There was, after all, no great scandal. No one, not even the *Chronicle*, was calling for Sir Edwin's head. In two or three weeks the contretemps would be almost forgotten as the voracious media devoured and forgot a succession of new stories. In six months' time it might as well never have happened.

However, if you are charging ten thousand pounds a day to the long-suffering shareholders of Entwistle Enterprises, it is as well not to state the blindingly obvious. Ambrose's face went through a medley of contortions calculated to convey the profundity of his thoughts. He blew out air and then took in a lungful again. He examined Sir Edwin's ceiling and rolled his eyes. He crossed his elegantly pinstriped legs at the ankles and then uncrossed them. Finally he came out with his advice costing about five hundred pounds a word.

'I think you should issue a statement saying that it is not, and never has been, your intention to sell the *Daily Bugle*.'

'That's not true, of course.'

'Of course,' agreed Ambrose.

Sir Edwin was not a man wedded to telling the truth but he was interested in knowing the advantage of telling a downright lie.

'It'll clear the air,' pronounced the PR man gnomically. 'And it'll cast some doubt on the veracity of the *Chronicle*'s account. I'll ring Simon Bindlap on the *Financial Gazette* and spin him a line.'

'And what happens if Po says he and I have been having talks?'

'He won't,' declared Ambrose confidently. He leant towards Sir Edwin as though imparting precious information to the Press proprietor that might carry a special premium. 'He'd lose face.'

Sir Edwin pondered his adviser's statement. He certainly didn't have unbounded confidence in him. There was the time when the media had been squawking about his multi-million-pound bonus – paid in a year in which the profits of Entwistle Enterprises had dipped. Ambrose had advised judicious donations to various charities, including the Bishop of Middlesex's fund for inner-city gangs that had turned to Christ. Far from calling off the hounds, this stratagem had provoked charges of tokenism and bad faith.

On the other hand, when one of Sir Edwin's hotels in Bermuda had collapsed, killing two elderly American guests enjoying a 'grey honeymoon' break, the PR man had successfully managed to direct most of the blame on to a hapless local builder. There was no doubting Ambrose's advice did sometimes bear fruit, though whether more by luck than judgement Sir Edwin was never sure.

'Won't me saying I've never had any intention of selling the paper, and never will, deter buyers?'

'Not at all. It'll have the opposite effect. They'll know it's a lie – a code for announcing that you're ready to sell.'

'I see,' said Sir Edwin, who did not really see at all. He was well aware that there was hardly a queue of would-be buyers clamouring to acquire the paper. He didn't want to put off a single potential suitor. Other publishers had too many financial problems of their own to wish to take on the *Bugle*. With Mr Po out of the frame, his best remaining hope lay with Boris Vrodsky, the Russian oligarch who had stolen and cheated his way from life as an out-of-work stevedore to being the richest aluminium magnate in the world. The only problem was that Vrodsky was wanted in the United States on seventeen counts of larceny and misappropriation of funds, and it would need all Ambrose's know-how, and much more, to represent him as an acceptable owner of the *Daily Bugle*.

'All right. Put out a statement saying I'm not a seller and never will be. Tell Bindlap I'll speak to him if it'll help.'

When Ambrose had left, Sir Edwin lapsed into ruminations about the *Bugle*. What should he do with Doodle? There was no doubting the editor was a safe pair of hands who had rarely caused him any grief. All the same, he was getting on and knew damn all about Bugle Online. That was why he had lined up Yapp to impress Po. Yapp looked as though he was the flipping future. The proprietor still suspected him of being behind the story in the *Chronicle*. Disloyalty was a terrible thing. On the other hand, you could never really trust any journalist, even one as accommodating as Eric Doodle. Betrayal was written into their DNA. You always had to remember that. Yapp was like an apparently well-trained Rottweiler who would gobble up your dinner when you weren't looking. So long as you weren't lulled into a false sense of security you could deal with such people. It was a question of knowing where you stood. If Vrodsky or anyone else was interested in buying the *Bugle*, Yapp, for all his faults, was a more effective advertisement than Doodle.

Sir Edwin Entwistle stroked his small moustache thoughtfully. Although not given to self-pity, he reflected that he was sometimes under-appreciated, even by Caroline. The life of a Press proprietor was not an easy one. There were politicians forever muttering about tighter controls of the media – look at that rascal Terence Glasswell trying to stir up the great and the good. There were guests at fashionable dinner parties grumbling to him about their treatment at the hands of the *Daily Bugle* and Bugle Online. There were the damned journalists, who behaved as though money grew on trees and thought they had a God-given right to write whatever they wanted, and hang the consequences. Worst of all, there were the bloody readers. They lapped up stories about sex and infidelity without ever troubling their soft heads as to the means by which they were obtained. Then they had the nerve to tell pollsters that they believed newspapers should respect people's privacy. Their idiocy was scarcely credible. It never seemed to occur to these halfwits that the production of a newspaper took time and money. Give them half a chance and they preferred to go online and read the stuff free rather than part with a fraction of the cost of a cup of coffee. Thank God the *Bugle* had some older readers who were too dyed in the wool to give up their old ways.

Sir Edwin again stroked his moustache, which Caroline had often urged him to shave off. Time does not wait even for a Press tycoon and he realised he was late for an appointment in Earls Court. Mrs Vera Potts, as he liked to think of her despite their relative intimacy, would be waiting in her flat with a pot of tea and a plate of éclairs, as well as her whips and the other accoutrements of her trade. The thought of that homely scene, and Mrs Potts clad in red lace suspenders and a black brassiere restraining her monumental bosom, brightened Sir Edwin's troubled mind, and he was able to banish all thought of Ambrose Treadle, Boris Vrodsky, Eric Doodle, Trevor Yapp, presumptuous journalists and the tiresome readers of the *Daily Bugle*.

Chapter Twenty-Four

Despite Ambrose Treadle's prediction, there were few who interpreted Sir Edwin Entwistle's statement as evidence that the press tycoon remained eager to sell. Even Boris Vrodsky rubbed his eyes in some perplexity as he sat on his private jet peering into his tablet to keep up with developments in a dozen countries. On the other hand, there were many who doubted the contention that Sir Edwin hadn't attempted to offload the *Bugle* to Mr Po. A seemingly authoritative piece by Simon Bindlap in the *Financial Gazette* suggesting that no talks had taken place – quoting 'sources close to Sir Edwin Entwistle' – was widely disbelieved. The *Chronicle* was particularly sceptical, with Edward Sneed in a waspish second leader coming close to calling the tycoon a liar.

The same issue reported that Terence Glasswell's Call to the Nation task force had been augmented by the respected retired High Court judge Sir Patrick Clapp, who had agreed to act as chairman. The *Chronicle* noted that Sir Patrick had proved himself a tireless critic of the excesses of the tabloid Press in a succession of libel and privacy cases. However, it did not mention that before being appointed to the judiciary he had frequently been retained by the *Daily Dazzle*, and sometimes the *Bugle*, to defend with great ingenuity and apparent conviction the very practices that he later abominated as a judge. The *Chronicle* was increasingly confident that, with a membership comprising the likes of Sir Patrick Clapp, the Bishop of Middlesex and Sir Archibald Merrick, the committee would make a valuable contribution to the debate on Press freedom. Glasswell was rightly taking no part in the proceedings of the task force, which was sensible in view of his well-known feelings about the media. But the paper thought he should be congratulated for focusing minds on what was undoubtedly an issue of public concern.

Down in the dungeon Benedict was far removed from these lofty considerations. He had been subjected to the first phase in a long series of punishments dreamt up by Trevor Yapp. This excluded the possibility of even occasional interchange with Suzy Wattle, whose husband Nipper Richards had been charged in Malaga, so it was reported that very morning, with forty-five alleged drug offences, as well as one of attempted kidnapping. Benedict's new task was to monitor the illiterate rants of readers posting comments on Bugle Online.

To start with, he had tried to impose some order on these splurges – inserting full stops and commas and capital letters in roughly the right places. But he soon realised it was a hopeless task. These torrents of unpunctuated nonsense would flow on until the end of time. He now restricted himself to removing obvious libels and vile abuse which readers unleashed against public figures, Bugle Lovelies, journalists and one another. This morning he had taken out some obscene observations about Suzy Wattle's breasts, a pledge to cut off the editor's testicles and two death threats directed at Adam Pride.

Although he hated the work, he was relieved still to be a free man. For fear of attracting the notice of police officers, he crossed roads only at traffic lights. After work he went straight home, avoiding public places as much as possible lest he be recognised from Glasswell's description.

Trevor Yapp stood at one end of the dungeon observing the young man with concentrated malevolence. He had accused Benedict to his face of being the MP's assailant and did not for a moment believe his stammering denial.

The deputy editor of the *Daily Bugle* was in high spirits. Sir Edwin Entwistle had just telephoned him in a friendly way and proposed lunch at the Fig Leaf in a few days' time. Yapp was confident that the proprietor intended to revive his offer of the editorship. One of his first acts on being installed behind Arthur Pepper's desk would be to sack Doodle's half-witted protégé, Benedict Brewster.

Two miles away, in her gilded bedroom in Eaton Place, Caroline lay on her bed, each eye covered with a thin slice of cucumber. On this occasion she had little fear of interruption from her husband, who she knew was lunching at his Mayfair club, which was also favoured by Russian tarts and, whenever he was in London, Boris Vrodsky.

Caroline was not happy. A disconsolate Sam had asked her a favour which she felt she couldn't perform. She had been glad to help her lover by passing on the details of Mr Po's loan to Terence Glasswell which she had learnt from Evelyn Wherewill. And she had been delighted to tell Sam about her husband's talks with Mr Po with the object of scuppering the deal. But this time it was different. She felt powerless to intervene.

Sam had suggested she persuade Madame Po to ask Mr Po to give him an interview. Caroline told Sam that Madame Po had cut her at a charity auction, and she could no longer speak to her. Sam then asked her whether she could think of any other way of approaching Mr Po. She had replied she couldn't. This was not absolutely true.

Caroline knew that in a couple of days the Pos were spending the weekend at Hastings Hall with Evelyn and her awful brother. The purpose was to persuade Mr Po to purchase the Qing vase to which the earl's ancestor had helped himself during the Second Opium War.

Evelyn was always helpful. If Caroline were to ask her to persuade Mr Po to grant an interview to Sam Blunt, she would do her best, though she would wonder why her friend was interceding on behalf of the drunken hack who had ruined her lunch party. But Caroline could have easily invented some sort of elaborate explanation.

She didn't like seeing Sam thwarted and unhappy, and longed to help him. What held her back was the possibility that any interview with Mr Po might cause further embarrassment to her husband. The Chinese billionaire might insist that talks publicly disavowed by Treadle Associates on behalf of Sir Edwin had taken place. God alone knew what other bombs he might detonate. Although Sam's mission was to expose Glasswell, he could hardly ignore revelations about Edwin when he wrote his story. He was no longer constrained by being a *Bugle* journalist, and might relish kicking Edwin when he was down.

Caroline did not love her husband. She was besotted

with Sam. But she was a woman of the world. She knew that she and Edwin were lashed together on the bridge of the same ship. She might be disloyal to him, and he to her, but in the end they shared a common interest, even if they had differed about the sale of the *Bugle*. She looked forward to the day when he would take his seat in the House of Lords and she would be able to attend state occasions in her tiara. Caroline expected the day would come when she would weep at his deathbed.

She also guessed that Sam was tiring of her. She was not surprised, though disappointed. She could see it was not in his nature to be true to any person, and that he was not wedded to any principle, other than that of disclosing the secrets of those who did not want them disclosed. She had loved him for the dangers he had passed. There was something restless and rebellious about him. He didn't belong to anyone. These were the things which had drawn her to him in the first place. Even in their most ardent moments of lovemaking she felt some part of him remained elsewhere.

Their brief liaison would not last. It was sad. She knew it was sad. But she closed her mind against the sadness.

Who can say Caroline wouldn't have interceded with Evelyn Wherewill if she believed Sam would always love her? She might sometimes appear to the world as a calculating woman. But Caroline would have given up the house in Eaton Place, the estate in Shropshire, the *Bugle*, even the tiara itself, if she had found a man who loved her as she loved him. It could not be Sam.

That evening they met as usual at the Metropolitan Hotel. They had always dined in their cramped room. Tonight Sam did not remove his clothes. He sat on the bed, his head in his hands. Caroline suddenly yearned to get out, whatever the danger. When she suggested to Sam that they go to a local restaurant for dinner, he readily accepted.

'What's the matter, darling?' she finally asked when they were seated in a dark corner of La Bastide.

'Nothing.'

'Tell me.'

'It's nothing. Just frustrated, I suppose.'

'By what?'

'I haven't got a job, remember.'

'If money is any problem—'

'It isn't. I can try PR if the worst comes to the worst.'

'But I can always help.'

'No thanks.'

'Why not? Don't be proud. Whether you have money or not in life is simply a matter of chance.'

Sam did not respond to this aperçu. He disposed of a glass of red wine in one go and poured himself another.

'Darling, are you drinking too much?'

'I expect so.'

Caroline looked cross.

'Have you had any more thoughts about Mr Po?' Sam asked after a while.

'You know Madame Po won't speak to me. I don't see what else I can do.'

'What about one of your friends? Don't any of them know him?'

'None that comes to mind. The Bishop of Middlesex knows Madame Po through her charity work, but I can hardly ask him.'

'I suppose you can't,' said Sam.

'How's Benedict?' asked Caroline. Though she had never met the younger son of Sir Cumming Brewster, Sam had sometimes made her laugh by regaling her with stories of his exploits.

'Slaving away, I expect. Still petrified of being arrested by the police.'

In choosing La Bastide, Caroline was not to know it was a favourite watering hole of Steve Rutt, the showbiz correspondent of the *Daily Dazzle* and author of the paper's daily Celebrity Diary, who happened to live nearby. He often entertained his girlfriends here, describing them as 'contacts' and putting the cost on expenses. Occasionally he dined alone, still contriving to charge the bill to his newspaper on the basis that he was on the lookout for stories.

Rutt knew everyone though not everyone knew him. He had recognised Caroline and Sam as soon as they came into the restaurant. The beautiful wife of the proprietor of the *Daily Bugle* was familiar to any reader of society magazines. Sam's 'mugshot' had been used in his newspaper when he was still covering foreign stories.

What could they be doing together? Rutt had heard that Caroline Entwistle didn't take her marriage vows entirely seriously. Of Sam's long trail of sexual conquests he knew nothing, though he had heard about his drinking habits. Could they be sleeping together? It seemed unlikely she would be interested in a hack. But what were they doing here? Blunt could hardly be interviewing her at such a time and in such a place. Rutt noticed that the two of them were not talking much and that there seemed to be a frostiness between them. He concluded they were close.

It didn't matter whether or not they were having an affair. Rutt would leave it to his readers to decide they probably were. He was already writing the paragraph in his mind. *Stunning Caroline Entwistle was spotted dining in upmarket Notting Hill eatery La Bastide with well-known ladies' man Sam Blunt* . . . He'd get a couple of free dinners from François for mentioning his restaurant. The only question was whether his editor would let him write about Caroline. There was an accepted convention, disregarded only by the *Chronicle*, that newspapers didn't carry disobliging stories about other editors and proprietors. Or their wives. Still, if he wasn't too specific he might get away with it.

Sam and Caroline were leaving. As they passed Rutt's table, he looked down. He did not see the tear in her eye or the look of indifference on Sam's face. He did not know that Caroline was returning to Eaton Place, where she would spend the night awake alongside the somnolent bulk of Sir Edwin Entwistle, or that Sam was going to his basement flat in Barons Court, where he would sleep alone. Nor, to be honest, did Steve Rutt care.

Chapter Twenty-Five

The third edition had gone. It was three o'clock in the morning. The once bustling newsroom was deserted. If a bomb dropped on Buckingham Palace now, it would be too late for the *Daily Bugle*, though not for Bugle Online. Down in the dungeon sat the lone figure of Benedict Brewster enduring Trevor Yapp's latest punishment. He was on 'late watch', which involved hanging around all night in case a stray bomb did fall on Buckingham Palace. In such an unfortunate event he would be expected to pass on the information gleaned from the news agencies to the avid insomniac readers of Bugle Online. Yapp was certain Benedict would be unable to discharge this duty with any competence. And he wouldn't have been surprised to learn that the young man had dozed off. But the risk of such an incident taking place was minuscule, and the joy of making him suffer was very great.

Dr Robert Munganwa was a hard-working cleaner. Near the end of his night shift he sometimes liked to sit on the deserted 'backbench' in the newsroom for a few moments and imagine that this was his paper and he its editor. When he was a small boy in Kangala he had wanted to be a journalist but then Moses Ovambo had mounted a coup and turned the country's three newspapers into government mouthpieces. Robert had done his first degree at Tepe University, where he had proved himself a brilliant student, before travelling on a scholarship to Lisbon, capital of the former colonial power, to do a doctorate in philosophy. He had returned to take up a post at his former university, married the lovely Carumba, and they had had a son. They were poor but in love, and he had enjoyed his job teaching philosophy and literature.

He often wished that he had not sacrificed this enchanted life and had avoided opposition politics. But travel in Europe had deepened his loathing of Ovambo. Zinc had been discovered in huge quantities in the Wali desert. The dictator had sold concessions to the Chinese and pocketed hundreds of millions of dollars that should have gone to the Kangalan people. It was when Moses Ovambo built a palace modelled on Versailles for his wife Stella that Robert decided he could no longer honourably resist the urgings of a colleague at the university to join the underground opposition.

Within a month he was arrested and thrown into Tepe prison where Carumba was not allowed to visit him. He was expected to survive on a bowl of thin soup a day. There were ten men, some of them murderers, in his stinking cell. Every morning he expected to be shot. Then he recognised one of the guards as a member of his own small tribe from the north of the country, and a bribe secured his escape. He made his way to South Africa and then to Europe, arriving first in Portugal, where he found no work, before travelling to England. There he claimed political asylum, which was denied him on the grounds that Kangala was classified by the United Nations as a democracy and Moses Ovambo recognised by Great Britain as a friend and ally in whose well-governed country Dr Munganwa would face no risks whatsoever when he returned, as he must do. He lodged an appeal which his solicitor said was unlikely to be successful. Before the court hearing, he elected to disappear.

Friends from Kangala had told him about opportunities for cleaning at the *Bugle*. At first he was wary, having heard the newspaper was ferociously opposed to uncontrolled immigration and fearing it might betray him to the authorities. But he was short of money and needed a job. The man who had interviewed him was himself a foreigner, seemingly from India or Pakistan, and didn't even ask to see Robert's papers, which was as well since, apart from an out-of-date Kangalan passport, he didn't have any.

There were three others from Kangala who were part of his cleaning team. Batista, who been smuggled into the country in the back of a lorry container, was an adventurer hoping to make money. Jacob, like Robert, had been refused political asylum and gone off the radar. Gorgeous Rachel was a student who had stayed on when her studies had ended. She flirted entrancingly with Robert. He was almost certain she wanted to go to bed with him, but the thought of Carumba and their little boy held him back.

The four of them had worked at the *Bugle* for nearly a year, going about their tasks unobtrusively. The journalists seemed not to notice them either in the daytime or at night. It was almost as though they did not exist. Only a pretty blonde girl called Dora, who was secretary to the strange editor Doodle, had smiled at him twice when he was on lavatory-cleaning duty. (Robert was appalled by the squalor of the lavatories used by the male journalists. They were almost as disgusting as the ones in Tepe prison.) Although suspicious when the map went missing, Doodle had subsequently been perfectly polite to him. The only really nasty person was the one who gave the orders to the journalists. Robert thought his name was Mr Yupp. This man had once complained about the noise as he was trying to empty a wastepaper basket as quietly as possible. He was not sure he had heard correctly, but he thought Yupp might have muttered: 'Why don't you fuck off back to Africa?' If only he could.

· As he was paid only just above the hourly minimum wage, his earnings were small, but they were made to go a long way. One third he transferred to Carumba every month. Another third he kept for his living expenses: he shared a bedroom in New Cross with three men from Kangala, and they cooked in a small microwave on which were balanced a few books of philosophy and a Bible. The final third he donated to the Movement to Free Kangala from Oppression (MFKO), whose global headquarters were located in the same over-crowded bedroom. He and his friends maintained a website, gave a few pounds to Kangalans living in London who had no other means of support and organised regular demonstrations outside the Kangalan embassy in Knightsbridge. They had mounted a protest during the recent visit to London of His Incomparable Excellency President Moses Ovambo and Her Magnificence Stella Ovambo which had been noted by Benedict in his derided, unpublished colour piece. A number of his friends, most of whom had been 'illegals', had been arrested by the police. They had been fed back into the immigration system, where they would be refused asylum again and vanish before they could be returned to Tepe.

Splash!

Robert had felt astonishment and sadness at the *Bugle*'s failure even to acknowledge Ovambo's fleeting presence in the capital. Didn't it know that he had locked up hundreds of political prisoners and driven thousands of Kangalans abroad? He reasoned that if his country had been a former British colony, rather than a Portuguese one, the newspaper might have shown some interest. The other papers weren't any better. The only time the *Financial Gazette* ever mentioned Kangala was to report further discoveries of zinc deposits in the Wali desert. The *Daily Dazzle* was apparently unaware of the country's existence. Even the *Chronicle*, which might have been expected to know better, was worse than useless. At the time of Moses Ovambo's visit, a columnist called Timothy Brown, who presented himself as an old Africa hand, had praised the President for the stability he had brought to Kangala, as well as for his development of the mining industry which was gradually enriching the country. Robert, who knew there was child malnutrition in his own tribal area, could not believe that a sentient human being was capable of writing such nonsense. The Movement to Free Kangala from Oppression dispatched a dignified though angry letter to the *Chronicle*, which Edward Sneed, or a factotum acting on his behalf, declined to publish.

Robert knew he should get on. All this thinking about the past would get him nowhere. He surveyed the empty newsroom from the backbench one more time, imagining journalists peering into their computer screens being answerable to him, not Yupp. He wondered whether he would ever be able to return to Kangala and teach his students again, and his heart was heavy.

Rachel was emptying a wastepaper basket far across the newsroom, outside Yupp's corner office. How beautiful she was. He longed to stroke her face, and to clasp his arms around her bosom. But these were bad thoughts. What would Carumba think? She was waiting for him, with their son, and he must wait for her.

By the time Robert got to the door to Yupp's office, Rachel had moved on, which was perhaps just as well. He went into the office, took out his duster, and began to flick it around Yupp's desk. How tidy it was. Pens were arranged in a row like sleepers on a railway track. There was a white notepad on which someone, presumably Yupp, had written, *Lunch – S?* Robert wondered who 'S' was, and how he or she could possibly want to have anything to do with a man like Yupp.

Then he noticed that a drawer in the desk was half open. He tried to close it, but it wouldn't budge. He pushed harder. He was about to give up when he noticed lying in the drawer what looked like a folded map.

Some instinct told him that this was Doodle's missing masterpiece. He extracted the map, opened it, and laid it out on the desk. No more than Yapp, or Yupp, could he make any sense of the intricate markings and numberings, but his sympathetic imagination grasped immediately that this was a work of love whose mysterious disappearance had caused so much pain to the poor editor Doodle. Robert folded up the map carefully and put it into his pocket. He would restore it to its rightful owner.

Chapter Twenty-Six

As Eric Doodle was driven by Ted Daws from Number Ten to Pepper House in Pimlico, he reflected that for once in her life Daphne might be pleased with him. Reinstated as editor, he had been summoned to meet the Prime Minister in the usual way. When he had informed his wife of this appointment, she had delivered one of her sternest lectures. This time he was on no account to leave Number Ten without securing a firm and irrevocable promise of a knighthood.

The Prime Minster had been his habitual plaintive self, complaining about his backbenchers, the machinations of the Home Secretary, the inaccuracies of the *Chronicle* and the downright lies of the *Daily Dazzle*.

Doodle played his allotted role. 'I can see it must be hard, Prime Minister. Your burdens are heavy ones. At least the *Bugle* remains loyal.'

'I'm grateful for that, Eric. And glad to hear you're staying on as editor.'

'Thank you, Prime Minister.'

The little man frowned. 'Eric, you don't happen to know anything about the Church of England?'

Doodle had been confirmed at his prep school. He attended his local Anglican church in Wimbledon with Daphne every Christmas.

'A little, Prime Minister.'

'I've got to make a choice for the next Archbishop of Canterbury. They've given me two names to choose from, and I'm damned if I can tell the difference between them.'

'I can appreciate the difficulty.'

'One is the Bishop of Bournemouth. The other is the Bishop of Middlesex. What do you think?'

Doodle did not think very much. It was many years since the *Bugle* had disposed of its last religious affairs correspondent, a defrocked canon with a weakness for drink and excursions on Hampstead Heath. He knew nothing about the Bishop of Bournemouth, but had read about the Bishop of Middlesex's noisy rallies, which were said to draw thousands.

'I gather the Bishop of Middlesex is quite a figure. A bit evangelical, perhaps, but he could be just the person to pep up the Church of England.'

'Do you think so?' asked the Prime Minister.

'Yes, I do.'

'Interesting.' The Prime Minister put a large tick against one of the names on a sheet of paper. 'I'm grateful for your advice, Eric.'

'It's a pleasure, Prime Minister.'

Doodle knew the moment had come. He hated asking this man for anything, but his fear of Daphne had become an even more powerful force.

'I'm glad you appreciate the *Bugle*'s support, Prime Minister. With an election looming, it must be good to know where your friends are.'

'It is, believe me it is. Wherever I look I see fools or traitors. At least I know I can count on you.'

'You can, Prime Minister.'

Doodle gave a slightly nervous cough before embarking on a script he had rehearsed in front of Daphne a dozen times with his wife playing the part of the Prime Minister.

'When I joined the *Bugle* as a young reporter, the editor was Sir William Enstone. A great editor in many ways. He was a fine gentleman of the old school. I don't know whether you've ever heard of him.'

'No,' replied the Prime Minister, who hadn't and quickly grew bored when discussing other people's affairs.

'Anyway, Sir William was editor of the *Daily Bugle* for – well, it must have been fifteen years, which is even longer than me. The interesting thing is that he was made Sir William – given a knighthood, I mean – while he was still editor of the paper. I believe it established some sort of precedent.'

'I see.'

Doodle doubted that he did. Daphne had played the PM's part in an exceptionally dim-witted way, which he had thought overdone in the sitting room of 2 Common View. He was now revising that opinion.

'What I'm getting at, Prime Minister, is that if the powers that be thought they wanted to express their gratitude for the unwavering support of the *Bugle* over the years by, well, by honouring me, there is the perfectly good precedent of old Sir William Enstone.'

'I see.' The Prime Minister uttered the words this time in a way that suggested the penny had finally dropped. 'I'll look into it, Eric.'

'Thank you, Prime Minister.'

'I suppose you've got a knighthood in mind?'

'That was certainly the way my thoughts were turning. I'm only thinking of the paper, of course.'

The Prime Minister frowned again. 'Sir Edwin is angling for a peerage. We wouldn't want to risk the charge of favouritism by obliging both of you at the same time.'

'I can see that. On the other hand, there could be a decent interlude. I dare say Sir Edwin wouldn't mind waiting. Besides which,' he added, 'there is no knowing how long he will own the *Daily Bugle*. Editors can sometimes last longer than proprietors.'

The Prime Minister looked keenly at his confidant, and Doodle thought he detected a look of respect he hadn't seen before.

'I'll do my best, Eric, you may be sure of that. As you know, it's not strictly in my gift, but I expect arms can be twisted, if you know what I mean. You'd hardly be a controversial choice. Leave it with me. I'm glad you mentioned it.'

Doodle relived this conversation several times as Ted drove him back to Pimlico. He hoped Daphne would be pleased. How could she not be? The Prime Minister had as good as promised him he would get a knighthood. Other than demanding that he put it all in writing, he did not see what else he could have done. Surely even Daphne would not have expected that.

When they got to Pepper House he went straight to his office. Dora brought him a cup of tea, closing the door as she left. He opened the centre drawer of his desk and pulled out the latest edition of *Rural Retreats*. Then he dug into his jacket pocket and extracted his new map.

Splash!

Doodle's feelings on losing his old map had perhaps been similar to those of T. E. Lawrence after he left the manuscript of *Seven Pillars of Wisdom* at Reading railway station. The idea of starting again was anathema. And actually, he thought, his predicament was worse than the writer's had been. Whereas Lawrence had had a reasonable expectation of remembering the broad gist of what he had written, Doodle could not possibly recall the precise location of symbols that related to houses he had already forgotten about. That map represented literally years of original research which was lost forever. He felt like Sisyphus, forever rolling a stone uphill only for it to tumble down again. The futility of it all was unbearable.

And yet there was no point in being imprisoned by the past. He had to move on. His search for the perfect country house was as pressing as ever. He must not give in to despair and despondency. The future had claims as exciting as those of the past. He looked at the virtually pristine document in front of him. At least he could be sure that no one would steal this version because he would always keep it in his pocket.

Doodle opened his copy of *Rural Retreats* at random. His heart missed a couple of beats. The picture was of a small Jacobean manor house of such exquisite proportions that he felt his eyes fill with tears. It was surrounded by its own small deer park. The price was high, perhaps too high for his pocket, but it might be negotiated down. Most extraordinary of all, this vision of perfection was located in the Lincolnshire Wolds, no more than a few miles from Sir Cumming Brewster's handsome seat.

Eric Doodle lay back in his chair and closed his eyes. He could hear his butler knocking on the library door – or was it a new, refashioned Daphne, miraculously enamoured of the countryside and all its ways? Yes, it was his wife. He could see her shining eyes and her seraphic smile, just as she once had been. 'Sir Cumming has arrived,' she announced with a hint of pride. He saw the baronet's good, open face and the two of them clasped each other's hands. 'Fine day for shooting, Doodle. We've got some decent guns too.' Oh, a fine day it was, the earth hard with frost and the trees splayed against the white sky, the dogs sweet and eager. His loader stood next to him, as he took aim and fired. 'Good shot, Sir Eric. A fine shot indeed. You got that one smack on, Sir Eric.' And after the first drive, when they were sipping sloe gin, his friend Sir Cumming Brewster came up to him. 'You've set the bar high for us today, Doodle.'

'Eric?'

What were those dogs? Were they springers or cockers? God knows, he should get himself a good dog book.

'Eric? There's someone to see you.'

Doodle felt the Lincolnshire Wolds receding, and the happy voices faded away. He opened his eyes.

'What is it, Dora?' he asked crossly.

'There's a man to see you.'

'Who is it?'

'It's one of the cleaners.'

'One of the cleaners? You know they're not my responsibility. Ask him to go and see the – er, the appropriate department, would you?'

'He says it's urgent. He says he's got something he knows you will want to see.'

Doodle hesitated. He didn't want to be bloody-minded but really it was too much to have cleaners barging in like this.

On the other hand, perhaps he did have something important to show him. He'd better see him. Then it occurred to him that the man might be violent. He might be one of those psychotic types sometimes featured in the *Bugle* who went up to strangers and stabbed them to death for no apparent reason.

'I'll see him, Dora. But you stay too. We might need you.'

Dora left the room and returned after a few seconds with Dr Robert Munganwa at her side. She beamed at him encouragingly as though they were old friends.

Doodle recognised Robert as the cleaner he had interrogated after his map had been stolen. He remembered that his comrades had called him 'Doctor', presumably a jocular reference to his distinguished appearance. For a moment the editor wondered whether he should rise to his feet and shake the man by the hand. He fancied that this was what Sir Cumming Brewster would have done, but feared he might lose dignity if he did.

'Do sit down, won't you? And Dora, why don't you grab a chair?'

Robert sat down in front of Arthur Pepper's portentous desk. He was not nervous in front of this strange man Doodle. He had slept alongside murderers in Tepe prison. He had left his wife and son behind in Kangala. He knew who and what he was. Nothing could frighten him now.

'My name is Dr Robert Munganwa,' said Robert. 'I come from Kangala. I have lived in England for more than a year. I am leader of the cleaning team in these offices.'

'Pleased to meet you again,' said Doodle rather idiotically.

'I do not wish to waste your time. The other night we were cleaning late, as we normally do. It is my duty to clean the office of Mr Yupp.'

'Yapp,' suggested Doodle.

'Yapp? OK. I was dusting his office' – Robert ran his hand around in front of him by way of offering Doodle and Dora a visual aid – 'and I saw that this left-hand drawer was opened. So I tried to close it but it would not close. I gave it a firm push but still it would not close. Then I looked inside it, and I saw this.'

Robert dug into his pocket and lifted out Doodle's map, which he held aloft as though it were something he had won in a prize draw. If he had produced the deeds to the Jacobean manor house in the Lincolnshire Wolds, he could not have had a more electric effect on Eric Doodle.

'My God, you found this in Yapp's desk?'

'Yes, sir. In the left-hand drawer, as I said.'

'Are you absolutely certain?'

'Naturally. I have told you what happened.'

Doodle's nimble mind was racing ahead. He had no reason to doubt this man. Why on earth should he lie? He must be telling the truth. Unless there were some incredible explanation which he hadn't thought of, Yapp had come into his office, stolen his map from his desk and then concealed it in his own desk. But why? It didn't matter why. Doodle realised he had been handed a weapon with which he could cut Yapp down to size, if not drive him out of Pepper House.

'Tell me, would you be prepared to testify in front of others?'

Robert had foreseen this. He realised that by coming forward he was risking exposure, and might be arrested by the immigration authorities.

'Yes. I will testify if necessary.'

Splash!

Doodle now got up from his chair, circumvented Arthur Pepper's desk, and stood in front of Robert, who rose to his feet. The two men shook hands. Robert gave the precious map to Doodle, who received it gingerly, as though it were a Dead Sea Scroll that might disintegrate into dust at the slightest shock.

'Thank you, Dr Munganwa. Thank you. I am forever in your debt.'

Chapter Twenty-Seven

Ambrose Treadle provides his wealthy clients with a daily cuttings service. Even in the age of the internet many of the older ones still appreciate hard copy. Any reference in a newspaper to their companies or the activities of their rivals is cut out by an industrious band of underpaid young people and placed in a folder which is then delivered by a motorcycle courier. Younger tycoons prefer to use Ambrose's online service. Boris Vrodsky, who is still in his early forties, monitors references to himself, some of which can be quite biting, on his tablet.

Sir Edwin Entwistle is usually too busy to examine the expensively assembled folders which he has elected to be sent, and one of his secretaries drops them unread into the wastepaper basket. On this particular morning, however, he had time on his hands as he sat in the Mayfair headquarters of Entwistle Enterprises. In an hour he would be driven the five hundred yards from his offices to the Fig Leaf, where he was due to meet Trevor Yapp for lunch. He had decided, despite everything, to appoint him editor of the *Bugle*. It would reassure Boris Vrodsky to have Yapp in charge. Doodle really was getting past it.

Splash!

As he waited, there was little for Sir Edwin to do other than to recollect his last session with the vigorous though undoubtedly good-hearted Mrs Potts, and to read the cuttings that had been prepared for him by Ambrose Treadle's minions.

He opened the folder, which was marked 'confidential' despite its entire contents having been filched from the free Press. There was a story from the *Financial Gazette* about the *Chronicle*, which had just reported losses even more staggering than the previous year's. Edward Sneed was quoted as saying that his paper had an exciting digital future, and he was not at all worried that it had shed nearly a fifth of its circulation in the past year. An article in the *Chronicle* itself reported that the *Financial Gazette* was encountering problems in launching its Peruvian edition. A further piece in that paper noted that the Commission looking into Press ethics was hoping to deliver a preliminary report in three months. It now had a genuinely all-party complexion. The *Chronicle's* financial difficulties provoked a degree of *schadenfreude* in the *Daily Bugle*, which also carried a column by Adam Pride about the Prime Minister's increasingly testy relations with the media.

Sir Edwin was on the point of closing his folder – really, Ambrose had a bit of a cheek charging him so much for this stuff – when he noticed a small item from the *Daily Dazzle*, next to which someone had made a red mark, presumably in the hope of attracting his attention. Beneath the headline TYCOON'S WIFE OUT ON THE TOWN, Steve Rutt had written: 'Stunning 40-year-old Caroline Entwistle, wife of billionaire tycoon Sir Edwin Entwistle, was spotted in upmarket Notting Hill restaurant La Bastide dining with scribbler Sam Blunt. Friends deny any burgeoning relationship, and suggest that much-loved Caroline is mentoring Blunt after his recent dismissal from his newspaper.' There was no mention that Sir Edwin was a Press proprietor.

Sir Edwin closed the folder abruptly so that it made a slapping noise not unlike that of Mrs Potts' whip. He was shocked and outraged. There was a solemn understanding between proprietors not to permit their newspapers to mention the activities of their peers unless to praise them. Only the *Chronicle* chose to stand outside the rule. Editors were expected to enforce it, come what may. It made little difference that his ownership of the *Bugle* hadn't been mentioned. He would ring that old crook Deever Bottle, the Canadian proprietor of the *Daily Dazzle*, and tell him to get lost. Bottle would get the message. He wouldn't want the *Bugle* trawling through his murky business affairs.

But what in God's name was Caroline doing dining with that low-life creature Sam Blunt? Though he had been unfaithful, and knew his wife had also been so on several occasions, it didn't occur to him even now that she might be having an affair with this loathsome specimen of his breed. There must be some sort of rational explanation, yet he couldn't imagine what had induced Caroline to spend a single moment with him. The wife of Sir Edwin Entwistle should not have been seen in public with such a person. It looked seedy. And whereas he, having come across Blunt, knew it was inconceivable that any impropriety had taken place, others who hadn't had the misfortune of meeting him might arrive at a different conclusion.

He was about to pick up the telephone to talk to his wife when it rang, and his secretary informed him that Eric Doodle was on the line.

'What is it, Eric? Can't it wait?'

'I'm afraid not, Sir Edwin. It's an extremely important matter.'

The newspaper proprietor made an irritable clucking noise. 'Fire away, then, but be quick.'

'I think we should meet.'

'Meet? What would be the point of meeting when I already have you on the line? Do get on with it.'

'Very well. I regret to tell you that Trevor Yapp has been caught stealing.'

'Caught stealing! What in God's name are you talking about?'

'He removed a personal item from my desk and concealed it in his own.'

'What personal item?'

'It was a map – a very special map – on which I had spent a great deal of time.'

'It doesn't sound very serious to me. He probably just borrowed it.'

'It's not the kind of map you would borrow. It's obviously very personal to me.'

'I can't follow you, Eric. You don't seem to be making any sense. Who says that Yapp stole it?'

'A cleaner.'

'A cleaner!'

'Yes, he happens to have a doctorate in philosophy from the University of Lisbon.'

'Oh.' Sir Edwin did not know what credence to attach to holders of doctorates in philosophy from the University of Lisbon. 'What does Yapp say?'

'He's confessed.'

'Confessed!'

'In a manner of speaking. He agrees that he took the map from my desk and put it in his, but he doesn't appear to regard it as stealing. In fact, I regret to say he called me a mad old fart.'

'Did he?' Sir Edwin bit his lip. 'Surely we don't need to get worked up about this, Eric. I'm sure Yapp has his reasons.'

'I am not getting worked up! I should tell you that I have spent years working on this map. Yapp must have known it, and yet he deliberately kept it from me. I regard it as an act of gross insubordination, and proof of a mean spirit. I can't ever work with him again.'

Sir Edwin had never heard Eric Doodle speak like this. He was a little taken aback. He could see this damn map mattered to him for some unknown reason, and he wasn't going to be sweet-talked into overlooking the matter. It all made his lunch with Yapp, and his plan to make him editor, rather tricky.

'Eric, can I suggest we all calm down?' Sir Edwin was speaking more softly now, like a marriage counsellor confronted by a particularly irate and intractable husband. 'I can see this map must be important to you. Let me have a word with Trevor and I'll get back to you.'

'I won't be persuaded that it doesn't matter. If necessary I am prepared to go public. I won't work with that man again.'

When the call had ended, Sir Edwin decided that the inexplicable matter of Caroline and Sam Blunt would have to wait until after lunch. He brooded over what he had been told. Had Doodle gone mad? Why would any sane person wish to steal a map? But then he reminded himself that Yapp was an odd character. There was something dark about him.

Hadn't he leaked his talks with Po? According to Doodle, he had confessed to taking the map and yet was unrepentant. It all seemed very odd. How he wished he could be free of all this journalistic bickering, and make an agreement with Boris Vrodsky to take the *Bugle* off his hands.

Sir Edwin noticed the time. He should be leaving for the Fig Leaf.

Ten minutes later he was cautiously making his way across the fashionable restaurant's polished marble floor like a novice at an ice rink. Lady Evelyn Wherewill smiled sweetly at him as he passed her table. The tycoon had momentarily forgotten about the account of his wife's dinner in Steve Rutt's diary in the *Daily Dazzle*. She had not.

Lady Evelyn was lunching with her brother, an unusual occurrence on account of his notorious tight-fistedness. He had felt his sister deserved some reward for having introduced him to the Pos. They had just spent the weekend at Hastings Hall, in whose crumbling drawing room Po had agreed to pay an enormous sum of money for the earl's Qing vase, thereby relieving him of the need to do questionable deals with his Middle Eastern friends. In celebration of the agreement, on which he and the billionaire had shaken hands, he had bought his sister a single glass of champagne.

She examined Sir Edwin's face carefully to see how the news had affected him. Although she was not a reader of the *Daily Dazzle*, a friend had drawn her attention to Rutt's item. She knew at once that its insinuation was well founded. Everything fell into place: Caroline's original request that the reporter be asked to lunch, as well as her eagerness to accompany him back to his flat after he had made such a spectacle of himself. Lady Evelyn was aghast that such a leading light of

London society should have had an affair with this common little journalist. And yet she accepted the world as it was. She had long believed there was no explaining the urges of lust and love. These were mysteries, which it was futile to attempt to unravel. For reasons she would never understand, her friend had found this odd man attractive, and there was no point in expressing either censure or wonderment.

At a nearby table Madame Po was lunching with the Bishop of Middlesex. She too knew about the piece in the *Dazzle* for the simple reason that Lady Evelyn had pointed it out to her that morning during one of their increasingly frequent telephone conversations. She was surprised because Caroline was rich and the journalist was poor. Madame Po was frightened of the poor even though (or was it because?) her parents had lived in a two-room corrugated iron shack in the backstreets of Chengdu. But she was no more censorious than Lady Evelyn. Being loyal to her husband, who bitterly maintained that he had been let down by Sir Edwin, she felt some satisfaction that the bloated and self-satisfied Press tycoon had himself been betrayed.

Her guest, Bishop Bob, had not noticed Sir Edwin Entwistle's entrance, and did not follow his slow progress to his table where Trevor Yapp was already sitting with a smug look on his face. The prelate was peering moodily into an exotic-looking cocktail which Madame Po had pressed on him as they began to discuss his latest initiative to bring inner-city youth to God. He was not a happy man. That morning he had received a hand-delivered letter from Number Ten informing him that, after much deliberation, it had been decided to appoint the Bishop of Bournemouth as the next Archbishop of Canterbury.

Splash!

Bishop Bob could not fathom it. Dick Akers, otherwise known as the Bishop of Bournemouth, was a mediocre time-server and devious high churchman who had never even half-filled a cathedral in his life. His unsoundness on women bishops and his avoidance of any intelligible opinion on the subject of homosexual priests suggested to the progressive Bishop Bob a timid and reactionary mind. His mission to re-evangelise England had been dealt a bitter blow.

What he did not know was that Dick Akers had been translated to the See of Canterbury as Primate of All England because a careless Prime Minister had put a tick against the wrong name after receiving expert advice from Eric Doodle.

No one in the world was fated ever to know the true reason for the Bishop of Bournemouth's elevation, though many in the Press, including the *Chronicle*'s Timothy Brown and even the *Bugle*'s Adam Pride, welcomed the appointment as inevitable, with both expressing the thought in their different ways that Dick Akers was by a country mile the stronger candidate.

Sir Edwin at last made it to his table and squeezed his bulk into the chair opposite Trevor Yapp. The deputy editor looked more pleased with himself than the Press tycoon thought he had a right to be. He felt himself siding more with Doodle in his dispute with Yapp. Without his quite realising it, the piece about his wife had put him in a bad humour. Most of lunch was spent discussing politics and the tribulations of other newspapers. It was only over coffee that Sir Edwin turned his attention to the affairs of the *Bugle*. Yapp was certain the moment of his coronation was imminent.

'I had a call from Eric this morning,' remarked Sir Edwin. 'He's got his knickers in a twist about a map he says you stole.'

Yapp smiled malevolently. 'I'm afraid our old friend Eric has lost the plot.'

'What do you mean?'

'Bellyaching about a map.'

'Did you take it?'

'I borrowed it, in a manner of speaking. It's no secret Eric hasn't been pulling his weight for some time. He spends half the day cooped up in his office with the door closed. I'd noticed him reading some sort of country property magazine. Then I found the map.'

'Found?'

'I was looking on his desk for a letter I'd sent him and he should have sent back,' lied Yapp, 'and I saw the map. I thought it had something to do with all the time he'd spent reading the magazine.'

'And did it?'

'It's difficult to say. There are all kinds of signs and figures and numbers. To be perfectly frank, I sometimes wonder whether Eric is all there.'

The Press magnate considered what had been said to him. The map business did undeniably sound odd. Maybe Eric had gone a bit loopy. On the other hand, he didn't like the idea of Yapp removing it from his desk. It smacked of dishonesty. Sir Edwin again recalled how he had suspected the deputy editor of leaking his negotiations with Mr Po to the *Chronicle*.

'Where is this map?'

'Eric's got it back.'

'I'd better take a look at it.'

Sir Eric Entwistle had an account at the Fig Leaf and had no need to ask for a bill. He now examined his watch whose gold strap encircled a formidable wrist.

'I have to go,' he announced, as he began to heave himself out of his chair.

'Go?' exclaimed a surprised Trevor Yapp. 'Isn't there anything else you wanted to say?'

'Nothing whatsoever,' replied the proprietor of the *Daily Bugle* emphatically. 'Except that I think you'd better stay away from Pepper House until I've had this out with Eric.'

Chapter Twenty-Eight

Sam Blunt was amazed to read Steve Rutt's diary item in the *Daily Dazzle*. Never in his life had he been on the receiving end of a disobliging story in a newspaper. It was he who asked the questions. He had interviewed Nipper Richards and his then newly acquired wife Suzy Wattle after the remains of her ex-husband Shifty Perkins had been discovered in a concrete block on the Seville-to-Malaga *autopista*. Closer to home, he had revealed Terence Glasswell's liaison with Lady Evelyn Wherewill. MPs, businessmen, foreign potentates, football managers, starlets and numerous crooks in every walk of life had at one time or another nursed feelings of resentment towards Sam because of revelations he had published about them. But until this moment no member of the Fourth Estate had deemed his affairs to be of sufficient interest to share them with the wider public.

Sam wondered how Sir Edwin Entwistle would react. At least he couldn't be sacked from the *Daily Bugle* as he no longer worked for it. The tycoon would presumably not resort to kneecapping or a contract killing, but he would expect his fellow proprietors not to employ him. And any idea, however unpalatable, of working for Ambrose Treadle was now out of the question. The only paper that would take no notice of the urgings of Sir Edwin was the *Chronicle*, but doubtless it had other reasons for not wishing to make use of his services.

He reckoned he had enough money to pay the mortgage on his Barons Court basement flat for another month. After that, unless he got another job, he would have to sell it. Ever since becoming a young reporter Sam had been paid enough to live as he pleased, with a little help from his expenses. For the first time in his adult life he faced penury.

What happened to destitute former journalists? There was old Wally Holmes, the alcoholic chief leader writer on the *Bugle* at the time Sam joined the paper. On one occasion the editor, Sir William Enstone, had come to look for him late in the afternoon in his office, and was told by the other leader writers that he hadn't returned from lunch. He did not realise that they meant lunch on the previous day. After many reprieves Wally had finally been sacked when he was discovered half an hour before deadline with his head resting on his typewriter and the first leader uncomposed. Six months later a former colleague had seen him lying on a bench in Kensington Gardens with a can of premium lager in one hand and a pristine copy of the *Daily Bugle* in the other.

Sam shivered momentarily. He did not want to end up like that. And yet he was not an introspective fellow. He had lived every day as though it were his first and his last. It was not in his nature to worry much about the future. Even now, most of his mind was focused on the single issue of how to corner the slippery, mendacious and insufferably self-satisfied

Terence Glasswell. The man had masterfully turned the tables so that he, Sam Blunt, was under examination. It was monstrous. It was an outrage. Sam felt like a general who has lost his army, his coordinates and any hope of ever engaging the enemy in battle. The only support he had was Benedict who, when not undergoing the series of tortures devised by Trevor Yapp in the dungeon, lived in a state of fear of being arrested by the Metropolitan Police, while fretting about the ever-elusive Sophia.

Did our hero spare a thought for the woman who loved him? A fleeting one. He wished Caroline all the good fortune in the world. She was a fantastic sport. But their affair had been practically over anyway. These things must be enjoyed while they can.

For Sam, Caroline was a sleek, self-possessed lady with a built-in escape chute. He would have been astonished to be told that she was gazing somewhat forlornly out of her bedroom window in Eaton Place in what she imagined was the direction of Barons Court.

Caroline was sad. And also very worried. Edwin was due back at any time. He would have been shown the piece in the *Daily Dazzle* and would want to know why she had been having dinner with Sam.

It was a reasonable question. Caroline had rehearsed a variety of answers. She could simply claim that Steve Rutt had been mistaken, but in that case her husband might suggest she seek an apology which Rutt, being for once in his life wholly in the right, would be reluctant to give. Another possibility was simply to admit her affair with Sam. Having once followed her husband to Earls Court, she knew that he visited the flat of a Mrs Potts, though she had no idea that whips and manacles were part of their encounters. Even allowing for the hypocrisy that always attends these matters, Edwin would find it difficult to mount a strong case against her if she invoked Mrs Potts. Nonetheless, she saw that such a course of action carried its dangers. They might establish a moral equivalence which gave neither of them the right to criticise the other, and still be left without a marriage. Caroline did not want that. She had thought of another stratagem.

Sir Edwin came up to their bedroom as soon as he got back. He had returned from Pepper House in a grim mood. An interview with the rather impressive Dr Robert Munganwa had fully corroborated Doodle's story. The significance of the map was still not at all clear to Sir Edwin but he could see that it mattered enormously to the editor, and surmised that Yapp had also grasped as much. Its removal by him was an indisputably hostile act. Nor did he believe for a moment that the deputy editor had come across it by chance while legitimately looking for a letter on Doodle's desk. He must have been deliberately poking about, and had stolen something that was obviously precious to the editor.

Doodle had got the bit between his teeth and was threatening to tell Edward Sneed at the *Chronicle* the whole story if Yapp wasn't summarily dismissed. Sir Edwin did not much like this aggressive new Doodle. He also wondered whether he could sack Yapp for stealing something which, though priceless to Doodle, was worthless to every other human being in the world. There was also the question of Boris Vrodsky to consider. Selling the *Bugle* would be more problematic with Yapp gone and Doodle still in charge.

What did it really matter that Yapp was a thief and a liar? All he wanted to do was to get the bloody newspaper off his hands as soon as possible.

He plonked himself down on their vast double bed and looked at his wife, who was sitting at her dressing table rubbing cream into her face.

'Why were you having dinner with Sam Blunt?'

Caroline continued to apply her face cream. 'I was doing it as a favour for someone.'

'A favour? What do you mean?'

'For a friend. I'd really rather not discuss it.'

The chairman of Entwistle Enterprises was not to be fobbed off so lightly. He waved a copy of the *Daily Dazzle*, which he had brought with him.

'I would like to discuss it, if you don't mind.'

Caroline stopped rubbing cream into her face and turned around, so that she was no longer addressing her husband in the mirror.

'My darling, if I tell you, can I swear you to secrecy?'

Sir Edward, though unsure that he should be accepting any conditions in these circumstances, reluctantly agreed.

'You mustn't ever mention what I am about to tell you to anyone.'

He reiterated that he wouldn't.

'You'll find this hard to believe, but Evelyn has been having an affair with Sam Blunt.'

Sir Edwin did indeed let out a sort of gulp of wonder.

'It's hard to credit, I know, particularly as Blunt was the journalist who exposed her affair with Terence Glasswell. But these things are never easy to explain, I suppose. They just happen, and there's no rhyme or reason.'

'But why Blunt of all people?'

'They met at one of her lunches. He's quite attractive, in a way. I dare say he's a snob. Anyway, she was drawn to him, and he to her.'

'And when did this start?'

'Oh – a couple of months ago, I should think.'

Sir Edwin was having difficulty in processing the information. Evelyn Wherewill, of all the people in the world, and Sam Blunt!

'What has all this got to do with your having dinner?'

Caroline left the dressing table. She sat down on the bed close to her husband, leant forward and lowered her voice.

'He became a little demanding. I think he fancied he was in love with Evelyn. She'd had enough. So she asked me to act as a kind of go-between.'

'Why couldn't she tell him herself?'

'She'd tried to, but he wouldn't accept it. She asked me to deliver the *coup de grâce*. I'd come across him once or twice at her lunches, and knew him from the *Bugle*. To tell you the truth, I was becoming a little worried for Evelyn.'

'So you delivered the final bullet at the restaurant?'

'That's right.'

'I see.'

Sir Edwin did not quite see. He thought it odd that a woman like Lady Evelyn Wherewill couldn't get rid of Sam Blunt herself. On the other hand, he still found it impossible to believe that his wife could have been attracted to such a grubby man. Here at least was an explanation of sorts. Evelyn Wherewill had always been an odd fish. She'd had that affair with Terence Glasswell, after all. There was no accounting for taste. He had heard that she was surprisingly frisky. This thought somehow put him in mind of Vera Potts.

'How very odd,' he said.

Caroline agreed that human behaviour contained very many puzzles.

'But why the secrecy? Why don't we ask Ambrose to give the whole story to the *Daily Dazzle*? It'd show what a rotten little hypocrite Sam Blunt is.'

'Edwin! You swore! Evelyn is practically my best friend. She doesn't want the whole world to know she's been having it off with a reporter.' Caroline leant forward so that her face was a few inches from her husband's and placed a hand on a thigh. 'If her brother found out that she's been having a fling with Blunt, he'd reduce her pitiful allowance to zero.'

'I suppose you're right,' he conceded.

'I know I'm right.'

Sir Edwin was aware that his wife, who appeared to be wearing only a thin silk dressing gown, was now very close to him. He looked at her and admired her beauty. At times like these he marvelled that he should have any need of Vera Potts. Caroline was so perfect and Vera, well, she was a fine-looking woman, but physically she occupied a different planet to his wife. But perhaps that was it. Caroline looked *too* perfect whereas Vera occupied a lower, more elemental sphere that was his own natural habitat.

'What a strange world it is,' observed the normally unphilosophical proprietor of the *Daily Bugle*.

'Yes, it is a strange world,' agreed Caroline Entwistle as her lovely hand rested on her husband's generously proportioned thigh.

Chapter Twenty-Nine

During quiet afternoons Geoff Dobbs, the doorman at Stride's Club, liked to watch television in his small cubicle just inside the front door. The Westminster Channel was a favourite. Prime Minister's Question Time and even the deliberations of the Welsh Assembly had provided welcome diversion. In recent weeks he had been entertained by the sittings of the Call to the Nation Commission. Geoff recognised several of the leading lights. Sir Archibald Merrick was a familiar figure as a member of Stride's. Sir Patrick Clapp had been a guest at the club. The Bishop of Middlesex was a constant presence on television. Terence Glasswell had accompanied Sir Archibald to the club only a month or so ago.

The Commission's remit slightly baffled Geoff. He regularly read the *Daily Bugle* (copies of which he removed from the library once they had been finished with) and sometimes bought a copy of the *Daily Dazzle* on the way to work to read its sports pages. Newspapers were often silly, of course, and sometimes unfair. But he couldn't understand why an inquiry into them was needed.

As it turned out, Sir Archibald was not often to be seen.

Sir Patrick Clapp asked most of the questions, with the Bishop of Middlesex and other members of the Commission chipping in. Geoff thought the retired judge rather pompous and pleased with himself. An exchange between him and a witness called Edward Sneed, the editor of the *Chronicle*, stuck in his mind. Both men seemed to agree about everything, especially the deficiencies of the *Daily Dazzle*. They tittered together about its vulgarities.

Glasswell's testimony, which had opened the proceedings, was in Geoff's view overdone. The MP described his encounter with the journalist who had followed him, and dramatically held aloft the microphone that had been smuggled on to his person. At one point his voice appeared to quaver as he recalled the effects that the horrible experience had had on his wife. Sir Patrick generously asked if he would like a short adjournment so that he could compose himself. Glasswell thanked him but said his personal feelings were as nothing compared to the Commission's vital work.

On this particular evening Geoff was reading a copy of the previous day's *Bugle* in his cubicle. He smiled at Sir Archibald Merrick – the financier, though ponderous, was a nice enough fellow – as he came into the club. But he had difficulty in maintaining his look of pleasure when he realised his guest was Terence Glasswell. Geoff had heard alarming rumours that the MP wanted to be put up for membership of Stride's. Surely it had not come to that.

He lowered his eyes to the *Bugle* and a column by Adam Pride, which he had been struggling with for some minutes. He couldn't work out whether or not the columnist was supportive of the Home Secretary's growing machinations against the Prime Minister. It seemed as though Pride was hedging his bets. Nonetheless, having embarked on the piece he felt duty bound to wade his way through to its conclusion.

'Evening, Geoff.'

The doorman looked up and saw the genial, weather-beaten face of Sir Cumming Brewster. He was fond of the baronet, who seemed to him to represent the heart and soul of the club. He saw he had his son with him, a tall gangly youth who could do with a bit of filling out, but seemed a chip off the old block.

'Good evening, Sir Cumming. Nice to see you, Mr Brewster.' He noticed that the young man had a somewhat hunted look.

Sir Archibald and Terence Glasswell were already ensconced in the dining room, with the MP halfway through his second glass of wine. Despite dining with Sir Archibald, who was frankly a bore, Glasswell was in a benevolent mood. That afternoon he and Finula had finally forsaken the constricting sofa in his office, and stolen into Mr Po's private suite on the top floor of Anglo-Chinese Investments. He knew there was no risk of their being interrupted because Po had just returned from another trip to Kangala and was spending the day at his house in Billionaires' Row. In his four-poster bed, never used in its new home since being purchased at Beasley's for an enormous sum, Glasswell and Finula had been able to make imaginative use of the space the sofa had denied them.

He looked at Sir Archibald and thought he had better ask a sensible question. Later he intended to push the old boy into putting him up for membership of Stride's.

'How's the Commission getting along, Archie?'

Sir Archibald winced. He did not like Glasswell using the abbreviation of his name, which was reserved for old friends.

'Pretty well, I think. Sir Patrick Clapp has been making some very useful interventions. It seems he knows the Press inside out.'

'When will you be finished?'

'Sir Patrick thinks we can deliver our preliminary report in a couple of months. I gather you have to have a preliminary report these days. It gives you two shots with the same barrel.'

'Will you be making any recommendations?'

'Very possibly,' replied Sir Archibald cautiously, having rather lost track of the Commission's proceedings. 'Of course, whatever happens, a free Press is absolutely sacrosanct.'

'I agree,' lied Glasswell.

'We just need to find a way of reining in its wilder practices.'

'Exactly.'

Without looking up from the table Glasswell knew something was wrong. During his jungle warfare training he had been taught to sense a hostile potential assailant at a distance of fifty yards. Feeling a foreign presence now, he unthinkingly took his knife off the table, and held it in front of him, much to the alarm of Sir Archibald Merrick. Then his eyes flicked around the room, darting over tables of middle-aged and elderly men, until within seconds he had identified Benedict Brewster as the man who had thrown a punch at him in the side street in Victoria.

'That's him,' hissed Terence Glasswell.

'That's who?' asked the bemused financier.

'The journalist who tried to plant a microphone on me a few weeks ago. I'd never forget that face.'

Splash!

Sir Archibald turned to inspect the alleged culprit on whom his guest's eyes were fixed in a rather scary way.

'You mean that young man with Sir Cumming Brewster? Most unlikely, I'd have thought. He's probably one of his sons. He'd never bring a journalist here.'

'I'm telling you. It's him.' Glasswell was still fingering the knife.

'Whoever it is, can I suggest we leave the matter for now? We don't want a nasty scene in the club.'

Glasswell thought of his chances of becoming a member, and loosened his grip on the knife, which he put down. He could wait. He would follow the young man when he left, and pummel him to pieces then.

The two men resumed their conversation, discussing the possibility of the Home Secretary mounting a coup against the Prime Minister, as well as the generosity of Mr Po as a benefactor. Glasswell shot frequent glances at Benedict to satisfy himself that his prey had not crept away.

The young man was beginning to relax after another arduous day in the dungeon, still tortured by fears that he might at any moment be arrested by the Metropolitan Police. Surely, though, he was as safe in the dining room of Stride's in the company of his loving father as he would be if he had taken sanctuary in the Vatican. The police would never come here. He took another sip of the delicious claret his father had ordered, wondering why he suddenly seemed rather preoccupied.

As was usual, Sir Cumming Brewster had observed other members and their guests when entering the dining room. A gentleman never stares, but it is natural in a club to see whether old and dear friends may be present. He had at once noticed Sir Archibald Merrick dining with a guest. A further glance, after he and Benedict sat down, established that this guest was Terence Glasswell, whom he had last seen in the flesh nearly forty years previously when both of them were eighteen-year-olds in the same house at Eton. What a rotter he had always been. He still bore a grievance against him for having stolen – there could be no other explanation for its sudden disappearance – an elaborate Swiss Army knife given him by his father.

Sir Cumming looked affectionately at his own son, who was wolfing down some potted shrimps. He felt his protective instincts welling up inside him. He knew that Glasswell would not create a scene in the club. But he also guessed that he would have recognised Benedict as his assailant, and would jump him, or try to get him arrested by the police, as soon as he left. A stratagem was needed. Sir Cumming thought of Geoff.

He waited until Benedict had demolished three hefty lamb chops and two helpings of syllabub before imparting news he knew would disquiet him.

'Benedict, old boy. Don't look, but our old friend Terence Glasswell happens to be at a table over there.'

Benedict turned to look, and his eyes met those of Glasswell. He felt like a wildebeest on the African plains who knows he has just been sized up by a famished big cat as a dependable dinner.

'What shall we do?' he asked.

His father had had most of dinner to devise a plan, which he now unveiled to Benedict. They would get up together, as though to leave. He would then appear to spot Sir Archibald for the first time, and would go over to his table, where he would engage the City magnifico in a spirited conversation, while recognising his old school mate, and creating as much hubbub as possible. While this was going on, Benedict would skedaddle, pausing only to instruct Geoff to use every means possible to delay Glasswell should he follow him. It was an utterly straightforward plan.

While keeping an unwavering eye on Benedict, Terence Glasswell had broached the subject of his possible membership of Stride's. Would Archie put him up? Archie was in a quandary. He knew the MP would attract a fusillade of black balls and that he, as his proposer, would then be obliged to resign. Having spent half his adult life trying to be admitted to Stride's, he did not want to lose his membership because of Glasswell. On the other hand, nor did he want to offend a man to whom he had just given dinner, and who served as a vital channel of communication with Mr Po.

As fate would have it, he was relieved of this insoluble dilemma. Appearing instantly as though via some sort of disembodied transference, Sir Cumming Brewster stood by their table. The baronet administered a hearty slap on Archie's back while simultaneously grasping Terence Glasswell's right hand, and refusing to let it go despite the MP making agitated attempts to extract it.

'Archie! You didn't tell me you had this old rogue in tow. It must be almost forty years, Terence. Good God! Time goes faster than it has any right to do. How have you been keeping body and soul together?'

Glasswell had rumbled the baronet's intentions. He couldn't see Benedict because Sir Cumming stood in the way, but he knew he must be in the throes of escaping. He gave a violent tug and this time succeeded in removing his arm from Sir

Cumming's grip. Then, in a sudden movement straight out of the ABC of jungle warfare which astonished the other two, he slipped noiselessly below the table, weaved his way through a forest of legs and knees, and emerged the other side of the table without any of the other diners noticing anything untoward. Before Sir Cumming could put out a restraining hand, Terence Glasswell was speeding out of the dining room like a greyhound.

Though he has often been justly accused of clumsiness, Benedict's keenest critics have never suggested that he can't move quickly when on the run from a bellicose MP. Some fifteen seconds elapsed between his leaving his table like a high-powered rocket and Glasswell shooting out of the dining room of Stride's Club. Everything being equal, it may be conjectured that the MP would have caught the journalist, if not within the confines of the club, at least somewhere in St James's Street. As it was, those precious fifteen seconds gave Benedict enough time to share with Geoff Dobbs the essential genius of Sir Cumming Brewster's master plan.

When Terence Glasswell rounded the corner into the lobby of Stride's, his soldier's instinct told him that his quarry could not be far ahead. He accelerated down the corridor towards the front door, which for some reason had been left open, presumably by his fleeing assailant. Unfortunately, as he sped past the little cubicle he did not take account of one unforeseen impediment, namely Geoff Dobbs' right foot.

This appendage, extended almost daintily at precisely the right juncture, had the effect of upsetting the MP at full pelt. He became airborne. For a moment, amid flailing arms and legs, it seemed as though the jungle expert might miraculously regain his balance, but that moment passed. Terence Glasswell flew out of the door of Stride's Club, clearing the head of an American tourist, before landing in the gutter with a painful thud.

Chapter Thirty

When the morning editorial conference was finished, Dora brought Eric Doodle a cup of coffee, closing the door behind her as she left. The editor of the *Daily Bugle* was happier than he had been for many years. Trevor Yapp was still under instructions from Sir Edwin Entwistle not to come into the office. In a series of conversations with his proprietor, Doodle had repeated his demand that his deputy be sacked. Sir Edwin had countered that, although Yapp had seriously erred in removing the map, it was not obviously a sacking offence. Eric Doodle begged to differ. As a result of his refusal to have Yapp back, and Sir Edwin's disinclination to get rid of him, the deputy editor was in limbo.

An even greater source of joy for Doodle than Yapp's absence was the restitution of his beloved map. It lay open now on Arthur Pepper's desk, partly covered by the latest edition of *Rural Retreats*. Since its miraculous return Doodle had had an inspiration. He had always rejected the idea of Cornwall as a county in which he might one day have his country house. It did not seem fully English. It even had a flag of its own, and some diehards were said to be reviving the Cornish language. Along with the more wholeheartedly Celtic nations of Wales and Scotland, as well as the counties of the south-east of England which had been excluded for financial reasons, Cornwall had been off limits.

A photograph of a delicate white Regency mansion in south Cornwall overlooking the wide reaches of the English Channel had encouraged him to think again. He loved the red roses curling around the portico and the palm trees swaying in the front garden. There were several acres of pastureland running down to cliffs, against which the ceaseless waves broke and plumed. It occurred to Doodle that such a house might deal with the Daphne problem. For although his wife had expressed distaste for every aspect of the rural life, she had never spoken in such vehement terms about the sea. Indeed, Doodle was sure she had once recalled a seaside holiday in Devon which she had enjoyed with her parents as a young child. She had also made some appreciative remarks about seagulls on a Dover-to-Calais cross-channel ferry. Might her opposition to his life's work be tempered were he to present their retreat as a house overlooking the sea which just happened, almost as though it were an afterthought, to be located in the country?

So Doodle's thoughts had been tentatively leading him. Of course, counties such as Herefordshire and Shropshire and Lincolnshire remained preferable for all kinds of reasons but there no longer seemed any justification for vetoing Cornwall. Small marks and shaded circles and crosses were beginning to colonise an area on the map which for years had lain empty.

A buzzer on Doodle's telephone buzzed. It was Dora.

'Eric, Adam Pride would like to see you. He wants to

discuss a trip to America to write about the presidential elections.'

'Tell him to come back later.'

'The arts editor wonders whether you and your wife would like two free tickets to see *Swan Lake* at the Royal Opera House next Thursday week.'

'Er, yes.' Eric quite liked ballet. Daphne loved it. 'Check to see whether my diary is free.'

'And an odd-looking man from the Immigration Authority is waiting to see you in the outer office.'

'Ah.' Doodle had quite forgotten about this meeting. 'Better show him in.' He began to fold away his map.

Dora waited fifteen seconds for Doodle to clear his desk of incriminating evidence before ushering in the official. He introduced himself as Albert Tether and sat down in a chair in front of the editor's vast desk, looking apprehensively to his right and left.

Unbeknown to Eric Doodle, Tether regarded the *Daily Bugle* much as an obscure, Soviet-era factory manager from Siberia would have regarded *Izvestia* – as the fount of ideological truth and the voice of political wisdom. His job was to identify failed asylum seekers who had disappeared after having had their applications refused. Once he had found them – if he ever did – he was supposed to arrange for their deportation to their home country. In this role he and his colleagues in a small and overworked department had many detractors, not least in the pages of the *Chronicle*, where sages such as Timothy Brown had questioned whether it was humane or practicable to pursue asylum seekers in this way. However, the *Bugle* was supportive, while often loudly complaining that more was not being done. Sitting in front of Eric Doodle, Albert Tether felt he was in the holy of holies.

'What can I do for you?' asked Doodle cheerily.

'Thank you for seeing me,' said Tether humbly. 'You may be aware that the Immigration Authority has begun a new programme to deport failed asylum seekers.'

Doodle nodded. He had indeed heard about it. Hoping for the support of the *Bugle* and the *Daily Dazzle* in his scheming against the Prime Minister, the Home Secretary had recently announced a new crackdown against those who had avoided the judgment of the courts by vanishing. The *Bugle* had welcomed the initiative, though not without expressing its fear that little would change.

'This is rather difficult for me,' confided Tether, as he leant over Arthur Pepper's desk towards Eric Doodle, lowering his voice. 'Naturally the last thing in the world I would wish to suggest is that any fault should be laid at the door of the *Daily Bugle.*'

'I'm sure not,' replied Doodle, uncertain of where the conversation was going.

Tether leant further towards the editor, lowering his voice almost to a whisper. 'We've received a tip-off that a group of Kangalan asylum seekers are working as cleaners here at the *Daily Bugle.*'

'Really? That sounds extremely unlikely to me.'

'Our intelligence is usually very sound, Mr Doodle,' said Tether unctuously. 'But of course I don't expect you'd know what a Kangalan asylum seeker might look like.'

'I don't expect I would,' agreed Doodle.

'Let me show you something.' Tether dug in his jacket pocket and produced a photograph which he pushed across the desk in front of the editor. 'This is their ringleader, Robert Munganwa. The Kangalan embassy says he's dangerous. He broke out of jail. Is he familiar to you?'

Eric Doodle picked up the picture and immediately recognised Robert. He looked younger, and was slightly fuller in the face, but there was no mistaking the man who had returned his map.

The *Daily Bugle* had often berated the Government for its inability to find and deport failed asylum seekers. It had suggested time and again that it could not be beyond the wit of a properly run organisation to round up the miscreants and put them on an aeroplane. And yet now that he was inspecting a photograph of his friend Robert, he knew he had to make an exception. He could not betray the man who had found his precious map and proved so solid a witness while being interrogated by a sceptical Sir Edwin Entwistle. Doodle disliked telling lies. He did not even do so to Daphne when she was on the warpath. This time, though, he had no alternative.

'I've never seen this man before,' Doodle declared, tossing the picture back to Tether as nonchalantly as he could. 'I'm sorry I can't help.'

'Are you absolutely certain?' Tether sounded disappointed rather than disbelieving.

'Completely.'

'Would you know all the cleaners in the building by sight?'

'I'm sure I would.' This was not strictly true since they were not his responsibility. Fortunately Tether seemed to have an exaggerated view of the omniscience of editors, and the scope of their responsibilities. 'I repeat that I've never seen this man before.'

'Oh.' Tether seemed lost for words. He could not doubt the keeper of the holy of holies. 'Is there anyone else I should speak to?'

Doodle's brain moved quickly. He didn't want this man talking to the person who really was in charge of cleaners. 'My valued assistant, Dora, whom you've met, knows everything that goes on in this building.'

Tether brightened. 'May I speak with her?'

'Of course.' Doodle pressed a button on his phone. 'Dora, will you pop in here a moment?'

Doodle beckoned Dora to come around to his side of the desk, having taken back the photograph from Tether.

'Dora, dear, this gentleman is from the Immigration Authority, as you know. He is looking for an asylum seeker from Kangala who is said to be dangerous. I want you to take a careful look at this.' Doodle displayed the photograph of the familiar face. 'Do you recognise him?'

Dora took a good hard look at it. 'No.'

'Now are you absolutely certain, my dear?'

'I've never seen this man in my life.'

'Thank you, Dora.' He tried to simulate a look of regret. 'I'm sorry, Mr Tether. If Dora hasn't seen him, you can be sure he hasn't been here.'

Albert Tether thanked Eric Doodle for his time, asking him to keep a lookout in case Robert Munganwa ever did decide to seek work in Pepper House. Dora escorted him to the lift.

It so happened that at the moment she pressed the button on Tether's behalf, Robert was ascending from the dungeon, with a bucket and mop in his hand, intent on getting off on the same floor. He had spent the past half an hour cleaning the lavatories in the dungeon, which that morning had been particularly foul and disgusting. There had been more than the usual number of unflushed bowls, containing mounds of clogged-up paper and faeces, and he had had to mop up a small lake of urine on the floor of the men's lavatory. He was looking forward to a recuperative mug of tea and a biscuit with his comrades, and a chat with Rachel. Every day he found himself looking forward more and more to seeing her.

It was fortunate for him, and possibly for the future of Kangala, that after some debate the architect of Pepper House in the 1950s had agreed to instal two lifts. So it was that Dr Robert Munganwa stepped out of one lift at the very moment that an oblivious Albert Tether disappeared into the other.

Chapter Thirty-One

Mr Po's palace in Billionaires' Row was built by a now forgotten multi-millionaire in the 1890s. David Lupine, later
ennobled as Lord Lupine, who sat in the House of Lords with
Arthur, Viscount Pepper, had discovered rivers of gold in
South Africa. With a small portion of his fabulous riches he
constructed a gloomy neo-Gothic castle in Kensington which
a hundred years later had been purchased, gutted and trans-
formed into a kind of overblown airport lounge by Mr Po.

The tutelary gods of humour who watch over us sometimes relish historical symmetry. When he bought his palace,
Mr Po was already far richer than Lord Lupine had ever been,
with a fortune based on construction, banking and mining.
The companies that he controlled through nebulous and
impenetrable webs employed tens of thousands of people in
China, Hong Kong and Africa. The zinc deposits of Kangala
would by themselves have made him a billionaire. But this was
not quite enough either for Mr Po or for the playful tutelary
gods. It was necessary that he find gold in the Wali desert, the
most arid and unpopulated part of the Republic of Kangala,
ruled over by His Incomparable Excellency Moses Ovambo.

Only a very few people knew of what was a very significant discovery: Madame Po, who could be trusted not to tell anyone, not even – in fact, especially not – Lady Evelyn Wherewill; a few of Mr Po's most intimate associates, who certainly did not include Terence Glasswell; a small number of mining engineers who seldom left the Wali desert; and Moses and Stella Ovambo, both of whom had reasonable expectations of increasing their vast ill-gotten wealth as a result of the find. Otherwise it was a well-kept secret. Ambrose Treadle did not know, and nor did the commodities editor of the *Financial Gazette*, who kept his ear pretty close to the ground. Boris Vrodsky, who had extensive mining interests in Siberia and parts of Africa, remained in a state of ignorance. The Movement to Free Kangala from Oppression (MFKO) and its London president, Robert Munganwa, were also wholly in the dark. So too was the Chinese government, Mr Po's often covert partner in a dozen African ventures, including the Kangalan zinc mines.

What could it profit Mr Po that he would be richer still? He had more money that he could possibly spend were he to live a thousand years. Adding a few hundred poorly paid Kangalan gold miners to his existing global workforce of tens of thousands would hardly increase his enjoyment in directing the lives of his fellow men. Presidents and prime ministers already genuflected in front of him. Why, then, did the thought of all that shining gold fill him with a sense of satisfaction? It was because from being reputedly the forty-ninth richest man in the world, several places behind Boris Vrodsky, he could now aspire to being in the top twenty.

Splash!

Mr Po exhaled a tiny amount of breath, as he stroked the Qing vase which he had recently acquired from Lady Evelyn Wherewill's brother. He marvelled at its delicate shapes and beautiful colours – the deep blue flash of a bird's wing and the grace of a Chinese lady's arm. Mr Po knew the earl was convinced that he had persuaded him to pay more than the vase was worth, but he would happily have paid ten times as much. What was a huge amount of money to the corrupt and miserly peer was to Mr Po almost nothing. Yet it irritated him that the so-called English gentleman should have asked him to Hastings Hall with the intention of duping him. Though his ancestor who had helped himself to the vase during the Second Opium War was doubtless no better a man, at least he wouldn't have sought to disguise his rapaciousness. He would simply have seized the vase from someone whom he regarded as his inferior.

What a humiliation the opium wars had been to his people. He felt that by regaining the vase he had in some small way reversed the shame which the English had visited upon his country. It seemed to him incredible that the race which had treated the mighty Qing Emperor Xianfeng as though he were no better than a tribal chieftain, and had looted and burned the Summer Palace, should have been reduced to this pitiable state. Where was the ruling class which had controlled half of Asia and a quarter of the globe? Their ignoble modern successors were men such as the greedy earl and Sir Edwin Entwistle and the crooked Terence Glasswell, who had the temerity and poor taste to fuck his secretary in Mr Po's own private suite in the Park Lane offices of Anglo-Chinese Investments. What astounded him was not so much that the English had changed the world, and altered the destiny of nations, but that they had wholly forgotten they had done so.

The billionaire rose to his feet and placed the Qing vase gently on a Louis Quinze console table for which his representatives had outbid Boris Vrodsky's at a recent auction at Beasley's. He sat down again and took out of his pocket a DVD which contained a recording (complete with sound) of Terence Glasswell's couplings with Finula, recorded by an automatic camera concealed above the previously unused four-poster bed, which he intended to view in a few minutes.

Glasswell had been useful to him for a time, running little errands in the City, and then serving as a conduit to Sir Archibald Merrick and the Prime Minister. Mr Po had been happy to make a small gift to help him buy a little house, largely because he had felt sorry for his wife, Cynthia, who exuded sadness and disappointment. But even this act of generosity had somehow been twisted against him in the mendacious pages of the British Press. That fool Sir Edwin Entwistle had revealed their talks about the *Daily Bugle* – not that he had ever been really serious about buying the paper, though his friends in Beijing had thought it a good idea. The suggestion that he, Mr Po Chun, was somehow unfit to own such a second-rate publication – of which the ludicrous Entwistle was considered an appropriate owner – had insulted him.

Glasswell had outlasted such usefulness as he had provided him. And yet Mr Po was reluctant to let him go without inflicting some retribution. The man must suffer a little. He was confident that he would think of something, given time.

Mr Po got up again and made his way across the marbled hall to the cinema and television room with its banks of chairs. He was glad that Madame Po was out, busying herself with her charity work with that strange bishop. He wouldn't want her to come across him watching this particular DVD. But he didn't regard himself as a voyeuristic person. He expected to feel more disgust than pleasure.

As Mr Po was settling down in the front row, Sam Blunt was crossing Notting Hill Gate towards Billionaires' Row, less than a quarter of a mile away. He had just had a few drinks with an old girlfriend in a pub near the Portobello Road. After they had finished a bottle of wine he had wondered whether they might go to bed together, but the moment had passed. When he left the pub he realised he was hungry, yet didn't feel like spending his dwindling resources dining by himself in a restaurant. He momentarily thought of Caroline as he passed the Metropolitan Hotel.

Sam walked a little unsteadily for a hundred yards down Billionaires' Row before recognising where he was. The sight of the monstrous houses made him think of Terence Glasswell for the first time for a few hours. He no longer had any strategy for turning the tables on the shameless MP. Sam was broke, jobless, and, for the first time in his adult life, he felt utterly powerless.

When he got to the railings outside Mr Po's residence he stopped to look at the grey looming mansion. Then an idea occurred to him – a mad idea, admittedly, but in its way no more far-fetched than bribing a Spanish telephone engineer in Malaga to bug Nipper Richards' telephone, or arranging for Detective Chief Inspector Nobby Walters and his mistress to have an all-expenses-paid holiday in the Algarve in return for the policeman having revealed the identity of the headless torso dredged up from the Thames not, as it happened, very far from Lady Evelyn Wherewill's residence in Fulham.

Sam was too tipsy to think of being daunted by Mr Po's vast wealth. He walked briskly through the open gate and across the gravel drive. Having bounded up the steps much as Terence Glasswell had done a couple of months earlier, he gave the front door a couple of sharp raps with a golden knocker shaped like a dolphin. After a few moments, the door was opened by a pretty Filipino maid wearing a neat uniform and a starched apron.

'Hello,' said Sam Blunt cheerily. 'I've come to see Mr Po.'

Chapter Thirty-Two

Angelica eyed Sam suspiciously. She knew Mr Po was not expecting any visitors. Strangers were not expected to call unannounced at the house. She fingered an electronic device in her apron pocket with which she could alert her husband Tomas, who doubled up as one of Mr Po's drivers and bodyguards, and at this moment was watching American wrestling on television in their small flat in one of the towers of the house. But there was something agreeable about the smiling, good-looking man who stood in front of her, and she took her finger off the button on her contraption.

'I don't think you have an appointment,' she said.

'I haven't,' admitted Sam. 'But I've got some information for Mr Po. I'm a journalist.'

Angelica did not like journalists, and she was certain that Mr Po would not. She put her finger back on the button.

'You should make an appointment through Mr Po's office,' she said.

'I'm happy to do that,' Sam assured her. 'But I think Mr Po might prefer to see me now, as I'm here.' He flashed a smile at Angelica which she thought disgracefully flirtatious. 'Would you do me a favour and tell Mr Po that my name is Sam Blunt? I used to be chief reporter of the *Daily Bugle*, and I want to talk about Terence Glasswell.'

'All right,' said Angelica, closing the door in Sam's face.

Mr Po was sitting in the front row of his cinema and television room. The DVD, which had lasted half an hour, was over. Terence Glasswell had done things with Finula which he would not have believed possible. The man must be double-jointed. The woman was undoubtedly broad-minded. Mr Po admitted to himself that he was slightly jealous, as well as appalled. It was many years since he and Madame Po had attempted one hundredth of what seemed to come naturally to this virtuoso couple. Nonetheless, it was an outrage for Glasswell to have had sex in his private suite. He would sack him.

He heard a knock on the door, and looked up to see Angelica. For the first time he wondered what it would be like to make love to her.

'There is a man at the door wanting to see you,' Angelica informed him. 'I tell him to go off?'

'Who is he?'

'His name is Blunt. He says he is a journalist.'

Mr Po had never had to do with a journalist outside China. He had known a few in Chengdu who were employ-ees of the state, and wrote down whatever he instructed them to.

'Tell him to go away,' he said. 'Ask Tomas to get rid of him.'

Angelica did not think it would be necessary to call on her muscle-bound husband to repel the handsome man on the doorstep.

'OK,' she agreed. As she turned around to leave, she remembered that she had not carried out all of the journalist's request. 'He says that he used to be an important reporter on *Bugle* newspaper and he wants to talk about Mr Glasswell.'

Ten minutes later Sam was sitting on an enormous sofa whose soft, undulating cushions seemed to want to suck him downwards. He looked at the ageless face of Mr Po, who was enveloped in an identical sofa the other side of a large glass table.

Sam knew how to tell a story. He told Mr Po much of what he knew about Terence Glasswell – from his original sighting of the MP in Billionaires' Row to his discovery that he had not declared a pecuniary benefit which Mr Po had been generous enough to make to him. He thought it prudent not to refer to the incident when Benedict had tried to plant a microphone on the MP.

When Sam finished his account the billionaire asked what he could do.

'Terence Glasswell is getting away with murder. The story is that he is a corrupt MP. But thanks to the *Chronicle*, all that really came out was that Sir Edwin Entwistle had spoken to you about selling you the *Daily Bugle*.'

Mr Po winced at the recollection.

'I'd like to redress the balance,' continued Sam. 'Prove that it's Glasswell who's the real rogue. But I need more information about him.'

With a superhuman effort Mr Po managed to extricate himself from the cushions that seemed to be trying to drag him under. When he reached the edge of the sofa he leant forward to press a button on an intercom on the glass table.

'Angelica. Bring two silver goblets and a bottle of the

special 1961 first growth from the cellar.' He looked at Sam. 'I bought the last three cases in the world.'

Sam brightened up. Things seemed to be going better than he could have hoped. He patted his jacket side pocket to confirm that his notebook was there, and checked that he had a biro.

'Mr Po, do you mind if I take the odd note?'

'Write whatever you please. But I can do better.' He strained to press the intercom button again. 'Bring a digital recorder from the top drawer in my desk.'

When Angelica had left the wine and the recorder, Mr Po relapsed into the cushions, clutching a silver goblet of claret with both hands.

'Terence Glasswell is not a good man,' he announced.

'No, he's not,' agreed Sam.

'A very greedy man. And not very clever.'

'Yes.'

'I employed him part time because he knows China and he is an important MP. Nothing wrong with that.'

'No.'

'He wanted money, so I paid him generously. I also helped him to buy a small house. Nothing wrong with that either.'

'Absolutely not.' Sam thought the wine tasted a little sour. He'd have sent it back if Marco had produced it at the Saraceno.

'Then Sir Archibald Merrick told me that the Prime Minister's party was short of money, and can I help? So I use Glasswell as a kind of go-between.'

Sam nearly lost control of his goblet of 1961 first-growth claret.

'Excuse me, Mr Po. Are you saying you gave money to the Prime Minister's party?'

'That is exactly what I am saying.'

'Did they declare it?'

'I don't know, but that is not my business. Perfectly legal to give money. I tell my accountants. It's written down somewhere.'

'Absolutely.'

'Only I am a Chinese, not British, citizen, so maybe they should not have accepted it. But still I did nothing wrong in giving it. The Prime Minister has never done anything for me. I don't even have any businesses in Britain.'

'So why did you give it?'

Mr Po shrugged. 'I live in their country. They ask for money. I give it to them.'

'How much was it?'

'Not much. Maybe two million pounds.'

'And Glasswell was the courier?'

'Not quite like that. After the first occasion, Sir Archibald Merrick did not ask for more money. Glasswell told me when it was wanted – three or four times – and I arranged for transfers to an account in the Channel Islands.'

'And you are perfectly sure that the Prime Minister knew about it?'

'Yes. When I met him at the *Bugle*'s centenary party a few months ago, he thanked me for everything I have done.'

Sam double-checked that the green light on the recorder lying on the table between them was still on. This was the story of a lifetime.

'Will you do something for me?' asked Mr Po.

'Of course.'

'Pour the rest of the wine into our goblets. You are much younger than me.'

When Sam had done this, and sat down again amid the shifting cushions, he asked another question.

'Why are you telling me all this?'

'Partly so you can tell the world what kind of man Terence Glasswell really is.'

'And also?'

Mr Po looked Sam in the eyes. He still held his goblet of wine aloft.

'When I was a young boy I thought Britain a great country. I knew she had lost her Empire. I realised there had been economic problems. But I thought she was still strong, deep down. Chinese politicians were a little wary of your country – maybe they still are. We have long memories. It is not much more than a century and a half ago that an English army marched to Beijing and humiliated the Emperor. Can you imagine the shock? For us, that is only yesterday. Then I saw what the British had done in Hong Kong, how the rule of law combined with Chinese enterprise had made it rich. Even when I came here to live I thought I would find some hidden secret that would explain what had made Britain great. But I found nothing. I found narrow, corrupt men like Sir Archibald Merrick and Terence Glasswell and Sir Edwin Entwistle and your weak Prime Minister. I was sorry and, I suppose, a little angry. So that is partly why I am telling you this. I want to tell the truth. I have done nothing wrong. I don't need to live here. I can return to Hong Kong, or go anywhere. I don't care what your newspapers write about me. My dreams of your country are over.'

'I'm sorry, Mr Po. I don't know what has happened to us. I can't believe there aren't some fine people here.'

'I expect there are. I haven't met them.'

'Thank you for telling me this.'

'That's all right, Mr Blunt. I'm glad we have met. I hope you write a good story. I'll look forward to reading it. I hope you will make a fair report.'

He put his hand into his pocket and took out the DVD. 'Here. You had better have this. And don't forget the recorder.'

That evening, when Mr Po lay in bed alongside the monumental figure of Madame Po, her black hair which in the daytime resembled a vibrant plant now constrained in a net, he told her about Sam's visit. After he had finished, his wife astonished him by disclosing that she had met Sam Blunt. She described how he had arrived late for lunch at Lady Evelyn Wherewill's minuscule house in Fulham, and how her friend the Bishop of Middlesex had led him into the dining room as though he was displaying a sinner.

'He was very drunk,' recalled Madame Po. 'And I think he must have wet his trousers. Then Caroline Entwistle took him away.'

'Silly man,' said Mr Po. 'I think that journalists are often pathetic people.'

'Yes, he is a silly man,' agreed Madame Po. 'But there was something else. There was something of the child about him. Unusual in a man of that sort. Perhaps that was what Lady Entwistle liked.'

'Did they have an affair?' asked Mr Po.

'That is what Lady Evelyn says.'

'What funny people.'

Madame Po Chun extended a hand across the bed to her husband. They lay still for several minutes, hand in hand. Then Mr Po eased his wife tenderly towards him, and began to do some rather unfamiliar, though surprisingly enjoyable, things to her long-neglected body.

Chapter Thirty-Three

Eric Doodle had not sat on the backbench of the *Daily Bugle* for many years. He seldom even ventured into the newsroom. Trevor Yapp had been in charge of news.

But Yapp lay banished at home and Doodle was running the show. The first edition of the paper was due to be completed in a few minutes.

Sitting on the backbench with his lieutenants around him – the night editor, the splash sub and, behind him on the news desk, the news editor – Doodle imagined himself on some gigantic intergalactic spaceship voyaging through space. He felt at one with his staff as he had not done since becoming editor – with the rows of sub-editors in front of their screens, with the few reporters who had not yet gone home, with the features desk putting the last touches to the comment pages, and with the sports department even now getting a report of a late football match on to the back page. They were all part of his domain, defined by their shared separateness from the rest of humanity, bound together in the great enterprise that is a daily newspaper. And they were about to inflict a deadly attack on the enemies of honest government and a free Press: the Prime Minister, the Home Secretary, Sir Archibald Merrick and, above all, Terence Glasswell.

Doodle hadn't informed Sir Edwin Entwistle of what he was about to do. He was almost certain that the former carpet billionaire would baulk at a story that would in all probability bring down the Prime Minister and the Government, thereby dashing his expectations of a life peerage. Perhaps later, when the *Bugle* was celebrated across the world as the cornerstone of a free Press, the proprietor would come around, but Doodle wasn't going to give him a choice now. If he was sacked, so be it. He almost gloried in the certain sacrifice of his knighthood. He, who had defended the Prime Minister through thick and thin, would not countenance corruption. A line had to be drawn somewhere and Eric Doodle was drawing it now. Surely even Daphne would realise that what he was doing was far more important than any knighthood could ever be.

He read the front-page headline on the screen in front of him which would pass into history as soon as he gave the go-ahead to the night editor. PM HIDES ILLEGAL PAYMENTS FROM FOREIGN TYCOON. The headline was so huge that there was only space for a hundred or so words before the story ran over to pages two and three. It contained a detailed account of undeclared payments made to the Prime Minister's party by Mr Po Chun, with its vice-chairman Sir Archibald Merrick and Terence Glasswell, MP, acting as conduits. On pages four and five there were profiles of the two men and of the Chinese billionaire, and a short piece about Anglo–Chinese relations. Pages six, seven, eight and nine were given over to the DVD that Mr Po had passed to Sam. Several grainy pictures showed Glasswell and Finula in various gymnastic positions, though Doodle had insisted on a liberal use of black strips to preserve their modesty and constrain the prurience of the readers of the *Daily Bugle*. Finula's possibly insincere endearments to the MP were reported at length, while some of Glasswell's exhortations were considered too fruity for a family newspaper and, again on Doodle's instructions, were replaced with asterisks so plentiful that it would have taken an expert in Linear B to have worked out what he actually said. On its centre pages the *Bugle* stepped into its pulpit and adopted a more high-minded tone. A full-page leader argued that the gifts which Mr Po Chun had made in apparent good faith had been illegally accepted by the Prime Minister, whose failure to declare them showed that he knew they were impermissible. The leader also reminded the readers of the *Daily Bugle* that both Terence Glasswell and Sir Archibald Merrick were associated with a campaign to curtail the freedom of the Press. Their hypocrisy was amply highlighted by these compromising revelations, as well as by the pictures of Mr Glasswell, who presented himself as happily married man, exploiting his young secretary in Mr Po's private suite in the Park Lane offices of Anglo-Chinese Investments.

On the other side of the centre spread there was a column by Adam Pride, who had been prevailed upon by a reinvigorated Doodle into writing things he might have preferred not to. He asserted that the Home Secretary could not plausibly dissociate himself from disgraceful behaviour by a government of which he was a leading light, or by the party of which he was such an important member. Everyone was complicit to a greater or lesser extent. Pride, who did not disclose that he was an occasional lunching companion of Glasswell's at the Fig Leaf and other expensive watering holes, also declared that the MP was politically a busted flush who would be fortunate to escape the attentions of the Metropolitan Police.

The deadline for the front page had been delayed half an hour so that the early editions of other newspapers could not pinch the *Bugle*'s story. Now it lay five minutes away. No one thought of mentioning this to Eric Doodle any more than they would have told him that he was approaching an alien planet somewhat too quickly for the structural well-being of his spacecraft. They were sure their editor knew what he was doing. He would give the go-ahead to the night editor when he was ready. Eric was a good chap, really. A bit aloof, and obviously not as hands-on as the grisly Trevor Yapp, but a decent enough bloke all the same. He'd do the right thing by the *Daily Bugle*.

Doodle had not yet told the night editor to send the completed front page because he did not want to spoil one of the most delightful moments of his life. He knew that once the button had been pressed something precious and unrepeatable would have ended. They would enter a new phase, exciting no doubt, but unpredictable too. He also knew that if he waited another quarter of an hour he risked Penzance and Truro not getting copies of the first edition of the *Bugle* in time for paperboys to collect them at the newsagents at seven o'clock to deliver with the other papers. He did not want that.

Doodle imagined copies of the *Bugle* being unpacked and distributed to a sleepy and pimply paperboy who was the last, vital link in a chain that started with Mr Po. Of course by that time Bugle Online would have been carrying the news for several hours. Radio and television would be spreading it to millions. The later editions of rival papers and their websites would have taken it up. A thousand blogs would have claimed ownership of it, and the story would be tweeted and re-tweeted around the world. But Doodle was a man of his time and he could not set aside the romance and excitement of hundreds of thousands of copies of his newspaper being driven across the country through the night to all the corners of the kingdom.

He looked to his left at Sam, who was sitting next to him. Reporters, even former chief reporters, did not normally sit on the backbench, but this was Sam's story. Doodle marvelled that he had misjudged him so. He had been influenced by Yapp, of course. Yet he was at fault, too. They hadn't used him properly and hadn't protected him from himself.

How astonished he had been the previous day to receive a call from Sam in the Half Moon suggesting that he join him there to discuss what he described as the story of a lifetime. Doodle felt that entering any pub in the vicinity of Pepper House was beneath his dignity as an editor, and had suggested that they meet in the office, or otherwise at Bright's Club later. Sam said he had no intention of returning to Pepper House until he had spoken with Doodle in person. If he wasn't interested in what he had to say, there were always other newspapers in the world such as the *Chronicle*, and other editors such as Edward Sneed. Eric Doodle arrived at the Half Moon within ten minutes.

Sam showed him his story, which survived almost unchanged as the *Bugle's* splash. Doodle knew at once that it was everything the ex-chief reporter had cracked it up to be.

'What do you want?' he asked.

Sam named a five-figure sum which Doodle readily accepted.

'There is another condition,' said Sam.

'If it's your job, you can have it back so far as it's in my power. Sir Edwin Entwistle may sack me after I have published this story.'

'It's not my job I'm worried about. I want Benedict Brewster to share the by-line on the front-page splash. And I'd like you to promise to take him out of the dungeon and give him a proper job in the newsroom.'

Eric Doodle had no difficulty in accepting such conditions in respect of the younger son of Sir Cumming Brewster. Even if he were dismissed, Sir Edwin would hardly notice the presence of Benedict in the newsroom, though Yapp certainly would if he ever came back to the paper.

'I can guarantee that,' said Doodle.

Now the editor looked to Sam's left where Benedict was sitting. The young man's expression was both proud and awed. He did not think he had a right to have his by-line on this story but Sam had insisted that it would not have been written without his cooperation and support. They had worked as a team. It was no time for Benedict to break ranks now. They were in this together. The young journalist wondered what Sophia would think to see his name above such a piece. He imagined his disbelieving mother putting the paper in front of his father. 'Cumming, dear, do look at this.'

Across the newsroom Doodle noticed the figure of Dr Robert Munganwa standing in a corner with that female

colleague of his. Robert was watching. He sensed that something portentous was about to happen. He did not know
that it concerned Mr Po, part of whose unimaginable wealth
lay beneath the Wali desert, beneath his native soil, in mines
where fellow Kangalans laboured in noise and heat and dust
for a fraction of what even he was being paid to clean the
lavatories at Pepper House.

Doodle looked interrogatively at the night editor.

'Sport all done?'

The night editor nodded.

'Leader page finished?'

The night editor nodded again.

Eric Doodle looked at the front page on the screen. He
read the headline for the hundredth time, and checked the
by-line. *Exclusive: By Sam Blunt and Benedict Brewster.*
Suddenly he wondered whether he had got it all wrong. He
could imagine his old friend the Prime Minister smoothly
claiming that it had been a mere oversight on the part of
junior employees not to declare Mr Po's gifts. They, like him,
had innocently assumed that the Chinese tycoon was a
British citizen. He could hear Terence Glasswell saying that
what he did in private with Finula was only his and her
business, and the unauthorised use of these pictures by the
Daily Bugle was another example of the abuse of power by
an over-mighty Fourth Estate. He had apologised to his wife
Cynthia and she was standing by him.

Then he conjured up the face of Sir Cumming Brewster
surveying his copy of the *Daily Bugle* over breakfast at Bassett
Park. What would the good-hearted baronet say? He would
say that devious and corrupt politicians were at it again.
He would say that Terence Glasswell was a bounder who

had brought only sorrow to his family and disgrace to his country. He would say that he was proud and honoured that his son had played a role in exposing these scoundrels.

Eric looked at the front page one last time and grinned at the night editor.

'Send it,' he ordered.

Chapter Thirty-Four

It is seven o'clock the following morning and there are approximately twenty people squeezed into the Prime Minister's bedroom in his flat above Number Eleven Downing Street. Newspapers are strewn all over the carpet. The Press Secretary is perching on the edge of the prime ministerial bed with a notebook in his hand. The Cabinet Secretary's large bottom is cushioned by a pillow. Special advisers sit on the floor. The Prime Minister himself frets, blames and curses as he weaves through obstacles of arms and legs and human bodies. Mobile phones ring and buzz; tablets are consulted; voices on a radio are barely heeded. On an unobserved television in the corner of the room, Timothy Brown of the *Chronicle* and Adam Pride of the *Daily Bugle* are agreeing that the Prime Minister may have some difficulty in convincing the country of his innocence.

Reporters have swarmed across the capital. The wonder is that there are so many of them. They are gathering in Downing Street, hoping for a statement, and waiting for the entrance or exit of a significant player in the drama. They are camped outside Terence Glasswell's house in Victoria, where the curtains are still drawn, as Cynthia swiftly packs her suitcase. They stand by the gates of Mr Po's mansion in Billionaires' Row, warily watched by Angelica and her muscle-bound husband from their tower. They have collected outside the offices of Anglo-Chinese Investments in Park Lane. A couple of them are loitering outside Sir Edwin Entwistle's house in Eaton Place, where Caroline is attempting to calm the agitated proprietor of the *Daily Bugle*. Far away, in the outer reaches of south London, Steve Rutt is ringing Finula's doorbell with the intention of offering her a small slice of Deever Bottle's billions to describe her sexual escapades with Terence Glasswell, MP, for the benefit of the *Daily Dazzle*'s several million readers.

Amid the hubbub in the Prime Minister's flat a desperate and implausible strategy is emerging. He hadn't known Mr Po was a Chinese citizen. He hadn't been told – either by Terence Glasswell or by Sir Archibald Merrick. He had naturally assumed he was British. His Press Secretary will not go so far as to tell the world that these gentlemen have deliberately misled the Prime Minister – only that, for whatever reason, they kept him in the dark. He did not concern himself with the details of party funding. For God's sake, didn't people know he had a country to run!

'Have you found the Home Secretary?' asks the Prime Minister for the tenth time.

No, they haven't found the Home Secretary. The Home Secretary has vanished. His mobile is turned off. His special advisers don't know where he is. He isn't at home. It is clear as can be that the devious man has done a bunk and is trying to put as much distance as possible between himself and Number Ten.

Splash!

'Bastard,' mutters the Prime Minister.

On the television news it is being reported that Sir Patrick Clapp and the Bishop of Middlesex have announced they are considering their positions as members of the Call to the Nation Commission inspired by Terence Glasswell.

On the radio news the leader of the Opposition is calling for an immediate inquiry and a Government minister is declaring that the Prime Minister is an honourable man whose integrity should not be impugned.

On the television there are pictures of a tear-stained Cynthia climbing into a taxi with a small suitcase before speeding off to an unknown destination.

In the flat above Number Eleven the Prime Minister is growing ever more plaintive. If they can't find the Home Secretary, he would like to speak to the Chancellor of the Exchequer. He feels let down by everyone – by the Home Secretary, by that ass Sir Archibald Merrick, by the ghastly Glasswell, by Mr Po and above all by Eric Bloody Doodle, who was supposed to be his friend and confidant. It all goes to show you should never trust a journalist. If Doodle thinks he will ever receive even an MBE were he to live for a thousand years, he can dream on. As for Sir Edwin Entwistle, his life peerage is dust and ashes if the Prime Minister has anything to do with it.

At 2 Common View Eric Doodle is breakfasting calmly. For once, he will leave for Pepper House a little late. Daphne has taken his waiting driver Ted a mug of tea and a copy of the *Daily Dazzle*. Sir Edwin has telephoned three times and on each occasion has been informed in no uncertain terms by Daphne that her husband is out on Wimbledon Common walking their dog Bobby, and may not return for some time.

Daphne does not mind telling him this lie. For the first time in many years she feels proud of her husband. It seems to her that Doodle has directed the destiny of the nation. She doesn't really mind about the knighthood.

Across the great city the man who started it all lies alone, asleep, in his bed in his basement flat in Barons Court. There are no reporters outside. No one wants to speak to Sam. His name is not mentioned in any of the hundreds of reports being disseminated by the internet, television, radio and newspapers. The story has acquired its own momentum and no longer belongs to him or Benedict. It is as though he has been the conduit of a greater force. By choosing to bound up Mr Po's steps on a particular summer evening when he had had too much to drink he has changed many lives. And yet almost no one will ever give him the credit. Not that he minds.

Sam stirs, looks at his watch, turns over and goes back to sleep. He isn't going to Pepper House this morning, and never will again. Our hero has other plans.

Across the great unfolding city the editor of the *Chronicle*, Edward Sneed, is wrestling with a quandary at his home in Islington. He is not a supporter of the Prime Minister or his party, though he is on good terms with the Home Secretary, with whom he occasionally lunches at the Fig Leaf. He is therefore not at all unhappy to hear about a scandal which will surely lead to the collapse of the Government and an early general election. On the other hand, he can't bear to see the vulgar *Bugle* setting the political agenda in so dramatic a fashion. And although he has no affection for Terence Glasswell or Sir Archibald Merrick, he bitterly regrets the now inevitable curtailment of the Commission looking into the excesses of the Press. He had hoped that at the very least it would clip the wings of the *Bugle* and the *Daily Dazzle*, and enable the *Chronicle* to stake out some more high ground for itself.

Sneed purses his lips as he looks again at the photographs of Terence Glasswell and Finula bonking in Mr Po's four-poster bed. It is not as though he is a sexual puritan. He and Mrs Sneed have an accommodating marriage in which both of them have enjoyed occasional excursions. The intrusive and prurient nature of the pictures simply appals him. However much at fault Glasswell may have been in his political judgement, it wasn't necessary to cover four pages with such lurid photographs. He takes a closer look. Then he begins to compose in his mind the leader which the *Chronicle* will publish the following day. 'Undoubtedly serious allegations which have to be answered . . . Difficult to see how the Prime Minister can remain in office . . . Revelations only underline the need for state financing of parties . . . Most unfortunate that the *Daily Bugle* has seen fit to publish salacious photographs that only detract from its coverage . . . When the dust has settled, the excesses of the tabloid newspapers will still remain an important issue, and it is to be regretted that the Commission examining issues of Press freedom has been an unwitting victim of a political scandal.'

In Eaton Place Sir Edwin Entwistle is telephoning Eric Doodle for a fourth time, and for a fourth time he is being told by Daphne Doodle that her husband is still out on the common walking Bobby.

In the flat above Number Eleven the Prime Minister is asking for the twentieth time whether they have got hold of the Home Secretary and for the twentieth time is being told that they haven't. If he is going down, he will take the bastard with him. But he intends to fight. He will invite the tamest television interviewer he and his Press Secretary can find to come to Number Ten, and he will repeat the lie again and again that he assumed Mr Po was British.

Come away from the frantic city, across the waking country, to a tranquil corner of Lincolnshire neatly marked on Eric Doodle's map. Most of the corn has been cut now and the hedgerows have spilled their last flowers on to the verges. A paperboy is pushing a newspaper through the ancient brass letterbox of Bassett Park. Sir Cumming Brewster has been waiting for it. As soon as it lands on the stone floor, he picks up the copy of the *Daily Bugle* and looks at its front page. He has heard the radio news and hopes that his son's name may be on the story. Now he sees it. *Exclusive: By Sam Blunt and Benedict Brewster.* He sits down on a chair in the hall and reads the splash.

When he has finished it, he folds up the paper carefully. Then he walks up the curving Regency staircase and down a long corridor to the bedroom which he and Celestine share. His wife is sitting upright reading a book and sipping a cup of tea which he brought her ten minutes previously. She looks up.

Sir Cumming walks over to the bed and reverently lays down the copy of the *Daily Bugle* by her side.

'Read this, my dear,' he suggests. 'I think old Ben may have brought down the Government.'

Chapter Thirty-Five

All over London people are making their preparations. In the flat above Number Eleven Downing Street the wife of the new Prime Minister is talking on the telephone to the new Prime Minister's diary secretary. A general election has taken place and another party is in government. There has been a merry-go-round of changing places. The old Home Secretary is the leader of Her Majesty's Opposition. The ex-Prime Minister, always a dependable ally of the United States, has been reduced to delivering lectures on political ethics to businessmen on the American lecture circuit at £100,000 a shot. Terence Glasswell has lost his parliamentary seat in Yorkshire and is currently open to offers. Cynthia has stopped crying. She will never return to him. Finula, whose unsparing revelations in the *Daily Dazzle* did not greatly delight the ex-MP, has become a glamour model. Their relationship is over.

All over London people are making their preparations. Lady Evelyn Wherewill's hair colouring in the hairdresser off the New King's Road known to the cognoscenti is nearly finished. Bishop Bob is composing a critical tweet about the latest welfare reforms. He is preparing to walk to the bus stop where he will take a bus to an underground station and a tube that will convey him towards Mount's. Boris Vrodsky is still drinking in his Mayfair club, an arm draped around the shoulders of a lady of Eastern European origin, but he has not forgotten the party. In his office at Pepper House Adam Pride is approaching the end of a column about the strengths and weaknesses of the new Prime Minister. Governments come and go, but columnists observe in safety the debris of ruined political careers and smashed reputations, before embracing a new cast of characters.

All over London people are making their preparations. Mr Po and Madame Po are not among them. They have been spending most of their time in Hong Kong. Their mansion in Billionaires' Row won't be sold, though. Angelica and her husband will look after it. Madame Po will make occasional visits to keep an eye on the charity projects she has set up with the Bishop of Middlesex. She will have lunch with her friend Lady Evelyn Wherewill, who is said to be learning Mandarin. But Mr Po's odd love affair with England is over. He does not intend to live in London again.

In her bedroom in Eaton Place Caroline has asked her husband to zip up her new blue dress. She looks at him with some affection. Sir Edwin has lost weight as a result of being put on a strict diet by his wife, and looks five years younger. He has shaved off his moustache. He has also agreed to put a stop to his weekly visits to Vera Potts' flat in Earls Court, where rather too many éclairs were eaten. There is a sense of a new beginning for Caroline and her husband.

It was she who persuaded him to hold another party to advertise his continuing – in fact, his reinvigorated – commitment to the *Daily Bugle*. For a few days after the paper's sensational front page Sir Edwin was half minded to sack Eric Doodle. When he eventually got hold of the errant editor he suggested that it had been highly irregular to run such a momentous story without first consulting him. Doodle invited Sir Edwin to dismiss him and he very nearly did. But Caroline pointed out to her husband that the *Bugle* was being celebrated in many quarters for its fearless and independent journalism. She urged him to hang on to Doodle. Quite soon the proprietor came to believe that he was in some way responsible for the scoop himself. He cheerfully accepted compliments for his courage in carrying such an earth-shattering piece. There was admittedly the matter of the life peerage, but actually there was no reason to suppose an understanding could not be reached with the new Prime Minister, who is expected at Mount's this evening.

All over London people are making their preparations. The film star Tray Nevada has been invited to the party. So too has Caroline's friend Annette Bustome of the *Chronicle*, who once fabricated an entire interview with him. He won't recognise her. Edward Sneed will be there too, as will Emmanuele Botti. Sir Archibald Merrick, whose public denial that he had ever withheld Mr Po's citizenship from the ex-Prime Minister has been quite widely believed, is also expected. They will have to drink non-vintage champagne rather than the vintage variety so liberally dispensed at the *Bugle*'s centenary celebrations earlier in the year. This will be a more modest affair. Sir Edwin is under no illusion that his paper's new-found notoriety will improve its profitability. Circulation continues to trickle away. No, he won't throw money around. But Caroline has persuaded him to remain a proprietor, and Boris Vrodsky has accepted with something like good grace that he will never own the *Daily Bugle*.

Eric Doodle's confirmation as editor has led Trevor Yapp to accept an offer of a job as editor of Dazzle Online, where he is parading starlets in even scantier clothing than he did at the *Bugle*. Suzy Wattle has already been induced to show off her artificially inflated breasts on the beach at Marbella. But Yapp thinks she may be getting past it. He intends, with the help of Steve Rutt, to persuade Finula to take her top off. Not that she will need much encouraging.

There are some who believe that Doodle's chances of becoming Sir Eric have actually increased as a result of his act of bravery. Who knows, he may be invited by the new Prime Minister for a chat in the little flat above Number Eleven. He may even be asked to give a few words of advice.

This evening it is certain that he will be expected to say a few words at Mount's. He and Daphne have been timing his speech, which Sir Edwin has respectfully suggested should not exceed five minutes. Daphne has bought a new digital clock to ensure that this time there will be no misunderstandings.

Eric can hardly believe the changes in his wife. If she still regards him as a fool, she does not say so. To his astonishment she has acquiesced in the proposal that he rent a cottage on Sir Cumming Brewster's Lincolnshire estate.

A month previously, early in the shooting season, he had received an invitation from the baronet to shoot at Bassett Park. Mercifully, there were no awkward questions about the relative merits of springer and cocker spaniels. Doodle shot three pheasants and one woodcock. As they trod across a rutted field, Sir Cumming happened to mention that he was having difficulty in finding a tenant for a cottage.

Splash!

'Young families don't want to live deep in the country, these days,' remarked the baronet. 'They prefer to live in the town.'

The editor of the *Daily Bugle* replied he had precisely the opposite inclination.

Ivy Cottage is not the kind of residence that features in the property pages of *Rural Retreats*. There is no library or billiard room. It is a small, whitewashed house with only two bedrooms. A tiny front and back garden together amount to no more than a tenth of an acre. But it looks down a sweeping field towards a wood where red deer roam and foxes bark. No other house is visible, though if you peer hard you can glimpse through the massing trees the tip of the flagpole on Bassett Park.

Daphne has said that she is prepared to go there to see what it is like. She thinks her hay fever is better and she will keep away from stinging nettles. Fortunately Sir Cumming Brewster does not keep pigs.

All over London people are making their preparations. One person who has not been asked is Benedict Brewster, though Caroline heard so much about him from Sam, and knows that he had a hand in the story which brought down a government and ruined Terence Glasswell.

Benedict is working in the *Bugle*'s newsroom. He has a lot to learn but Eric Doodle is beginning to think he might possibly make a reporter after all. His father is enormously proud of him. 'My younger son is a journalist,' he tells almost everyone who does not already know. 'On the *Daily Bugle*.'

In a few minutes Benedict will join the glacial Sophia in the Half Moon. It can't be denied that she was impressed to see Benedict's by-line on the momentous splash. As she is a little bit of a snob, and rather less socially elevated than she might wish others such as Trevor Yapp to think, she was gratified to discover that her admirer is the younger son of a landed baronet. The auburn-haired beauty is an ambitious and gifted young woman. Eric Doodle has wondered whether she might not end up as an editor, if there are any newspapers left to edit. We will have to leave her and Benedict to fate and the temper of their desires.

All over London people have made their preparations. The champagne is cooled to just the right temperature. The oysters are ready. The waiters are waiting. Cameras click and flash and whirr as Caroline Entwistle steps out of her husband's limousine. Her beauty would take your breath away. It might make your eyes prick with tears. If only Sam could see her now.

But Sam is not there. He is in a battered aeroplane which rolls and shivers and wheezes as it begins its descent towards Tepe airport over the desert kingdom of Kangala. Sam is chatting up a beautiful African woman, with a gin and tonic in his hand that is certainly not his first since leaving Johannesburg nearly two hours ago. He has not returned to the *Bugle*. He does not work for any newspaper now. He has sold his flat in Barons Court (making a net profit of five hundred pounds) and given his old furniture to charity. Most of the money Doodle paid him for his scoop will be used by Sam to investigate Mr Po Chun's mining interests in Kangala and his relations with the autocratic Moses Ovambo and the extravagant Stella. He knows there is a big story here, though he does not yet know that Mr Po has struck gold. A big foreign story of the sort the *Daily Bugle* is no longer interested in. He hopes a rich American magazine will be. And maybe even the *Chronicle*.

Splash!

Dora told Sam about Robert Munganwa working as a cleaner in Pepper House, and his narrow escape from Albert Tether of the Immigration Authority. Before leaving London, Sam had a drink with Robert in the Half Moon. The two men liked each other. Robert told Sam about the Movement to Free Kangala from Oppression, his imprisonment in Tepe jail, and his separation from his wife Carumba and his son. He later handed Sam a small present which he asked him to give Carumba.

His Incomparable Excellency Moses Ovambo and Her Magnificence Stella Ovambo will not last for ever. Perhaps Mr Po and the Chinese will tire of them and find a replacement. Or maybe a lucky grenade tossed by a member of the small armed wing of the Movement to Free Kangala from Oppression will one day blow up the tyrant's motorcade. Such people are not immortal, though they may seem to be. The time will come when Robert Munganwa will be able to put down his bucket and mop to return to Kangala and see his wife. But how old will his young son then be?

The aeroplane lurches forward and the engines roar. The wheels grind as they are lowered. Sam looks out of the window and sees a straggle of huts with roofs of corrugated iron, and little figures walking endlessly across the sand.

Five thousand miles away Sir Edwin Entwistle is about to say a few words. Eric Doodle has spoken, and on this occasion came comfortably within the prescribed five minutes thanks to Daphne's scrupulous timekeeping.

It may be the memory of the centenary party all those months ago, or perhaps it is some intimation beyond our understanding. Caroline suddenly thinks of Sam, and to her surprise feels a gentle pull of sadness in her heart. She wonders where he is and what he is doing now.

The aircraft bucks and the engines screech as the pilot lines up the ancient machine to approach the runway. Sam looks out of the window again and sees miles of golden sand.

Sir Edwin is talking about the freedom of the Press. Of how newspapers have a sacred duty to speak truth to power. Caroline sets off a round of applause which is taken up by Lady Evelyn Wherewill and the Prime Minister, and then amplified by the Bishop of Middlesex and Sir Archibald Merrick and Ambrose Treadle and even Boris Vrodsky so that it becomes a roar of powerful people who categorically do not want the truth about them ever to be told.

'Rest assured that Arthur Pepper's great newspaper will always be safe with me,' declares Sir Edwin Entwistle. The applause starts up again. The proprietor of the *Daily Bugle* stretches out his hand palm downwards as though to quieten it. Edward Sneed scowls.

Sam looks again at the beautiful woman next to him, and notices how her tight white dress emphasises the gentle swell of her stomach. He wonders whether he should invite her to dinner at his hotel. He smiles at her, and she smiles back.

The exhausted aircraft tilts and groans. Sam reflects that it is not as straight as it should be for a landing. He and the black woman stretch out their hands to one another. At the last moment the pilot manages to level the machine, and Sam can feel the wheels bump heavily on the hot tarmac, beneath which lies the rich soil of Kangala.